OPERATION WINTERSET

OPERATION WINTERSET

By Mona MacDonald Tippins

Copyright © 2015 by Mona MacDonald Tippins

This book is a work of fiction. Any resemblance of characters to persons, living or dead is unintentional. Places are real, although used fictitiously. Businesses, buildings and street names are either imaginary or used fictitiously.

ISBN-13:978-0692428955
ISBN-10:069242895X

Edited by Carol Carroll

Cover photograph: *October Snow* by Susan Collins
Cover design by D.R. Dalton

Dedication

To my brother, Eddie Lawrence McDonald

Acknowledgments

I owe a debt of gratitude to the friends and family members who assisted in the making of Operation Winterset: Tim Tippins, D.R. Dalton, Shane Tippins and Ian Tippins.

Proofreaders: Kamie Tippins Keller, Loretta Tippins-Dalton and Diana Nixon.

As always Herb, thank you for your encouragement.

Contents

Chapter 1

Bad Kreuznach, Germany

Amber was the only soul taking the shortcut over the old stone bridge so close to midnight. The huge cross with a figure of the dying Christ loomed high above the bridge and the eerie blackness of the river below. She slowed her pace to survey the area as she approached the toy shop.

Her contact sat hunched in the doorway on a burlap sack, feigning sleep while clutching an empty wine bottle. He was wearing an old military overcoat. His toboggan hat was pulled down over his ears. The odor of cheap wine permeated his clothing. His cover was perfect. Amber leaned down, slipped a package into his overcoat pocket, and then headed back across the bridge toward her hotel on *Kaiser-Wilhelm-Strasse*.

Sensing a presence behind her, she turned and saw a masked figure stretching a length of rope between two rods. *A garrote!* Was her worst nightmare coming true? Adrenaline surged through her. She ran as if her life depended on it. Maybe it did.

She felt sure she had outdistanced the man, but she didn't stop to look back. The only sounds she heard were the staccato beats of her own footfalls. Still several blocks from her hotel, she cut across the pedestrian zone hoping to find help. Finally, she came to a hotel with its bright lights still on.

The man with the garrote stood on the bridge in the shadow of the cross waiting, watching until Amber disappeared into the night. He peeled the ski mask back from his face, dropped it into the river, and then walked softly toward the toy shop.

Amber's contact rolled the empty wine bottle under a bench and shuffled down the alley that leads to the stairs up to the castle. Before he reached the first step, a man holding a slim metal rod in each hand came up behind him. He stretched out the attached rope, looped it around the contact's neck and pulled it taut. Without hesitation, he twisted it until all gasping and struggling ceased, and then let the body slip onto the cobblestones. He took a package from the dead man's overcoat pocket, and then walked back over the bridge, pausing to make the sign of the cross as he passed the figure of the dying Christ.

At the *Silber Schwan Hotel,* Amber sat in the lobby wondering about the man with the mask. *Could it have been a woman? No, the stance was definitely that of a man.* She looked up in fear when a man entered the lobby. The receptionist gave him a key. He was a guest. On a hunch, Amber approached the receptionist. "Will you be on duty all night?"

"I will close in one hour."

She thanked him and went back to her chair. Her thoughts ran rampant. *I can't go back to my hotel. The man on the bridge might know I'm registered there. What if he breaks in and finds my room?* There was only one thing left to do and it was as a last resort. She would have to contact the only safe house in the area being used by PDI, the Potomac Decorating Institute, a cover for an intelligence agency based in Washington, D.C.

She called the safe house from the lobby phone.

A woman answered promptly.

Amber used the code. "I want to take the waters at Liebig. Can you arrange it?"

"Yes. When would you like to begin your stay?"

"I plan to leave as soon as you secure the reservation. Please send the ticket to the Silber Schwan."

"I will make the arrangements immediately. You should have the ticket soon."

"Thank you for your help. Goodbye."

The waters at Liebig were mentioned in an old German travel book. No one in modern times has been able to find out where Liebig is or was. Therefore, the phrase, "Take the waters at Liebig" is used as a code for assistance by agents and couriers in the area. "Take the waters" is a British phrase for going to a spa.

An agent would arrive at the hotel soon. Amber didn't want to be taken to the safe house. She only needed protection for the night. Tomorrow would be the last of the meetings, pick ups, drops and deliveries for this assignment.

Fifteen minutes before the closing hour, Emil Bingert came in and sat next to her. He was the "ticket." He is blond, bronzed and tall. Amber had dubbed him the "Golden Giant." She leaned toward him. "It's almost closing time. We can't talk here. We'll have to rent a room."

They registered and paid for a room on the second floor. Emil handed her a Bersa, eased the door open, and then checked the window and the balcony. He put a Glock 17 down on the nightstand next to the bed by the door. Amber perched on the edge of the other bed and examined the Bersa, a semi-automatic 380. *It's fully loaded, seven rounds and one in the chamber. That should do.*

"Emil, do you have a car here?"

"Yes, the Citroen, my old gray mare. Where shall we go?"

"I have a pick up in Lucerne tomorrow. There won't be any more trains leaving here tonight."

"We'll take the Citroen. I'll check the parking lots and streets around the hotel. If I'm not back in twenty minutes, call the safe house. If you don't get through, call the police. Don't mention me. Say that a man was following you and you are afraid to stay here. Ask to spend the night at the police station. I'll find you." He slid the Glock into his pocket, went over to the door and pressed his ear against it, listening for footsteps or breathing. "It's quiet out there. I'm going."

"The hotel office is closed. Take the lobby key."

Amber splashed cold water on her face and arms, washing away the perspiration. Fear makes you sweat even with a chill in the air. She turned off the light and listened for footsteps.

Two minutes before the twenty-minute panic time, Emil came back to the room. "Hurry, it's clear now. Let's move."

Amber grabbed the Bersa and they hurried down the stairs and out to the street. She slid into the passenger seat of his familiar old Citroen. She had hitched a ride with him before, when a train was deemed unsafe. Trains were her usual mode of transportation, and they were a part of her cover as a travel writer.

"I have to go to my hotel for some things. I'm staying at the *Abendstern*, on *Kaiser-Wilhelm-Strasse*. I have a lobby key."

Emil parked across the street from the *Abendstern* and scanned the area. "It's clear. I'll go in with you."

"My room is on the third floor. We'll take the stairs. I don't want to get stuck in that old elevator."

She led the way up the staircase. They felt their way along in complete darkness until someone opened a door above, letting the light shine down. Emil eased her down to a sitting position. They pressed their bodies against the wall until the door closed, and then continued up to the third floor.

In the room, Emil checked the balcony and the walkway along the river below. "We're okay. Hurry it up."

She grabbed her gear from the closet. "I'm ready."

Lucerne, Switzerland

Emil pulled over to the curb. "We're here. What's next?"

"We say our goodbyes. I need to go on alone from here." She returned the Bersa to him. "Thanks for the rescue, friend. I'll be seeing you."

"You're welcome. For now, goodbye and take care."

"I will. Bye." She got out, looked around, and then reached back in for her gear. *I've got a package to pick up and another train to catch.*

Train #2470 to Basel would leave at 2:30 p.m. Amber lifted her backpack onto the overhead rack.

She was thinking about her next delivery when a tall dark-haired man broke into her thoughts. "Excuse me, is this seat free?" He pointed to the seat opposite her.

Amber smiled and nodded. "Yes, it is. You're an American, aren't you?"

"Yes, I am. I'm Mike." He shoved his backpack under the seat, hung his jacket on the peg under the rack, took a pair of black-rimmed glasses from his pocket, and then sat down. "I've been traveling for three weeks and I've covered a lot of territory. Now, I'm heading to Paris."

"I'm Amber. I'm going to Paris too. I've been traveling for a couple of weeks and it's been great. I'll be glad to get back home to my husband, though. Are you married, Mike?"

"I was divorced two months ago. My wife has custody of my kids and I really miss them. That's the reason I took this trip. I needed some time away from work to sort things out."

"And have you?"

"Yes. I've decided to take my wife to court. I'm going to fight for the custody of my kids."

"That calls for a celebration. Let's go to the bar car. We have about an hour until our transfer point at Basel."

Basel, Switzerland

As the train slowed, Amber pulled her backpack down from the rack. Special documents or disks are carried in a pouch strapped around her neck, hidden beneath her blouse. Subconsciously, she put a hand to her chest. The pouch was secure. "Mike, I'll meet you on the platform. I need to make a quick stop."

She made the drop, and then joined Mike to board the train to Paris. Her instructions had been to choose a seat in any first-class compartment. The contact would approach her.

In Basel, her contact had always been "The Turk."

Mike sat across from Amber. "I see you're keeping a journal of your trip."

"This isn't a journal. I'm scribbling notes for a travel book."

"When will it be published?"

Before she could reply, a slim gray-haired man entered. He glanced around before taking a seat next to the door. He carried only a briefcase, which he placed on his lap.

The Turk eased the compartment door open and doffed his corduroy cap to Amber. A slight nod of her head was enough to let him know she had taped the disk under the shelf in the designated phone booth. He slid the compartment door closed and hurried back down the corridor to exit the train.

The gray-haired man rose, looked over at Amber and said, "Excuse me. I must meet someone in the bar car." When he reached the end of the corridor, he sprinted to the next car and stepped off just before the train pulled away. Pausing on the platform, he watched as the Turk approached a phone booth.

5

The Turk lifted the receiver, held it to his ear as if making a call, and then with one slick motion, removed the disk and slipped it into his pocket. Turning his head to view the platform area, he saw only a gray-haired man, facing the other way. Assuming all was well, he left the station.

He turned at the first intersection, slowing down to check out the area as he approached the Baseler Kaffeehaus. *If I was being tailed, I would have noticed it by now.* He sat down at the counter, ordered an espresso coffee, and then relaxed until time for the bus that would take him to his next contact. *Things have gone according to schedule. No suspicious characters hanging about.*

The clock above the counter reminded him that it was time for him to pay and head to the bus stop. *Barring intervention, this assignment will soon be completed. Maybe I'll take some time off. Travel a bit. Go somewhere far away from this jungle of deceit.*

A long line of passengers had formed by the time the Turk arrived. He took his place at the end of the line.

The gray-haired man stood in the shadow of a building. As the first passengers in line were boarding, he took a step forward, eased a blowgun from his briefcase, placed his lips around the mouthpiece, and then blew the dart into the neck of the last man in line. The Turk felt only a deep pinprick before drifting into nothingness. The poison on the tip of the dart needed only a couple of seconds to send a man to eternity. The gray-haired man reached in the Turk's pocket, removed the disk and slipped back into the shadows before the body hit the pavement.

Paris, France

The train pulled into Paris at seven-thirty p.m. Mike said, "I haven't booked a hotel. Do you mind if I tag along and ask for a room at yours?"

"No, I don't mind. I'll speak to the receptionist for you." The *Armande,* Amber's hotel is directly across from the station. Getting across that street was like running a gauntlet. After a lot of dodging and darting they made it to the other side.

Amber asked about vacancies for Mike but no rooms were available. She suggested the Evangeline hotel, a few blocks up the

Boulevard Magenta.

"I'll check it out. Which way?"

"It's to the left, on the same side of the street. Walk about three or four blocks and you'll see the neon sign flashing."

"Thanks. I'd invite you to dinner, but I've planned to meet one of my French cousins. How about tomorrow night? We could go up to Montmartre."

"No, thank you. I'll be leaving first thing tomorrow morning. My holiday is over."

"It's been a pleasure meeting you. I wish we had met sooner along the way. Good luck with your book."

"Good luck with your custody fight!"

The Armande serves as a safe house, always reserving a couple of rooms for agents or couriers. Amber didn't need to register. Yusuf, the Algerian receptionist asked her to step outside. His message was frightening; the disk had gone missing in Basel. He motioned for her to follow him back inside.

Her room was one floor up the spiral staircase. The old wood creaked with each step she took. The only view from the window in her room at the back of the hotel was of the red-tiled rooftops above the cobbled alley. She checked for escape routes. Unlike the rooms in most safe houses used by PDI, hers had no balcony or fire escape. When she leaned out the window to check the alley, thick dark wings flapped hard against her face, stinging sharply. She stifled a scream when a fat pigeon settled on her head. It took patience and dexterity for Amber to release her hair from its claws. *Ah, Paris!*

She sat in the rickety rattan chair and thought about the man on the bridge. *Who was he? Why didn't he follow me to the Silber Schwan or to the Abendstern? Why did the agency trust me with something so valuable? I'm just a courier. They should have sent a real agent who wouldn't have to call for assistance.*

Amber wouldn't be watching the twinkling lights on the Eiffel Tower tonight. She wouldn't be having dinner on board one of the *Bateaux Mouches* on the Seine. Instead, she bought a package of potato chips and a can of cola from the vending machines in the lobby. She didn't feel safe enough to venture out, although it was unlikely that the man on the bridge had followed her all the way to

Paris. Her evening would be hiding in her hotel room, praying not to dream of a man standing on a bridge holding a garrote.

Tomorrow she would be on her way back to Washington but tonight she needed to sleep.

The quilted bedspread was threadbare in places and some of the batting had lumped up from multiple washings. Its fleur-de-lis pattern was barely discernible. She stretched out on the narrow bed and thought about the way things had gone down in Basel. She could find no fault with the delivery. *How could the disk be missing? Did someone discover it before the Turk arrived? Was he followed? Was I?*

Thinking about the man with the garrote was the catalyst to Amber's nightmare. She reached the middle of the bridge as he caught up with her. She screamed. She felt the roughness of the rope as he slipped it around her neck, pulling it tighter and tighter until the breath left her body. Then, featherlight, she was drawn upward over the dark river.

Yusuf ran up the stairs and opened Amber's door with his passkey. She was lying on the bed holding a pillow over her face. He pulled it away and shook her shoulder. "Hey! Wake up! Wake up!" He slapped her gently on the cheek. Only then did she stir. She sat up and wiped the beads of sweat from her forehead.

"What are you doing here, Yusuf?"

"I heard you scream when I was down in the reception room. Were you attacked?"

"No. I was in a deep sleep and I must have been dreaming. I'm sorry for the disturbance."

"Don't worry about it. You would be shocked at some of the things that have happened in this old hotel. Go back to sleep."

"I don't dare go back to sleep after that nightmare. Thanks for coming to my rescue. Will you bring me some coffee, please?"

"Sure. One pot of freshly brewed … coming right up."

When Yusuf left the room, Amber made a decision. *I'll give my notice to the agency when I get back to Washington. It's time for me to live a normal life again. Every night I'll sleep safely in my own bed next to my husband. No more nightmares.*

Chapter 2

Washington, D.C.

After the flight from Paris, Amber took a taxi to the Potomac Decorating Institute (PDI). The unpretentious, three-story brick building sits on an ordinary street, in an ordinary neighborhood, just five blocks from an elementary school with its swings, seesaws, sliding boards and a set of monkey bars. Ordinary.

Inside the Potomac Decorating Institute things only appear to be commonplace. Clients are served on the main floor, although a designer showing fabric swatches or wallpaper samples might be an agent waiting to be summoned upstairs for a briefing or a debriefing. The elevator in the foyer on the first floor is disguised as a janitor's closet, operated by a code, which is changed often.

Reece Willoughby is the Chief Director of PDI. His private office and several briefing rooms are on the second floor. The attic and the rooms on the third floor are used only by a few top agents. As a courier, Amber had never been invited above the second level.

She waited until Willoughby finished a lengthy phone conversation. His snow-white hair and a slight stoop to his shoulders make him appear older than his sixty-eight years. She had known him all of her life. He was godfather to her and her twin sister, Arianne "Ari." Amber had always called him Uncle Will and it had been difficult to get used to calling him Willoughby.

As soon as he hung up the phone, she said, "I'm quitting and nothing or no one can make me change my mind. I'm just a courier anyway."

"Things have changed. Sit down and listen up."

She sat in the armchair across from his desk, but she didn't stop talking. "I'm not a real agent. I'm a housewife, paid to carry things across borders and deliver them. Something went haywire near the end of my assignment. Why was that man on the bridge after me? What happened to the disk at the drop in Basel?"

"I'll get to that in a minute. The agency considers you as a

9

potential agent and that's almost the same as an agent."

"How could I almost be an agent? I don't have a number like double-0-something-or-other."

"No, you don't. You'll have a code name, which you'll be given before you go on your first assignment as an agent."

"You still haven't told me why the man was after me."

"He wasn't. Maybe you were just in his way. Emil reported the incident in Bad Kreuznach. I heard about the Turk from our man in Basel."

"Was the disk delivered to the final contact?"

"I'm sorry. The Turk was murdered. We assume the disk was taken by the killer."

She leaped from the chair. "I slipped up! I didn't think that man in Bad Kreuznach could have followed me to Paris."

"Maybe he didn't. He probably followed the Turk or he knew where all of the drops and pick ups were."

"Wait a minute! What about the package I passed to my contact in Bad Kreuznach?"

"Your contact didn't make it either. He was strangled near the steps to the castle. The package was missing."

"It was that maniac on the bridge with the garrote. I caused my contact's death!" Remorse flowed over her. She held her head in her hands and shook it from side to side.

"Amber, stop! Don't punish yourself."

She moved her hands away from her face. "My cover may be blown. They know me! And they can find me in a heartbeat. Whoever *they* are."

Willoughby stood, went over to her and put his hands on her shoulders. "They have the disk. Why would they be after you? It's highly unlikely that they know who you are. The man in Bad Kreuznach only saw you briefly in the dark."

"If he was the one who sat in my compartment on the train, he knows me. It wasn't dark on the train. He left immediately after the Turk did."

"If he didn't follow you to the hotel, then how could he have followed you to Lucerne? Did you notice a vehicle tailing the Citroen after you and Emil left Bad Kreuznach?"

She paused, her mind going back over the hours on the road.

"No, I didn't. Neither did Emil. I suppose one of us would have spotted it."

"Then someone else supplied the information. You didn't pick up the disk until Lucerne."

She moved his hands away from her shoulders and walked to the door. "Whether the man in Bad Kreuznach followed me or not, I feel responsible for the deaths of my contacts."

"Don't blame yourself. That agent must have known where all of your contacts would be. They have their ways, Amber. You did your best, I'm sure."

"This time my best wasn't good enough. I quit, Willoughby. You can consider this my resignation. I quit!" She took the elevator down to the main floor and went into the cafeteria.

Cotter, an agent she had known for five years was in the line ahead of her. As they sat together over coffee, Amber asked him if he could take a couple of hours off.

"I'm free for the rest of the week. Do you want to go sightseeing?"

"Not today, thanks. I just need a ride to the airport in about fifteen minutes."

"Sure. I don't have anything planned for the rest of the day. Meet me here when you're ready to go."

She went back up to Willoughby's office. She had left her backpack by his desk.

He stood when she entered. "Amber, I have something to tell you about your husband."

"What's happened to Brian? Where is he?"

"He's at home. Nothing has happened to him. It's just that you won't be Mrs. Haworth much longer."

"What do you mean? Is this some kind of a joke?"

"Brian left you. He wants a divorce."

"I'm going home right now and straighten this out!"

"I know you're hurting, and I'm sorry. Maybe getting back to work will help you forget him."

"Work? I can't work! I have to get back to Brian. I'll catch the next flight out. There must be some mistake. Someone told you a lie. This can't be true!"

"It's true. He wants to marry someone else."

Amber grabbed her backpack, ran out the door and caught the elevator back to the cafeteria where Cotter was waiting. She rushed him out to the parking area. As soon as the car doors were closed she said, "Please take me to the airport."

"Washington or Baltimore?"

"I don't know. May I use your cell phone?"

He nodded as he handed it to her.

After the calls, she leaned her head against the window and began to tremble. "I've changed my mind. I don't feel like flying out tonight."

"What's wrong? Can I help?"

"Not right now, thanks. Take me to a hotel. Any hotel. Tell Willoughby where I'm staying and that I'll see him tomorrow. There's something he and I have to iron out."

"I'll tell him. Buckle up and we'll be on our way."

Amber gathered her things and got out of the car in front of the Riverdale Hotel. "Thanks. I'll call you soon."

She checked in, went up to her room and dialed her home phone number. Brian answered. Amber said, "It's me. I'm in Washington and I'll be home tomorrow. You won't believe what Willoughby told me!" She waited for a response. She could hear him breathing, so the lines weren't disconnected. "Brian! Are you there?"

"I'm here. We don't have anything to discuss. It's over! We're done. Don't call me anymore. Willoughby can fill you in on the divorce arrangements."

She slammed the receiver down. The tears came quickly, then the sobs … the kind that hurt at first, but when they're over you just feel numb. Then anger took over and she called Brian again. "Don't hang up on me! I deserve to know what's going on."

"We'll get together soon. For now, just let us be."

She hung up the phone. *Just let us be.* The walls seemed to close in on her. *It's true. Brian is with another.* She refused to cry again. She called Cotter. "It's Amber. Could you come to my hotel later, please? I need a friend."

"Hey! I'll be there right around dusk. Shall I bring takeout?"

"No. I'll call room service when we're ready to eat. Bye."

She called her mother, Genevieve. "Mom, it's me. I'm back in Washington now. How're you doing?"

"I'm fine. I'm worried about you, though. About the breakup with Brian, I mean."

"Everything will be okay, so don't worry. I'm staying at the Riverdale Hotel and I need some time right now. I just want to think it all out for a couple of days. Then I'll come to Burbank and we'll talk."

"I understand. Take care of yourself and come home soon."

Amber came out of the shower and looked for something to wear. Most of the clothes she had brought back were either dirty or wrinkled. She found a clean pair of jeans and a not-too-wrinkled striped shirt. She tied her wet hair back.

When Cotter called from the lobby she invited him up to the room. He greeted her with a kiss on the side of her forehead. She liked the way his light-brown hair always looked slightly tousled and how his brown eyes twinkled when he smiled. She sat down in the chair. He sat on the sofa. A man on the radio was singing "Don't Let the Teardrops Fall." That was appropriate. Amber just had to dance or maybe she just needed to be held. Dancing seemed to be the safe way. She rose from the chair, pulled Cotter up from the sofa and led him to the middle of the room. "Let's dance."

All too soon, the song was over and the deejay was giving a commercial. She slipped out of Cotter's arms and sat down on the sofa, knowing he would join her.

"Amber, what's going on with you?"

"Brian is divorcing me. He found someone else. Please hold me. That's all I need right now."

Cotter leaned over and kissed her.

She pulled back. "Wait! I just need a stand-up hug."

"You mean a friendly, teddy bear kind?"

"Yes. Just for a moment. That's what everybody misses when they've been alone. It's a traveler's kind of thing."

They stood and he put his arms around her.

Amber had missed having Brian's arms around her. She would never feel his touch again.

Cotter didn't want to let her go. He put his hand on her chin, lifted her face up toward his and touched his lips to hers.

A light knocking on the door gave her an excuse for not responding. The waiter wheeled a cart in, set their dinner on the table, and then rolled the cart out again.

Amber changed the station to classical music.

When they finished the meal, she told Cotter more of what she had heard about Brian from Willoughby.

"I'm sorry, Amber. That guy doesn't know what he's letting go. Anytime you want to talk or go out for the evening, just give me a call. When you need a friend, I'll be here or wherever."

"I know. Thank you, Cotter. I'll get back to you after I figure out what my next step will be. I'm tired now, and I'm planning to fly home tomorrow after I talk to Willoughby."

He touched her cheek. "I understand. Goodbye, for now."

She was about to doze off when Willoughby called.

"Amber, I need to see you right away."

"I'm in bed already, what's up?"

"We have to talk. Can I come over?"

"Can it wait until tomorrow?"

"No, it can't. I think you need to know that Brian's girlfriend is pregnant. Now, do you want to talk?"

"Pregnant? Brian is sterile!"

"Some things shouldn't be discussed over the phone. Now, get up. I'm coming over."

Within thirty minutes, he called from the lobby and said he'd be right up. She dressed in her jeans and striped shirt. "Come in. Whatever you have to tell me, just spit it out!"

"You know that Brian is sterile. He doesn't. His mother thought she was doing the right thing by not telling him. He thinks it was your fault there were no children. Anyway, his girlfriend convinced him the child is his."

"That's a real jolt."

"Brian wants the house. He wants to buy you out, and he has asked me to handle the paperwork for him because he doesn't want to see you again."

She was stunned. It was as if all the breath had gone out of her lungs at once. *Brian doesn't want to see me again.* She stood staring, unfeeling, as if she were made of stone.

Willoughby put his hands on her shoulders. "You won't need that house. You'll be traveling a lot. Work for us and we'll find you a place, anywhere you want. Please think about it. You need a life."

Amber pulled away, stepped back and looked up at him with tears streaming down her face. She made a barely audible choking sound before she spoke. "You don't know how happy I was to be coming home to my husband. I don't have a home now and I don't have a husband. You say I need a life? I had a life!" She dabbed at her eyes with the cuff of her sleeve. The tears didn't stop. She wiped her eyes on her shirttail and waited for him to speak.

"Let it go, Amber. Let *him* go."

"Let him go? He's gone."

Willoughby kissed her on the cheek and left her to her grief.

Chapter 3

Burbank, California

Amber was flying home. *I'll have to check into a hotel. No, I won't. Surely Brian wouldn't have his woman there. Not until the house is truly his ... theirs.*

Now, it was half hers and she intended to sleep in her own bed one more time. *Brian can sleep on the sofa or he can go to a hotel. Or go to Hell!*

On arrival at the airport in Los Angeles, she took the shuttle to Burbank. From there, it was only a few minutes by taxi to her house. She went to her front door as usual. Her key didn't work. *Brian must have had the locks changed.* She knocked. No answer. She put her finger on the doorbell and held it down for a few seconds. Still no answer. She would have to wait until morning to confront Brian. *Why didn't I tell the driver to wait?* She walked up to the convenience store and called for another taxi.

"Take me to the most famous hotel on Ventura Boulevard, please." *It's the least I can do for myself after all I've been through these last few days.*

The spacious lobby of the Hotel Nova Victoria is exquisite and so is Amber's room. The bedspreads are puff-stitched with irises and dark-green leaves. A pale-green sofa stretches along one wall. The drapes across the sliding glass door are subtly striped with green and off-white. It was the room she needed now. She had never stayed here with Brian, so there would be no memories plaguing her tonight. She stood out on the wrought iron balcony and felt the slight, cool breeze on her face. The lights on the boulevard below weren't as spectacular as those on the Eiffel Tower, but they were beautiful. In spite of her problems with Brian, it was good to be back in California again.

She still hadn't done her laundry. She hurried to catch one of the stores on the boulevard.

Back in her room, she poured a packet of lilac-scented bubble bath into the tub. The bubbles came up to her chin, tickling her in places she had never been tickled in.

An idea popped into her mind. *A singles' bar tonight! Do I dare?* She had never been to one before. She had never been single before, either. After the news about Brian, she might as well be single. She couldn't bear to spend the evening alone in the hotel room tonight. *A little music and maybe a dance or two will do just fine.* She called for a taxi before she could change her mind.

The ruby-red dress she'd bought was made of a silky crepe that clings yet flows. The color was a striking contrast to her dark hair. She slipped into it, and then went down to the lobby to wait for the taxi.

The young driver suggested the *Club Chez Moi.*

As Amber approached the bar, she imagined that everyone was staring at her. She ordered a glass of red wine and took it to a tiny round table.

There was no shortage of dance partners.

In between dances Amber drank margaritas. It wasn't long before they caught up with her.

She waited for a young black woman to finish a conversation on the pay phone. Amber wondered who the pretty woman was calling. *She already has someone to go home with. Of course, she has. Her big ol' boobs are about to pop out of her slinky dress.*

When the woman hung up, Amber dialed the special number and asked to be put through to Willoughby. He would be alone in his bed. Rowena, his wife died six years ago. He answered on the first ring. "Yes, what is it?"

"Hi, Uncle Will. It's me, your little Fairy Goddaughter. I just knew you were gonna answer your phone. When I'm drunk, I have that extra … sensory … per … something."

"Where are you? What has happened?"

"I'm in one of those fancy singles' bars on the boulevard. Nothing's happening yet, Uncle. *Nada!*"

"Tell me where you are and I'll send a car for you."

"No! You can't send anything for me, because I'm not going to tell you where I am." She hung up without saying goodbye and went to the main lounge. Taxis were lined up in front of the door

17

and so were waiting customers, mostly couples. *It seems as though I'm the only one that nobody wanted to take home.*

Amber managed to catch the sixth taxi in line. She settled back for the ride.

At the bar in the hotel, she bought a bottle of red wine and took it to her room. She called Willoughby to apologize and to let him know that she was safe.

Nearly half a bottle of wine and a lot of tears later, she heard a light tapping on her door. *Who can it be? No one knows I'm here.* She staggered to the door and yelled, "What do you want?"

"It's Volendam. Willoughby sent me."

She opened the door and fell forward into his arms.

"Amber, you sure need help. What is the matter with you?"

"I'll just tell you what the matter is. I didn't find anybody who wanted me. So, unless you want me, get out of here!"

"I'm married, didn't you know that?"

"No, I didn't or I wouldn't want you to want me."

"If I didn't have a wife that I love very much, I'd choose you above anyone else. I mean it. Does that help?"

"No, it doesn't." She picked up the bottle of wine. "This is what helps me and I'm gonna drink the whole thing."

Volendam paused to take off his jacket. "Put the bottle down, please. You've had enough. I'm going to have to poke some strong coffee down you."

"There's only one thing I want poked at me right now and yours is married, so just leave me alone!" She started crying again. He took her gently in his arms. "C'mon, Amber, do you want to be known as the Spy Who Cried?"

"It's a heck of a lot better than being known as the Spy Who Couldn't Get Laid!"

"You're drunk. I'd better go down to the bar and get you a gallon of coffee."

Volendam came back and tapped lightly before he opened the door. Amber was dozing on the sofa with the wine bottle in her hands. He eased it away and shook his head. *Jeez, she is lucky to be alive. This may be an all-night vigil.*

Willoughby had told him that her husband was divorcing her. The guy must be crazy, Volendam thought, as he studied her face.

He remembered that her eyes were blue-green. Her long, dark hair was just a shadow away from black.

Abruptly, as though she sensed he was watching her, she sat up and asked him the time.

"It's two-thirty. Are you planning to go somewhere?"

"No, I'm too drunk to go anywhere. I just wondered what he'd be doing now, that's all."

"Who?"

"That jerk I'm married to!"

Volendam tried to give her some of the lukewarm coffee. She turned her head away and laughed. "It's real funny. I mean it's a lot funny. Hey! You look just like Humphrey Bogart!" Her words were beginning to slur. She slid forward across the coffee table. He picked her up, carried her to the bed, slipped her shoes off and covered her with a sheet. He drank a cup of the coffee, and then stretched out on the sofa.

Volendam woke at 5:00 a.m., as he was accustomed to. He tiptoed out to get a thermos of fresh coffee.

By seven o'clock Amber began to stir. Finally, she sat up and groaned. "Yikes! What a head. I probably deserve it."

He poured a cup of the coffee and offered it to her.

"No, thanks, I'd just barf."

"The feeling will pass. You'll be okay. I have to go now, but I'll check with you later."

"Sure, friend, you've done enough already. Go on home, I'll be fine. Are you going to call in?"

"No. Willoughby will know things are okay if I *don't* call him. You're not the first PDI agent to get plastered, Amber."

"I'm not an agent. I'm not important, just used."

"Hey! C'mon, we're all important and we're all used."

"It doesn't matter anyway, because I'm quitting. I'm sorry that I came onto you, Volendam. I was drunk and I felt alone and unwanted. My husband is in love with someone else. I came home, only to find that I no longer had a home and that another woman would be sleeping in my bed."

"It must seem like the end of your world right now but soon, all the hurt will fade and you'll find a new life, without the man who didn't deserve you." He reached for his jacket. "I want to see my wife before she leaves for work. Let me know if I can help. I'm not far away, you know."

"Thanks. You're a good guy."

She was alone again. It was time to think things out. *I should give Brian the house. Things are beyond repair now. The little bitch can have him! They deserve one another.*

She called Willoughby at PDI. "It's me. Can we talk?"

"Yes, it's secure. I switched you over. So, you're still alive. How's my girl?"

"I'm not your girl anymore, Willoughby. For the first time in my life, I'm my own woman. And you know what? I think I'm gonna like it! I want my back pay. All of it. I want the bonuses, the out-of-pocket expenses and whatever else is due me. The plan is to take off right after you cut the red tape for me. I'm thinking about spending a year somewhere else."

"Why the haste? Think about your future. Don't quit because one mission went awry. Those things happen."

"Oh, right. Killers strangle contacts. Couriers like me cause the murders of their contacts. I won't be the cause … ever again. I want a new passport, in my maiden name. I won't be Mrs. Haworth anymore. I'll be myself again, Amber McFarland. Brian's little whore can take over my role now and the Haworth part of my name too. How soon will you have the new documents and all of my money for me? I need to be ready to travel."

"Don't you want a new job? You won't have enough money to travel around the world forever, you know. You'll eventually have to work. Why not work for us? We'll give you the special training for agents."

"I'll think about it. I still want my money, my maiden name and a new passport, as soon as possible."

"If you insist, I'll get on it right away. You'll hear from me in about three days. That's as soon as it gets."

"Okay. Bye." Amber called her friend, Claire Forsythe. "It's me. Let's go out to dinner tonight."

"Sure. How about going to Roxanne's?"

"Okay. I'm at the Hotel Nova Victoria on Ventura Boulevard. I don't have my car here, so pick me up around eight, please. Bye."

She dialed her home number. A woman answered, "Hello, who's calling, please?"

Amber didn't respond for a moment. *It's her, Brian's whore. What is she doing in my house?* "Who's speaking?"

"This is Barbie Sue."

"Barbie Sue, who?"

"Haworth. Who do you want?"

Amber slammed the receiver down and threw the phone as far as the cord would allow. *That did it! How can she use the name Haworth? They aren't married. Brian isn't divorced yet! What in the hell is that dumb bitch thinking?*

Claire arrived just before eight o'clock. "This place is super. Shall I spend the night?"

"Yes. I'm so lonely. I'll tell you about it after dinner."

Amber changed to her new red dress. A black silk pantsuit enhanced Claire's diminutive figure.

At Roxanne's they were seated by the marble fountain in the center of the dining area. The bubbling sound of the water soothed Amber's frayed nerves.

Back in the hotel room, Claire stretched across one of the beds and tucked her straight, chin-length, chestnut-brown hair behind her ears. "Tell me what has happened with you and Brian. Maybe I can help."

Amber sat down on the other bed and faced Claire. "No one can help but thanks for the offer. It's over between Brian and me. He's in love with someone else. And she's pregnant."

"Do you know who the woman is?"

"She answered my phone! Her name is Barbie Sue. I didn't get her last name. She's claiming the Haworth name already."

"A woman named Barbie Sue Ashlocke used to work in the editing department at Tech-View. I wonder if it's her. Not too many grown women would still be calling themselves Barbie Sue."

"What does Ms. Ashlocke look like?"

"She's a short blonde with a deep cleft in her chin."

"I'm going home tomorrow to get some of my things. Maybe

she'll be there. I'll let you know what she looks like. I might even find out her last name."

"Okay. I'll call you after I get off work tomorrow. Amber, Brian couldn't have been your Mr. Right."

"I should have known that. Fate wouldn't just plunk Mr. Right down in my own neighborhood! That would be too easy. We have to go through a maze to find each other. A maze that zigzags around the world. Do you think you'll ever meet your Mr. Right?"

"I don't know. I've checked out a lot of guys. Maybe some of us have to settle for Mr. Good Wrench."

"At least he'll keep your engine in tune."

"Yes. Maybe my body too."

Claire left the hotel at seven. Amber lazed in bed until nine. The dreaded encounter with Brian or Barbie Sue was unavoidable.

The taxi driver let Amber out in her driveway. A young woman answered the door. Her curly, bleached platinum-blond hair framed a pasty face and there was a slight cast to one of her big blue eyes. Her long-tailed blouse hung loosely over baggy jeans.

Amber looked closely at the woman's chin. *Oh, Lord! There's a deep cleft in it. She must be Ms. Ashlocke.* "Did you ever work at Tech-View in Burbank? Is your last name Ashlocke?"

"Yes, to both of your questions." The woman spoke with a cigarette dangling from the side of her mouth. "This is not your house anymore!" A clump of ashes dropped onto the plush blue carpet. "What do you want?"

"I want my grandmother's Damask Rose dishes, my clothes, my car and a few other things. I'm the lady of the house. What in the hell are you doing answering my door?"

"I'm the new lady of the house. You've been replaced. Come in and get your stuff out of my way. Hurry! I don't have all day."

Amber fought a desire to throw the woman out and lock the door. She pushed past her and ran upstairs to collect her things from the bedroom. She didn't recognize any of the clothes on her side of the closet. "What have you done with my clothes, you slut? You'd better come up here and talk to me before I come down there and punch your lights out."

Ms. Ashlocke took her time climbing the stairs. "You can't hit me! I'm going to have a baby!"

"Look, Bitch, just get me my clothes, my pictures and my grandmother's Damask Rose dishes. Then you can have Brian! Whose baby are you having? Or do you even know?"

Barbie Sue began to cry. "It's Brian's. It *is!*"

"Just give me my things, Girl! Cry on your own time."

Barbie Sue pointed to a cardboard box at the end of the hallway. "That's where I packed your clothes. Help yourself."

"I will! There should be a lot more clothes and other things here that belong to me and I want them all. Soon! Right now, I want my pictures and you'd better hurry it up!"

"Brian will sort them out later and send them to you. They're stored around here somewhere."

"Fine, just show me where the dishes are and give me the keys to my car. That would be the Mustang."

"Brian said not to tell you where your car keys are because some of his keys are on the ring too. You'll have to wait for him to take them off. I don't know where the damned dishes are. Come back tomorrow. I'll ask the maid to find them."

Amber picked up the box of clothes, pitched it down the stairs and hurried after it. *The heifer has a maid? I never had a maid. Maybe I didn't deserve one since I couldn't figure out how to get pregnant by my sterile husband.*

As she started walking down the driveway, she glanced back. Barbie Sue was standing on the porch.

Amber called out, "Please call a taxi for me or let me in and I'll call." She walked back toward the house. When she got near the porch, Barbie Sue yelled, "Here! Take your stupid old dishes." She threw a cardboard box at Amber. It grazed her arm before it hit the ground. Hearing the sound of breaking glass, she cringed. She sat down on the grass and opened the box. The teapot and several plates were broken. Barbie Sue ran back in the house and slammed the door.

Bailey, the postman came up the driveway. "Mrs. Haworth! Are you hurt?"

"No. I'm not Mrs. Haworth, though."

"Oh, are you the sister?"

23

"I'm Mrs. Nobody." She closed the box and stood up. Bailey picked it up and put it in his truck. Although it was against the rules, he offered her a ride. Amber handed him the box of clothes. "I don't want to cause you any trouble, so just take my boxes up to the convenience store on the corner and leave them. I'll walk up and take a taxi."

"You bet. I hope things will soon be okay with you."

Amber knew that things would never be okay again.

At the store, she called a taxi to take her back to her hotel.

She unpacked the clothing, set the box of dishes on the closet floor, and then dialed Brian's cell phone number. "I want my car, all the pictures of me and of my side of the family and the rest of my clothes, Brian!"

"Fine, if that's all you really want from me. Just don't think you can get away with coming around here anymore, causing trouble for Barbie Sue. Stay out of our lives!"

"Gladly! Mail my keys to my mother's house right away. Then you'd better send all the rest of my things to her too. I don't have a house anymore. Remember?" She hung up the phone, sat down on the bed and cried.

Claire called after work. "Shall we go out tonight?"

"I don't feel like going anywhere. Can you come to the hotel?"

"Sure. I'll be there in five minutes. Bye."

Claire kicked off her shoes and plopped down on a bed as soon as she came through the door. "Did she tell you she was Barbie Sue Ashlocke?"

"Yes. And she worked at Tech-View. She's the right whore."

"A woman is only a whore if she charges for it. She sounds like a real bitch, though. Barbie Sue is married! Her husband is in the military, somewhere overseas. The last man she was dating is from Thailand or some place in Asia. What if he's the father of her child? Brian would know the baby wasn't his if it looks Asian."

"It can't be his. He's sterile. I can vouch for that."

"What a mess. Shall I stay with you again?"

"No, I'll be okay. I need to plan my next step anyway."

After a breakfast served in her room, Amber called Willoughby at his office. "I want to come in."

"I'm glad. Book yourself on a flight whenever you're ready. We'll reimburse you."

"Okay. I'm going to see Mom first."

Genevieve McFarland hugged her daughter as she came into the living room. "It's good to see you, Amber. I'll take your things up to your old room. The coffee is ready to go, just push the button on the pot."

When Genevieve came back down, she brought out a plate of poppy seed cake and set it on the coffee table. "I slipped on this tacky shirt and old jeans but if you want to go out, I'll do a quick change."

"Mom, I just want to sit here and talk with you. Brian wants a divorce and I'm really hurt and confused. I always thought we were happy. I know I was."

"He didn't deserve you. I couldn't believe it when I heard what he had done. He wouldn't have told me if I hadn't called him to ask if he'd heard from you. His girlfriend answered the phone, so he had to explain."

When they finished their coffee and cake, Genevieve took the dishes to the kitchen. When she came back, she sat with Amber on the sofa and put her arm around her shoulder. "Someday you'll find the one who was meant for you."

"Yes, Mom, someday my prince will come. With my luck, someone else will be riding with him on his white horse. She'll probably be a blonde with a cleft in her chin!"

They spent the rest of the afternoon talking about happier times and looking through old photo albums. Genevieve handed Amber a picture of her with her sister Ari. "You two sure looked alike. You were a lot different in your ways, though. She was the quiet one and you were the one with a wild streak."

"Yes, I know. And where did I get it from? You and Dad had your moments. You always paid more attention to Ari. Was it because she was so quiet?"

Genevieve put the picture back and closed the album. "I only paid more attention to her because she needed it. You were out

25

with your father on weekends, doing your rough riding. Someone needed to be with Ari."

"You didn't know how to fly a plane or ride a motorcycle. Dad had to be the one to teach me. Ari didn't want to learn. Her idea of fun was going to the mall."

"I'm sorry I couldn't have been a Harley Mama for you."

"Lighten up. I'm glad you were the way you were. You were the best mother anyone could wish for."

"I was just teasing about the Harley Mama. I'm glad you're so tough and strong. You'll make a good agent."

"Reece Willoughby has a big mouth! If I had even hinted to you about my new status, he'd write me up for insubordination. That reminds me, Mom. I'll be leaving for Washington tomorrow."

Washington, D.C.

Amber took a taxi from the airport to her hotel. She called to let Willoughby know that she had arrived. They would wait until morning for their meeting.

Just as she was stepping out of the shower, the phone rang. She wrapped a towel around her waist and answered. "Hello."

"It's Emil. What about a late dinner?"

"Not tonight, thanks. I'm getting ready for bed. Anyway, I've had dinner. What are you doing in Washington?"

"Oh, they let me out of my cage once in a while. Can I come by for a drink? In the bar downstairs, I mean."

"Yes, ring my room when you arrive. I'll meet you. Give me at least a fifteen-minute notice."

When she hung up the phone, Willoughby called. "Emil is in Washington and he wants to see you. Has he called yet?"

"Yes, just a minute or so ago. Why?"

"He knows nothing about the breakup. I don't think you should mention it. Otherwise, he may come on to you. Right now, you're vulnerable."

Amber laughed and thought, *Vulnerable? How about horny?* "Whatever you think is best, Willoughby. If you were worried about my call from the singles' bar, that was just the booze talking.

I'm sorry about that. You should have known I wouldn't have gone home with a stranger. I just needed someone to want me. I'll see you tomorrow. Goodbye."

Amber lay sprawled across the bed with the damp towel still wrapped around her waist. Her arms were thrown back over the pillow, pulling her breasts taut.

She was almost asleep when Emil called back. She reached for the phone. "I'll be down in ten minutes." Not taking time to put on underwear, she slipped into the emerald-green pantsuit she had bought on her shopping trip and went down to the bar.

Emil stood and pulled a chair out for her.

After two drinks and three slow dances she invited him up to the room. When she switched the radio on, the song, "I Remember You" was playing. She asked Emil to dance, and for the first time since she'd known him, she noticed the color of his eyes. They were such a light hazel that they were almost golden, like his hair. He held her close against his body as they danced. Braless, Amber felt the gentle pressure against her breasts. She was ashamed of her feelings. *How can I feel drawn to Emil after being with Brian for so long? Maybe knowing that my husband is sharing our bed with Goldilocks has something to do with it.*

Emil pulled away when the song was over. "I should leave, because the way I'm feeling about you isn't right."

"Maybe it *is* right. My husband is divorcing me but now is not the time for us to be more than friends."

He took her hands in his. "I understand and I don't expect anything other than friendship. I want you to know that I've always been attracted to you. Sometimes, I imagined what it would be like to hold you in my arms. Not only while dancing, either."

"Brian and I were married right out of high school. I had never even dated anyone else. I have a meeting with Willoughby at PDI early tomorrow morning, so we'd better call it a night."

Emil let go of her hands, touched her lightly on the cheek and kissed her on the forehead. "Okay. I'll just be a friend, for now. Good night and take care."

Chapter 4

Biochemical Research Center
Sixty-three kilometers outside of Moscow

There was no death rattle. Just one shallow breath that sounded like a sigh and Alexei was gone. Doctor Sabine Heitbrock willed the monitor to show new movement. It only displayed the dreaded, final *flatliner*. She tried to revive him but Alexei was dead. Her son was dead because she couldn't save him, as she had saved others. Clasping his hands in hers, she cried. She cried for the little boy he had been and for the man he was and for the man he would never be. She removed the needles from his arms and took down the feeding tubes and containers. Sabine was angry. She was angry with the world, a world where illness and death prevailed. She wanted to smash the vials and grind the shards into powder with the heel of her shoe.

She went to her private lab, sat down at the long steel table, buried her face in her hands and let the tears flow.

When she could cry no more, she wiped her eyes and went back to Alexei.

Soon she heard a light knocking on the door. She opened it. Doctor Pavel Demidov was standing there with outstretched arms. His silver sideburns are a stark contrast to the coal-black color of the rest of his hair. Sabine stepped back until he entered the room.

"Oh, Pavel ... Alexei...."

He put his arms around her. "I know. He is gone."

"Please don't say he is better off, even if he is."

"I won't. I just want to hold you and try to comfort you."

"Alexei was only twenty-seven years old, the age that I was when I gave birth to him."

"I am so sorry. You need to report his death to the authorities immediately."

"I will. Then I'm coming back to be with him."

"Okay. I'll meet you here."

Sabine made the call, and then went back to Alexei. She spoke aloud. "What could I have done in my life that caused my son to suffer and die this way?" She hadn't heard Pavel return and she jumped up when he said, "I know you were not speaking to me, but I want to remind you that you have done nothing except work all of your life to make this world a better place." He took her hand and held it against his cheek. "Someone should speak to Svetlana about Alexei. I have a lot of work to do. I'll leave you, for now." He took his hand from hers and went back to his lab.

It was Sabine's sad duty to relay the news to Doctor Svetlana Antipova, Alexei's fiancée. She paused at the door of the main lab, phrasing the words in her mind before speaking. "He is gone."

Svetlana screamed out, "God in Heaven!" She began to wail and wring her hands.

Sabine moved close to her and whispered, "Control yourself. Someone may hear you."

Svetlana wiped her eyes. Grief for the dead must wait. There was work to do for the living.

When Sabine's work was finished for the day, she sat with her son's body. The heat had been turned off in the room and a deep chill hung in the air.

At midnight, Svetlana took over. She touched Alexei's hand and felt the stark cold of death. A feeling of utter despair enveloped her. Alexei Heitbrock was the love of her life, the only love she had ever known.

Just before dawn, Sabine glanced at the clock. It would soon be time to give the medicine to Cassandra. The last time she had checked, the little four-month-old girl lay in her crib, sleeping soundly, but now she was awake and hungry. Her sparse, almost platinum hair was damp, and lay flat against her head as if she had a fever. Sabine checked the baby's temperature. It was normal. She changed her diaper and gown. Then she crushed half of a Potassium Iodide tablet and mixed it with the formula. She held her close in her arms and talked to her while she fed her. Cassandra had been diagnosed with congenital hypothyroidism. She was one of the lucky ones, brought to the medical center soon after her birth, early enough to begin the treatments in time to prevent the worst of cretinism. There had been no motor rigidity or jaundice so far, although Sabine was concerned that Cassandra was sleeping a little too much. Sabine called for a nurse to take over.

Alena was there in five minutes. "How is our little angel this morning?"

"She had a restful night, finished her entire bottle and seems in a happy mood." Sabine kissed the baby's forehead and handed her to the nurse.

She carried a mug of coffee to the main lab and placed it on a table. Just as she was about to take a sip of her cooled coffee, she was startled by the sound of a gurney rattling toward her. Her hand shook. She spilled most of the coffee down her freshly laundered lab coat, knocking over a glass beaker in the process.

They were coming for Alexei. She would never see her son again. She jumped up, opened the door and looked out into the hallway. Two men were rolling the gurney. One of the men saw her and asked, "Where is the body that is to be removed?"

Holding back her tears, she led them to one of the anterooms. *Removed? Removed, as if my son were only an object.*

Svetlana was holding Alexei's hand and whispering to him. Wisps of her long blond hair had escaped the barrette and lay matted against her cheeks, wet with her tears. She began sobbing uncontrollably when she saw the gurney. Sabine coaxed her away from Alexei's bed and tried to comfort her even though her own heart was breaking.

They turned away as the men eased Alexei onto the gurney. His body now belonged to the government and there was nothing Sabine could do to change it.

She couldn't concentrate on her work. She went to the dining room to check on Cassandra and Darya, her six-year-old patient.

As Sabine entered, Alena looked up. "We'll be finished eating in a few minutes. Then I'll take Cassandra to the nursery."

"That's fine. I have some paperwork to do. Send Darya to the sunroom whenever she's ready."

Sabine put her papers aside when she heard the tinkling sound of a music box. Darya came waltzing in and set her music box down on a table. A tiny ballerina in a pink tutu was twirling around and around in the center. One arm had been broken off and it was always stored in the velvet-lined drawer of the box.

"Darya, did you finish your breakfast?"

"Yes, Doctor. I am ready to dance for you."

Sabine opened the brocade drapes, letting the sunlight filter through the wall-to-wall windows.

Darya began to dance, holding the chain of her Mona Lisa cameo pendant between the forefinger and thumb of her right hand, as she usually did when she danced. At bath time or bedtime, she always placed it back in the drawer of the box, next to the doll's arm.

She finished her dance with a flourish. Tipping her head to one side, she held her skirt out, spinning like a Whirling Dervish, while ignoring the beat of the music. After the final whirl, she tumbled onto the floor, laughing.

Sabine applauded vigorously and gave her usual, "Bravo!" She motioned for her to sit beside her on the sofa.

Darya touched the pendant. "I always had this." Then she pointed to the image of Mona Lisa. "This may be a picture of my mother. She may be dead, you know. That is why we cannot find her."

"She may be alive. We will keep looking for her."

Darya jumped up and squealed. "Doctor! There is a strange man peeking in the window at us."

Sabine looked out the window. The man had vanished. She took Darya by the hand and led her to the sitting room. She spoke to the nurse who sat working on the schedule. "Please keep Darya here with you. I'll be right back."

Sabine searched the immediate vicinity. There was no one to be seen. She went back to the sitting room. After the nurse walked out, Darya looked up, smiling. "Was that my father looking in the window?"

"No, Darya. Your father would have come in the front door and he would have asked for you."

Darya tugged on Sabine's sleeve. "Where is my father? He should be here with me."

31

"We don't know where he is. Maybe he doesn't know where you are either. Someday your father will find you and I know that he will love you as much as I do."

"I will dance for him when he finds me. Or maybe we will find him! I think I would like some hot chocolate, please."

"That's a good idea. I would like some too. With cream. Let's go back to the dining room."

Before taking Darya to the sitting room to study for the rest of the afternoon, Sabine took her to the lab for her medication.

After four years of living in foster homes, Darya was sent to an orphanage. Later, she was diagnosed as showing the first stages of cretinism and brought to the Research Center. They were told that Darya's mother had died in childbirth.

Sabine had checked her for signs of cretinism but found only a slightly low thyroid condition. Darya only needs the minimum dose of the medicine. She had seemed a little slow when she first arrived but now, with all the love and attention, she was approaching the expected level of mental growth for her six years. If the authorities knew she was in such good health they would send her back to the orphanage.

Sabine was not going to let that happen.

Chapter 5

Willoughby was waiting for Amber in his office. "Are you ready for the briefing?"

"Yes. Where will I be going next? And when am I going to get paid?"

"You'll be paid when I've finished talking to you and you'll know what your assignment is when the time comes. Please sit down." He leaned back in his chair as he spoke. "Any more questions before we send you to spy school?"

"Yes. Are you with the Langley group?"

He shook his head. "Absolutely not."

"Are you better or worse?"

"Neither. This is not a marriage contract, Amber. It's national security."

"Do you kill?"

"No, we leave that to the big boys from an agency you've never heard of. You won't be given any wet work to do."

She shook her head. "I would rather have it written in my contract, if you don't mind."

"We don't do contracts, we do dossiers. I can write it in yours if you like."

"I like."

"You may have to kill in self-defense. That's not wet work."

"Of course, I would kill anyone who was going to kill me! I'll see you after I've enjoyed a few days of R&R."

"No, Amber. We don't want a replay of L.A. Our singles' bars in Washington may have a few nosy agents lurking about."

"One trip to a singles' bar was enough. I was thinking about an innocent boat ride on Chesapeake Bay."

Willoughby took an envelope from the desk drawer. "Here's your new passport and payment for your last assignment. Report here tomorrow by seven a.m. You'll be taken to a training camp."

Training Facility Number 3
Somewhere in Virginia

Amber's room in the women's dormitory was furnished with four cots, a card table and four chairs. Closets lined the halls. She unpacked and went to the library, which doubles as a classroom. Her three roommates were already there. Only first names were used in the introductions. Belinda and Dahlia are tall, blonde Caucasians, Janelle a dark-haired, hazel-eyed black woman.

The instructor introduced himself, gave each person a few sheets of paper stapled together and left the room.

Most of the safety instructions listed for agents were things Amber had learned from her courier days. Only the first two rules were new to her.

1) Carry a concealed backup weapon when on a covert operation.

2) Do not take the first taxi in line.

3) Sit with your back to the wall or face a mirror in public places.

4) Always check for at least two escape routes before relaxing in a hotel or any public place.

The list went on and on through six pages.

When the instructor came back, he gave a demonstration on figuring compass direction without a compass, and then showed two films on martial arts and one on gun safety.

After the films were over, he went to the back of the room and pushed a button on the wall. Double doors slid open, revealing a gymnasium. It was definitely not a lose-pounds-get-fit type of gym. Several thick ropes dangled from the high ceiling. A huge wrestling mat lay in the center of the room. Boxing gloves were piled up against a wall.

The wrestling with each agent in turn wasn't easy for Amber. She won against Belinda, Dahlia kicked her butt and Janelle outdid her at the finish. Amber stood her ground for a few minutes against a couple of the men but lost to all five of them.

After dinner, Dahlia asked Amber if she wanted to go with them to the men's dormitory. "It's not what you might think! We just talk, dance and drink beer but not enough to slow us down the next day. You're welcome to join us if you like."

"Thank you. I'll see you there."

Amber took a quick shower, ran a brush through her hair, dressed in jeans and a T-shirt, and then joined her roommates. Music was blaring from a CD player.

Porter, a stocky blond, shook her hand and asked her to dance. Soon, a tall skinny guy cut in. "Hi. I'm Bubba. I'm pleased to meet you." The next song had such a fast, steady beat Amber could hardly keep up with Bubba. His ponytail flipped from side to side as he danced. Amber was relieved when the music ended. Dancing was not one of her strong points.

Stebbins stood and shook hands with her. He seemed too shy to be training as an agent. The dancing came to a standstill after Bubba brought in the beer and sodas.

Raleigh, a dark-haired, blue-eyed black man stretched out his hand to Amber and grinned. "Welcome to Basic Training."

"Gee. I thought this was Camp Peary!"

A tall redheaded man, with a matching goatee brought Amber a beer and a grape soda. "Take your pick or drink them both. I'm Warren."

Everyone took their drinks to a table and sat around talking. Amber said, "I was wondering why we give only a first or a last name. Does that mean we're all loose cannons here? Or can I know that?" No one answered. "I get it. Forget I asked."

Then Janelle spoke up. "I don't mind revealing my status. My last name is Brentwood and I spend most of my time in an office. I'd like to know why each of you joined."

Warren spoke first. "I needed money, but I didn't want a regular nine-to-five job. I guess I wanted intrigue and some time off in between." He looked at Stebbins. "You're next."

"I joined because I had nothing better to do. I don't have a family, so I guess I'm pretty good agent material. That's it. End of story. What about you, Janelle? Why are you here?"

35

"I'm following in my dad's footsteps. He didn't expect his little girl to enter the field that he had trained for. I surprised him by joining up after I finished college."

Dahlia said, "Come on, let's eat! I brought sandwiches and cookies." She opened a large box. "Dig in. We can talk in between mouthfuls. I'll go next. My boyfriend told me I was indecisive and couldn't stick with a job. He wanted me to find a job that I could turn into a career. I did. Now, he complains because he doesn't see me often enough. Serves him right! Raleigh, you're next up."

"Can it wait? That's my song and it makes me wanna boogie. Who's ready to start shaking?"

All of them danced with him through his special song. Then he took a cream soda from the cooler, popped it open and took a sip. "A guy from a well-known agency came to my university and spoke to a few of us about joining the company. I took him up on his offer. That's about it."

Belinda said, "I lost my husband last year. The big lug didn't die on me. I lost him to a long-legged super model. After the grieving period was over, I stopped feeling sorry for myself and decided I'd become a super spy." She reached for a sandwich. "How about you, Bubba?"

"I lived in a little country town in the Ozarks where the only real industry was a cotton mill. We had a comb factory, but it went bust. Most of the folks in the area were farmers. My family had a big peach orchard, a strawberry patch and plenty of vegetables growing on sixty acres. I wanted out. Out of town and out of a boring life. Pass the cookies, Porter. Tell us your story."

"I've got a sad story. Are you sure you want to hear it?" Every one of them nodded and cheered him on.

"I was a cop. One night, my partner and I were asked to respond to an emergency call. A woman had reported a possible break-in. When we arrived, weapons drawn, my partner went to the front door, while I checked out the back of the house. The woman came out of a sliding door, pointing a gun toward me. I told her to put it down. She didn't. She kept walking, stammering and waving the gun back and forth. Then she pointed it straight at me. I shot her. I shot the victim! She is paralyzed from the waist down. I resigned that night. I have never gotten over what I did. I still see her in my dreams. So, here I am, still trying to forgive myself."

Amber didn't go into detail about herself. "I'm newly divorced and I just needed to get away. Boring, huh? It sure is good to know all of you, but I think I'm gonna hit the sack. We've got a long hike tomorrow. I heard that our path is peppered with mudholes. That should make it interesting."

Day 2

The morning began with a five-mile hike with full packs. No one passed out or gave up, although there was a lot of grumbling. The way back was on a different road. Toward the end of the last mile, the agents all sank deep into the mud. Their boots made squishing sounds as they slogged through the muck. Amber almost made it back to camp before she slipped and fell. She got up, wiped her face on her sleeve, and marched on.

Day 3

After breakfast, the trainees were subjected to a ten-minute pep talk, and then taken to a field for a running contest. Running was Amber's forte. She had entered a dozen marathons and had placed second in a couple of them. *I've got this contest aced!*

The women lined up to race. When the signal sounded, Amber sped off, gaining ground almost immediately. Janelle ran a close second. Belinda and Dahlia were not even close. It wasn't more than a couple of minutes before Janelle caught up to Amber and ran neck in neck with her.

As they neared the last lap Janelle made a wild dash and passed her. Amber tried to catch up, but she didn't make it.

Janelle won, although she stands just five-feet tall.

Amber shook Janelle's hand and congratulated her. *So much for all those marathons! Maybe I'll never be a winner.*

Before the starting signal was given for the men to run, Amber was sent back to her barracks. Without explanation, she was told to pack up. She was to be taken back to Washington for a briefing.

Washington, D.C.

As soon as Amber stepped into Willoughby's office, he closed the door. "Keep your backpack on. Your first mission requires special training. You'll be taken to a different camp for five days. Escorts for the flight are waiting in the cafeteria. I'll go down with you and introduce you."

He led her to a table near the far wall. "Gentlemen, I'd like you to meet your passenger. This is Amber."

A tall thin man stood and offered his hand to her. His brown hair was streaked with silver. "I'm Dietrich. I'm glad to meet you."

The other escort, a dark-skinned man with curly black hair stood and pulled a chair out for her. "We'll have a short wait before we meet our driver. My name is Parkins."

Amber turned to Willoughby. "Goodbye."

"See you later. Have fun." He chuckled and walked away.

Training Camp for Foreign Operations
Somewhere in Nebraska

On arrival, Agent Parkins rented a car for the drive to the camp. At the entrance gate, a man in a military jeep escorted Amber through, leaving the two agents on the outside. The narrow road leading into the camp was extremely bumpy. The driver let her out in front of a wooden building. "Someone in there will get you started."

A soldier in a khaki uniform filled her in on the routine, and then issued her three sets of fatigues and a pair of combat boots. "You're in the third row of barracks, number twenty-seven. Unload your gear and report to the library." He pointed to the first building on the left. As Amber walked toward the barracks, a line of men marched past. One of the men looked at her and started whistling "When the Swallows Come Back to Capistrano."

She knew he was smarting off because she was a female trainee. He was referring to the former Soviet female agents called "Swallows," who during the cold war were sent to seduce foreign agents, with the intention of trapping them into divulging vital information, resorting to blackmail if all else failed. The male agents trained to seduce were called "Ravens."

Amber couldn't resist a retort. "I see the Raven has landed!" She heard laughter as the troops filed by. She walked on to the barracks. There were four beds in her room but no sign of a roommate. She went to the library and sat down at a table, waiting for someone to show up.

A lanky man with a bald head came in and sat down at a desk across the room from her. "I'm Corporal Renard. I'll go over your schedule with you." He took a file from a wire basket on his desk. "You will awaken each day at five o'clock and be at the chow tent by five-thirty. You will have forty minutes to load your tray and eat. Then you begin your training. Each morning you will find a note under your door stating where you are to report." He marked the file in red and put it back in the basket. "Dinner will be at six p.m. You are dismissed."

She went back to her room and unpacked the few clothes she had brought. She glanced at her watch. *Twenty-five minutes until chow time.*

Amber quickly bathed and dressed, then went to dinner. She followed the other trainees to the food line and on to the only table that wasn't covered with a tarp. *Oh, great. I have to sit with that rude marching guy?* She nodded as each of the men introduced themselves. The marching guy was Greg. *He's more like Mr. Gregarious.* The others were Chugger, Wycliffe, Blevins, Martin, and Raol. There wasn't much socializing going on. It had been a rough and tiring day for most of them.

When Amber stood to leave, Raol said, "I'll see you tomorrow morning at the library. I'll be your first date."

Day 2

Amber rushed through her breakfast to meet Raol. He was waiting in front of the library. "You're going to learn how to load, aim and shoot to kill." She followed him to the firing range. "I already have sharpshooter status."

"Professionally speaking?"

"No, but I've earned a few medals."

"Have you fired a Makarov or a Kalashnikov lately?"

"Kalashnikov, ten years ago, Makarov, never." *I must be going somewhere in Russia.*

Raol held up a Makarov. "This little gem is a blowback-action, semi-automatic Pistolet. Its 9-millimeter cartridge has a floating firing pin, without a spring or FP block. It operates as a double-action or single-action." He demonstrated it. "Take this baby and show me your stuff."

She checked it out and moved toward the target. Her first shot missed the bulls-eye by a few inches. After several more tries she hit it dead center.

Raol nodded his approval. "Good going." He took the Makarov from her and replaced it with a Kalashnikov. She checked it, loaded it, aimed and fired. Bulls-eye, dead on. She turned back to Raol. "Shall I keep on firing?"

"No. You're okay for today. In a couple of days, you can try with a real target, the silhouette. Where the heck did you train, anyway?"

"My father started training me when I was twelve years old. Practice was always part of our weekend."

"Smart man." He took the weapon from her. "My next trainee will be here shortly. You're going to get some real exercise now." He pointed to a group of men that were walking toward the gymnasium. "Catch up to those guys. They're in your exercise group."

The calisthenics were easy, then came the rope climbing. Amber remembered it from her high school gym class. She did okay, although her hands got sore from rope burns.

The next stop was in a wooded field in front of a long line of tall trees. In turn, they climbed each tree, and then slid back down to the ground. Next was climbing more trees and jumping from the lowest branches. Amber was first. She made it to the top and back down to the lower branches without effort. As she jumped, she scraped her hand against the rough bark. She looked at her bloody hand and winced.

Greg held up a hand. "Oh, dear, broke a nail."

She laughed, although she resented the remark.

Amber was called back to the library and given tools for picking locks. *What? I'm training to be a burglar?* She was taken to a group of buildings to practice unlocking different types of locks on keyholes, briefcases and safes. Then she pried open a few windows and a glass sliding door. *What could my mission be?*

Then she was taken to test her driving skills. Her instructor led her to the first vehicle. "This is an older model and year of the Chaika. The keys are in the switch, so let's do some tricks." He slid into the driver's seat of another Chaika and took off with a lurch.

She followed his lead, making sharp turns, sudden stops and playing a game of chicken.

He stopped next to her and got out. "You're pretty good. Now let me see how fast you can drive without wrecking it. Its top speed is a hundred and fifty-eight kilometers per hour. That's pretty close to a hundred miles per hour."

She pressed down on the pedal and floored it. She got it up to a hundred and thirty kilometers per hour before she slowed down, stopped, and then drove back to the starting point.

The instructor grinned. "Not too bad. You almost hit eighty miles per hour. Now let's see how you do on one of our Russian motorcycles." He opened a shed to reveal four Urals. "Choose your weapon."

Amber had driven Urals on many occasions. She hopped on the first bike and took off, taking only a couple of minutes to get it up to its top speed. She surprised him with quick turns and stops. Jumping over ramps was nothing new to her.

He put an arm up to stop her and motioned for her to head back.

She drove slowly back and stopped beside him. "Well ...?"

"Well, well! You get an A. You're done for the rest of the day."

"Good. Thanks for the lessons. I'll see you around." She went back to the barracks to clean up.

She barely had time to shower and dress before she heard a loud knocking on the door. *Now what?* She opened it and found Corporal Renard standing there with an attaché case. "Your agency has requested your immediate return to Washington. I'll drive you to the airport."

She grabbed her things and stuffed them in her backpack.

Washington, D.C.

Amber arrived at PDI, both tired and hungry. Willoughby met her in the second-floor hallway. "We're going to talk in one of the larger briefing rooms today. Come with me." He opened the door to a room Amber didn't know existed. A table was laden with sandwiches, pastries and a platter of cheese and fruit.

She grinned. "It's not your birthday, so what's the occasion?"

"You are the occasion. I thought you might be hungry after your flight. I'm sorry we had to rush you back here. Let's sit at the table so you can get started on the food." He sat down across from her. "Soon, you'll leave for your first mission." He poured a cup of coffee for her. "One of our top medical scientists, Doctor Sabine Heitbrock, has recently been taken from a highly classified medical laboratory complex in Maryland. We have learned that she is working in a research center near Moscow. Your job will be to get Doctor Heitbrock out of Russia."

"Why would the Russians take her? They must have plenty of scientists of their own."

"She has discovered something the Russians haven't. They found out about her discovery and spirited her away. One of our agents-in-place, Doctor Ludmila Nikolaevna Kirsinova, has been accepted for employment as Sabine Heitbrock's assistant at the Biochemical Research Center in Russia. Posing as Doctor Kirsinova, you will work alongside Sabine Heitbrock until you find a way to get her out of Russia. Ludmila will give you a passport and any other documents you need when you meet her in Finland."

"Why doesn't she take the mission?"

"She has had no training as an agent. She only advises us on certain issues and developments in the medical field. That's all you need to know at this time. Your final briefing will be in this office, just before you leave for Finland." He opened the top drawer of his desk and drew out an airline ticket and a folder. "Tomorrow you'll fly back to California. I'm sorry I have to rush you. Medical journals for you to study are in the folder."

Amber glanced at the titles of the journals and frowned. She put the journals down on his desk. "Embryology? Genetics? Am I a medical genius?"

He put the journals back in her hands. "Read them. Then destroy them. I'll meet you in Burbank in a couple of days."

"Just for the record, why was I taken out of camp?"

"It was because of your record. The report said you didn't need any more of that type of training."

"I was expelled from spy school for being too capable? Will I get a bonus for that?"

"Don't be absurd, Kid. You weren't *that* good. Anyway, I had asked them to send you back because we need to speed up this mission. After it's completed, you'll be sent to another camp for several weeks of surveillance training before your next assignment. I've already reserved a room for you at the Riverdale hotel for tonight. Go get some rest. Don't oversleep. You have to catch that plane tomorrow."

Arianne "Ari" Cosgrove got out of a taxi in front of the Potomac Decorating Institute and entered the building. She felt a keen sense of excitement. She had been summoned to her first briefing at PDI. She'd been taken aback when her godfather first approached her about becoming an agent. After she accepted the offer she spent six weeks at a training camp. Now she was about to embark on a career that would prove to be much more exciting than her job as an instructor at a posh health club. Using the code, she took the elevator up to Willoughby's office and knocked lightly on the door.

He opened it and motioned for her to enter. Before closing the door, he raised his voice slightly. "It's good to see you, Amber." He placed a finger to his lips to shush Ari as he escorted her into the office. "Sit down and rest." He pointed to the armchair. "There is a debriefing in progress down the hall. I'm sorry about calling you by your sister's name but no one in the agency is to know that Amber has a twin. I couldn't risk having you both around here at the same time, so I rushed her back to California. I haven't told her that you'll be working with her. You can tell her. You'll just be in Washington for a couple of days. I'm expecting another agent soon, so come back tomorrow around noon for a few pointers. There'll be a briefing with you and Amber together when I come to California."

"What if someone thinks I'm Amber and stops to talk to me? Can I see pictures of the agents who know her?"

"No pictures. I'll describe the agents you might run into. Slaney is forty-five years old. He has a mustache that matches his slightly long, sandy-colored hair. You probably won't run into Emil, but you need to know what he looks like, just in case. He is twenty-five years old, tall and blond. You won't see Cotter, an old friend of Amber's. He's away on an assignment. I've got you booked on a flight back to Los Angeles for the day after tomorrow. Until then, you are registered at the Riverdale Hotel, under Amber's name. Give me a call if you have a problem of any kind. There'll be a taxi waiting by the time you get downstairs." He handed her the plane ticket and walked her out to the hallway.

Ari went to dinner in the hotel restaurant soon after she checked in. She thought about ordering a steak. Then she remembered that she was impersonating her twin, a vegetarian. Dinner would be pasta and a salad tonight.

Just as she finished her shower and was ready for bed, the phone rang. Assuming no one else knew she was there, she figured it must be Willoughby. It wasn't. A stranger's voice came over the line. "Hi, Amber, it's Emil. I saw you take the elevator as I was going into the bar. Can I come up?" Ari moved the phone away from her ear for a second. *What a disaster! My first night as an agent and someone found me. And he thinks I'm Amber!* She felt obligated to see him. "Give me a couple of minutes." She dressed in jeans and a black sweatshirt.

When Emil walked in, Ari felt an immediate attraction to him. He put his arms around her and kissed her. Guilt swept over her. This was the first time she had been kissed since her husband, Evan had been killed. She needed to be an actor now. She returned the kiss and feelings of desire that had lain dormant engulfed her.

Four years is a long time to be celibate.

Ari eased out of his arms and suggested they order a bottle of wine. On the phone to room service, she almost slipped and used her own name. She'd have to remember that tonight and as long as she was covering for Amber, she *is* Amber. She sat down on the sofa and motioned for him to join her.

Emil sat beside her, reached across to the end table and turned the radio on. "How about a little music?"

"Sure. Whatever you want to hear is okay with me."

He turned the dial to soft romantic music, and then pulled Ari up from the sofa to dance to "When I'm With You."

When the music ended, Emil kept his arms around her, drew her closer and kissed her. Ari *needed* him to make love to her. She wouldn't resist.

She was ready when he danced her over to the bed, ready to accept any and all of the pleasure he could give her. He undressed her and began kissing her neck and shoulders, moving slowly down to her breasts. She felt the warmth of his breath against her. There was no need for foreplay. Ari was as soft as Emil was hard. He undressed and lay beside her.

When he could contain himself no longer, he took her in his arms and entered the pink velvet.

Chapter 6

Burbank, California

Genevieve was waiting by the window. She opened the door before Amber could ring the bell. "Welcome back!"

Amber dropped her things onto the hall table. "I'm glad to be home, Mom."

Genevieve put her arms around her. "I'm not supposed to ask about your work, but I worry about you being so far away."

"Don't worry about me. My work is easy. Let's sit and talk." She sat down on the sofa.

Genevieve sat beside her. "You probably know that Ari has been away too. I've been lonely without either of my girls."

Amber patted her on the shoulder. "I'm here, now. Anyway, that's enough about me. Tell me what you've been up to since I've been gone."

Genevieve hesitated a moment. "What would you think about me moving away from California?"

"Where to?"

"Washington. Reece Willoughby has asked me to marry him and I have accepted."

Amber rose from the sofa and picked up the photo of her parents from the mantel, taken on their wedding day. She sat back down next to Genevieve and handed her the photo. "Dad has only been dead for two years. How could you fall in love with someone else so soon?" She stood and turned her face away, masking her anger.

"Please look at me. Willoughby and I were in love long before he met Rowena. We had an affair."

"Oh, my God, Mother! My godfather? How could you?" She reached for the nearest chair and somehow landed in it. "That was a big surprise."

"Your father had been having affairs for a long time. I stayed with him because of you and your sister."

"Is the whole world sex crazy? My own parents? I must have had my head in the sand all these years. I'm not Uncle Will's daughter am I, Mom?"

"Of course, not! I would never have had sex with someone that I wasn't married to. You should know that!"

"You just said you had an affair with him."

"In my day, an affair didn't always mean sleeping together. It could just mean going out to dinner with someone you weren't married to."

"Ari and I have been adults and on our own for a long time. Why didn't you leave Dad?"

"By then Grandma Lilia was ill. After I used my inheritance for her treatments, I didn't know where to turn so I stayed with your father. I quit my job to care for her."

"I remember when she died. It was so sad."

"She was so frail by then that I could hold her on my lap in the recliner, as if she were a little girl. She died in my arms in that chair. She had been telling me about her life and love as a young woman in Russia. Then suddenly she was gone." Genevieve started crying.

"Mom, you were always a wonderful daughter for Grandma. You did your best for all of us."

Genevieve wiped her eyes. "I never told your father that I knew about his affairs. By then, it didn't matter, but I was lonely. That's why I started going out with Willoughby. He accepted the situation and was always a friend to both of us. He didn't ask me nor expect me to break my wedding vows, although he knew that your father was breaking his."

"I understand now, Mom. If I had known, I would have been more of a help to you. You should have confided in me."

"You girls loved your father so much. I didn't want you or Ari to change your feelings toward him." She put her arms around her daughter. "Amber, I need to be with Willoughby. Please give me your blessing."

"I give you my blessing. Grab some happiness. I love you."

"Thanks. I love you too." She moved back and looked at Amber. "I just needed to know the marriage would be okay with you. Ari already knows and she said she is happy for me. Now, how about ordering a giant pizza and a salad?"

"Okay. Sounds good to me!" Amber reached for the phone to

place the order. Just before she touched it, it rang. It was Claire. "Barbie Sue's divorce came through today. They are going to be married as soon as your divorce is final. She's in Saint Agatha's hospital and she's about to have the baby. I heard this through the grapevine at work. Gotta go! My break's over. Bye."

After their dinner order had been called in and delivered, Amber sat with her mother in the living room while they ate. They finished up the meal with a fresh pot of coffee.

Amber sat down in the recliner and tried to relax after Genevieve went to bed.

Brian called. "I want you to know I'm going to get a restraining order against you. Stay away from Barbie Sue. I have written a letter to your boss, telling him to warn you to keep away from us. I faxed it this morning."

"Go fax yourself!" She dropped the receiver onto its cradle and went to the kitchen. *I need a chocolate fix. It's Hershey Bar time!*

Amber woke early and called the hospital. Barbie Sue had given birth in the night. When Amber finished dressing, she ran down the stairs to the kitchen. "Mom, can I use your car for a couple of hours?"

"Sure. The keys are on the mantel."

Amber drove to the hospital and went directly up to the maternity ward. A nurse stopped her in the hall. "Who are you looking for?"

"I'm here to see the Haworth baby."

"Are you a relative?"

"It's rumored that I'm to be the godmother." *It is a rumor. I just started one.*

"Follow me." The nurse led her to the glassed-in nursery and pointed out the Haworth baby. There in the second crib from the left lay a tiny baby wrapped in a blue blanket. *It must be a boy. Brian should be happy.* There was no tinge of yellow to the baby's skin. No one would suspect that Brian wasn't the biological father. Barbie Sue had won.

Amber felt a constricting deep in her chest. *Brian has a son, but he may never know that he is not the biological father. Maybe the son will never know either.* As she was walking to the elevator, Brian came out of it with a bouquet of flowers in his hand. "What the hell are you doing here, Amber?"

"Just looking at your son. So?"

"I asked you to stay away from Barbie Sue!"

"I didn't go near the bitch. I just wanted to see the baby."

Raising his voice to a fever pitch, Brian pointed his finger at her. "You were not supposed to see him! That's the main reason I was getting the restraining order. Barbie Sue was afraid you would try to steal the baby."

"Do I look like some desperate, crazy woman who'd want to steal a baby? I certainly would not want Barbie Sue's! Give me some credit."

"Then why did you come here?"

"This may be hard for you to understand. I wanted to see if the baby looked like you." She couldn't tell him that she only wanted to see if the baby was part Asian.

"He does look like me, doesn't he? I'm sorry I treated you so badly. I didn't intend to hurt you. Barbie Sue promised me kids and I have always wanted a son to carry on my name. I didn't plan for any of this to happen. I swear. Now, I want a new life."

"Oh, you were bored with the old one?"

"Something like that."

"I gather you weren't bored with the old house!"

"If you really want the house I'll sell it back to you."

"The hell you say! I sure wouldn't live there after Goldilocks has been sleeping in my bed! Not to mention her cigarette ashes falling all over the place and the house smelling like stale smoke."

"I don't want to argue with you." He started walking away. Then he turned back. "I did love you, you know. Really love you."

"That was a lifetime ago."

Back at Genevieve's house, Amber thought about her life. She didn't want to stay with her mother or Ari for long. She'd had her own home with Brian since she was eighteen years old. Life as she had known it for so long was to be a memory. *Eleven years of loving someone. Eleven years of life down the drain.* She brought in the mail and found her car keys in an envelope from Brian. She opened the priority letter from his lawyer, knowing she would find the divorce papers inside. Brian was free to marry Barbie Sue. It was really over. "Mom, can you drive me to get my car?"

"Sure, Honey, let's go."

As they approached the house, Amber felt as though her past had been erased. She had known and loved Brian for as long as she could remember. Now, she must forget him and move on. The house was not hers anymore. Her Mustang was in the driveway. She had been dismissed from Brian's life.

She followed Genevieve back to her house. Genevieve suggested that they go out for dinner. Ari had returned. The three of them could make it a girl's night out.

"That sounds like fun, Mom. I haven't seen Ari since I came back. I'll pick her up."

After dinner, Amber dropped Genevieve off before driving on to Ari's house in Toluca Lake. She told Ari about the breakup with Brian. She hesitated a moment before telling her about the baby.

"What if the baby really is his? Maybe that doctor lied about Brian being sterile."

"Why would the doctor lie? Anyway, if Brian wasn't sterile wouldn't I have gotten pregnant at least once in all of those years?"

"I guess. Do you think you'll ever marry again?"

"No! I just want to be myself. I don't need anyone. I'll be just fine with a little romance, a candlelight dinner and someone to dance with and maybe an occasional bedtime story. What about you? Are you seeing anyone?"

Ari's face turned ashen. She opened her mouth but no words came out.

Amber asked, "What's wrong?"

"I have something to tell you and I'd give anything if it hadn't happened."

She walked over to the window and opened the curtains, pausing to organize her words.

"I went to Washington for a quick briefing with Uncle Will. I am to go on assignment with you because I can cover for you."

"Why wasn't I asked before he talked to you?"

"He had to talk to me first. He wasn't sure I'd want to work for them. Anyway, that's not the worst part. There's more."

"If it's worse than that news, I don't want to hear it."

"I don't want to tell you, but I have to because I'm your sister. When I was in Washington I met Emil. I had a one-night stand with him."

After the initial shock, Amber recovered. "Why did you think you had to tell me about it? That's your business, Sis."

Ari walked away from the window and sat down on the sofa. "He thought I was you."

Amber was aghast. "And you didn't tell him different?"

"I couldn't, because no one in the agency besides Uncle Will can know you have a twin. I'm so sorry. You aren't in love with Emil, are you?"

"No, I'm not. We just work together and I consider him a friend. Don't worry about it. Maybe Emil has a secret twin too. Let's just pretend you slept with the twin. Enough serious stuff. Turn on the music and bring out the booze!"

Ari turned the stereo on, and then went to the kitchen. She checked the cupboards and found a bottle of white wine. She called out, "Hey, Amber. What about a glass of wine with a couple of scoops of vanilla ice cream?"

"A wine float, huh? That sounds good."

Ari brought the drinks to the coffee table. "There is one more thing I need to confess."

Amber threw her hands up. "Do I look like a priest to you?"

"No, you don't, but you need to hear this. Do you remember Waldo Farnsworth? He was in your math class in tenth grade."

"Was he the guy with kinky red hair?"

Ari nodded. "Yes. One night after a school dance we drove up to Bristol Point, where all the kids went to neck."

"Not all. I never did. Get to the point, Ari."

"Waldo couldn't tell us apart. None of the kids could. I lost my virginity to Waldo that night. It was you he had a crush on … so I just let him think I was you."

Amber snorted with laughter. "You lost *my* virginity and I never knew it. That's twice you have used me as an excuse for your indiscretions. It had better be the last time, Ari!"

"Why were you laughing? Aren't you angry?"

"Yes, I'm angry! I laughed to keep from smacking you. Anyway, tomorrow is a big day for Mom. I'm going to get some sleep."

Genevieve slipped the golden topaz ring that had belonged to her mother onto her right hand. It would be her "something old." The yellow rosebud tucked in her dark-brown hair was "something new." She called out to her daughters who were still upstairs getting dressed for the wedding. "Amber! Ari! I need some advice. Would one of you come down here for a minute?"

Ari went downstairs. "Mom, how can I help?"

"I need something borrowed and something blue."

Ari unfastened the locket with the pictures of her husband and her son. "What about my gold locket? You can borrow it for today. It will look good with your outfit."

"It's perfect. Thank you. I still need something blue."

"Your contact lenses are blue."

"Oh, yeah, right. So, I guess I'm all set now. Set to make a big change in my life."

"Life goes on, Mom."

"Yes, it does. What about your life?"

"I don't know. Sometimes, I think I want to find someone, although it would be hard to replace a man like my Evan and I could never, ever replace little Roddy."

"Oh, Honey, I'm so sorry. We'd better change the subject or we'll both be crying! Anyway, it's time to leave."

Reece Willoughby arrived at the Los Angeles International Airport wearing a white tuxedo. A limousine was waiting at the curb and Willoughby was on the way to his wedding.

Genevieve and her daughters were waiting at the office of a justice of the peace. The bride was wearing a yellow silk suit. She carried a bouquet of orchids with touches of fragrant yellow plumeria and white stephanotis.

After the wedding ceremony, Amber and Ari were invited to a champagne brunch to celebrate.

Before it was time to say goodbye, Amber asked her mother to go to the powder room with her.

When they were alone, she held Genevieve's eyes with her own. "Mom, I hope you'll be happy in this new life. I know Dad couldn't have been the right one for you or he wouldn't have cheated on you." Genevieve took her daughter's hands in hers. "Amber, I have come to the conclusion that some of us have to marry the wrong person in order to have the right children."

Two days later, the honeymoon was over. It was time to hold the briefing at Ari's house.

Amber asked Willoughby what their code names would be.

"You are Jonathan. You both are."

"Am I Jona or Than?"

"Share it. *We* know who Jonathan is. Until this assignment is over, only Slaney and I will know your code name."

"Why give us a man's name?"

"It's also a bird's name. Do you remember the book about Jonathan Livingston, the seagull? I picked the name Jonathan because you are like him. You want to fly free."

"I guess those days are over for me."

He shook his head. "Not necessarily. I chose both of you to work this operation because you are identical twins and can cover for each other. Thanks to having your Russian grandmother in your home when you were growing up, you speak the language without an accent. This is not a milk run. Use extreme caution every step of the way. The code name for this operation is Winterset. Amber, get Doctor Heitbrock out before winter sets in." He moved his chair closer to them and continued. "Always check the mirror in hotels and public restrooms. Place your forefinger with the tip of your nail touching the surface of the mirror. There should be a gap between your nail and the image. If your nail is flush with the image, then it is a two-way mirror. Leave the area. You may hear it called a one-way mirror. Either is correct."

Amber asked, "Will I have a contact in Moscow?"

"All messages are to be given and received through our cobbler in Sergiev Posad, a town just a few kilometers from the research center. The cobbler will be your contact."

Ari cut in. "A cobbler? What does a cobbler have to do with this operation?"

"I'm sorry. I assumed you were told at camp. In intelligence jargon a passport is called a *shoe*. So, the experts who forge passports, visas and other documents are called cobblers. Don't you read spy novels?"

Amber laughed. "She reads romance novels."

Willoughby frowned. "C'mon, Amber, cut it out!"

"Sorry. Is there a code when approaching the cobbler?"

"Yes. Ludmila will give you the code when she briefs you. You will get a message to Ari when and if you need her to cover for you. If the operation goes bust, report it as *Gone Humpty Dumpty.* Then both of you get the heck out. Technically, you are illegals. For this mission PDI will consider you as legals, which means that no matter what happens, we will not abandon nor disown you when you are on the mission."

Amber said, "I'd hate to be disowned by my godfather!"

Willoughby growled. "Don't think I haven't thought about it more than once over the years! Now, how about making us some coffee? I need to speak with your sister."

After Amber had gone to the kitchen, Willoughby said, "Ari, in a few minutes someone is coming here to meet you. He's the man you are going to marry."

Ari stared at Willoughby in disbelief. "What in the world are you talking about? That's not funny!"

"No, it isn't. It just happens to be your job on this operation. Your cover will be as a newly married woman who accompanies her husband to Moscow, where he is employed in our embassy. The marriage ceremony or certificate won't be authentic. You are in no way obligated to be his wife."

Ari was shocked. She couldn't think of a retort. She went back to the kitchen. "Amber, please take the cups and spoons to the living room. I'll bring the coffee in when it's ready."

When the guest walked into the living room, Amber said, "Slaney! What are you doing in Surfin' Land? You've cut your hair and shaved your mustache. What's the special occasion?"

Slaney didn't answer. He just shook his head and grinned.

Willoughby called out, "Ari, will you join us, please?"

She put the coffee pot, a sugar bowl and a pitcher of cream on a tray, carried it to the living room and set it on the coffee table.

Willoughby introduced Slaney to her. Ari felt her face turning pink when Slaney took her hand and said, "I'm happy to meet you. May I have your hand in marriage, Mademoiselle?"

Although her heart was pounding and threatening to exit her chest, she managed to whisper, "Yes."

Amber stood stock-still, waiting for one of them to explain the joke to her.

Willoughby told her about the cover plan.

When the meeting was over, Amber walked out to his car with him, leaving Ari and Slaney to get acquainted. "Willoughby, I need to ask you something. Mom told me that Dad had had affairs. You were close with him and I know he confided in you. Did he ever have a child with any of the other women?"

"I had planned to tell you someday, but I think you need to know now. Greta Faulkner was his only long-term affair and she had a daughter by him." He paused, dreading to disclose the identity of the daughter. "It's Barbie Sue, Brian's wife. She is your half-sister. I'm sorry."

Amber felt as though her heart had stopped. She couldn't feel it beating. She stood motionless without expression.

Willoughby put his hand on her shoulder. "Snap out of it. You've had a shock, I know. I had to tell you. It's your right to know. Your mother doesn't know, so keep it that way."

She spoke softly in a voice that was not her own. "I hope there will be no more earth-shattering news for me. What has happened to my world? First, I find out my husband has left me, and now you tell me that the woman he married is my half-sister. That means the baby is my nephew! I have to get away from here. After I talk to Barbie Sue."

Amber drove to the house that now belonged to another. A thick cloud of cigarette smoke wafted across Amber's face as Barbie Sue opened the door. "Come in. You know, don't you?"

55

Amber nodded. "Yes. I'd still like to hear your side of the story if you don't mind."

"Have a seat."

"I'll stand. Please refrain from smoking while I'm here. Anyway, do you know how much you're hurting your baby?"

"Don't try to get me to stop smoking! I have been smoking since I was thirteen years old and I'm doing fine."

"Then keep on killing yourself and maybe your baby too. While I'm in this house, do not smoke!"

Barbie Sue grimaced, sat down on the sofa and crushed the cigarette into a half-eaten slice of toast on a paper plate. "If it's any consolation, I went after Brian. I stalked him. I had seen you two together a few times at Paddy's Irish Rose Club where some of us from Tech-View hung out. I decided that I would try to take him away from you because I wanted to hurt you. You don't know how much I wanted our dad to be with my mother and me, but he would never leave you girls or your mother. She never knew about me."

"So, you stole my husband to get even with me because my father wouldn't desert us for you and your mother? Do you know how ridiculous that is?"

"I'll admit it was a rotten thing to do. I'm not sorry, though. Dad came to visit us every other weekend and on holidays. I still treasure the porcelain doll he bought me for Christmas when I was six years old. She has a blue silk dress and her eyes are blue like mine and her curls are like mine were then. Dad said he chose that doll because it looked like me. He started calling me his little porcelain doll after that Christmas day."

Amber turned pale. "May I see the doll?"

"Sure. I keep it on my dresser in our bedroom. I'm saving it for the little girl we hope to have someday."

Amber grimaced at the thought. *Lots of luck with that! Your husband can't give you one.*

Barbie Sue came back with the doll.

Amber forced back a scream. "This conversation is over."

"Wait, please. I need to tell you something."

"I'll come back about five. I really have to go. This minute!"

She ran out to the car and drove to Ari's house. She could hardly keep from crying. Her Father had given all three of his little girls a doll that looked like Barbie Sue. *How could he?*

Amber pulled into Ari's driveway, stepped out of the car, ran up to the porch and banged on the front door with her fist.

Ari opened it and said, "Come in! What's wrong?"

"Give me your porcelain doll with the pink dress!"

"What are you going to do with it?"

"Just give me the damn doll!"

"Okay! Do I get the doll back?"

"Not unless you want her with a crushed head!"

Ari took the doll down from a shelf in the hall closet, wondering what was going on. Amber grabbed it from her hands and ran out with it. She put the doll down in the driveway. Then she backed her car over it. The doll made a loud popping sound as it cracked open. Amber backed up a few feet, then she jumped out and picked up the broken doll. Its body was split wide open. One eye dangled down what was left of its cheek. Ari screamed out the window, "Have you flipped your lid?" She ran out to the driveway and watched as Amber shook the doll, causing its dangling eye to flop around like something out of a horror film.

"Look at the doll's eyes, Ari. Barbie Sue's eyes. Dad's eyes!"

"You killed my doll and her name is not Barbie Sue!"

Amber shoved the doll into Ari's arms. "So, bury her!"

"You're acting crazy."

"Maybe I am crazy! And maybe you're not ready to hear this. Barbie Sue is Brian's new wife and she is Dad's daughter. That makes her our half-sister! The baby is our nephew and Dad is his grandfather. How's that for our family tree? One Christmas Dad gave each of his three little girls a doll that looked like Barbie Sue. Merry Christmas!"

Ari ran into the house, her heart racing. She slammed the door behind her. Amber followed her in and put her arms around her. "I'm sorry, Sis. Please forgive me for springing it on you that way. I have to go. I'll check with you later."

Amber drove to her mother's house. She used her key, relieved that Genevieve wasn't home. She stumbled on the top step leading to the attic, grabbing the rail just in time to keep from falling back down the stairs. She opened the metal trunk marked "Amber's Treasures." *Treasures? Ha!*

When she lifted her doll from its wrappings she looked at its wrinkled lavender dress. The golden curls were bedraggled. *I loved that doll!* Looking down at it, she realized that destroying another doll that some other little girl would love was a selfish thing to do. She drove with the doll lying on the seat next to her. She stopped at the first bus stop she came to and put the doll down on the bench, knowing that someone would take it home with them.

It was time to listen to Barbie Sue again. She was waiting by the front door when Amber arrived. "Come in. We'll talk in the living room. I was afraid you wouldn't show up. Would you like something to drink?"

Amber shook her head. "I'm running short of time today but this time, I think I'll sit." *Yeah, I'll sit on the furniture that Brian and I picked out together on our last anniversary!*

Barbie Sue sat down on the edge of the white recliner and motioned for Amber to sit on the matching sofa. "Please think of a little girl with a mother who was slowly dying of cancer. I was only eight years old when she was diagnosed. My mother lived and suffered for four years longer. The State provided her with a nurse and a housekeeper since we had no help from Dad. I don't expect you to feel sorry for me. I just want you to know why I became so bitter toward you and your sister."

"I was in no way to blame for what my father did or didn't do. I was also a child then. You and I are about the same age, so my father must have been proud of himself, getting his wife and his mistress pregnant the same year! Now you are sitting in my recliner, in my house, which you have stolen from me. You are living with my husband. You have taken everything from me. You are living my life. My life! And you want me to sit here and listen to you whine about my father not leaving me for you?" It was hard for Amber to restrain herself from dragging her off the recliner.

Barbie Sue went on speaking as if she hadn't heard Amber's words at all. "When my mother died, I was twelve years old. I had believed her when she told me Dad would tell his wife and girls about me. Then I would be part of the family. I had always wanted a sister and I thought I would have two." Tears welled up in her eyes. She wiped them away, and then continued. "After the funeral, my mother's sister told me to pack my things because our house

58

would be sold and I was to live with her. I started to cry then and said that my daddy would take me home with him. He didn't even come to the funeral! My aunt had to be the one to tell me my father didn't want me. I was devastated. I never saw him again, although he did call my aunt a few times to see how we were doing. By the time I was a teenager, he had stopped calling us. I read about his death in the obituary column."

Amber clenched her fists and gritted her teeth. "None of that entitled you to take my husband from me! Why didn't you do something against my father instead?"

"I loved him! I didn't want to hurt him."

"So, you wanted to hurt me? I never knew you existed yet you punished me because of my father. That makes no sense!"

"Maybe it doesn't, but you need to acknowledge me as a McFarland and accept me as a sister."

Amber stood, went to the door and flung it open. She turned back, shook her fist at her and sneered. "The best I can offer you is not to call you a bitch anymore, Mrs. Haworth!"

Chapter 7

Biochemical Research Center

Sabine looked up from her work as a man wearing a black overcoat and hat strode briskly toward her. His demeanor marked him as a man of authority. "Doctor Heitbrock, we were aware that the death of your son was imminent. Now that he is deceased, we will take your daughter as security. Men from my agency are now in Gdansk to apprehend her. She will be taken into Russian territory and held in our custody until your work here is completed."

Before Sabine could reply, the man turned and left the room. She cradled her head in her hands and cried. _My son is dead and now my daughter is to be unjustly imprisoned._

Gdansk, Poland

Vasily Shubinsky eased the sleek black Mercedes to a silent stop across from the _Café Polska._ A cold, damp breeze from the Baltic wafted over the lagoon and through the open windows of the car. He ran a comb through his slicked-back blond hair, then leaned back against the seat and sipped coffee from a thermal cup.

Arkady Malenkov dozed intermittently in the passenger seat. Only a narrow brown fringe of his short-cropped hair showed from beneath his black fedora hat.

Their assignment was to take the daughter of Doctor Sabine Heitbrock across the Polish border into the Kaliningrad Oblast, Russia. Dead or alive.

The cafe door swung open. Sara paused in the doorway and eased one strap of her backpack from her shoulder.

Vasily shook the sleeping Arkady. "Wake up! There she is!"

Arkady roused and held a photograph under the faint glow of the streetlight. The woman had the same thin frame and the same dark-blond hair as the one in the photo, but her hair looked longer and hung down in little curly twists like corkscrews. Still, she had to be the one. The first surveillance team had reported that the cafe had been her last stop.

Sara walked toward the center of town. She had seen no one on the street.

Arkady stepped out onto the sidewalk, staying a short distance behind her. She looked back at him. Feeling uneasy, she walked faster. At the end of the block she turned right, toward her hotel.

Vasily drove along slowly, and then accelerated as his partner closed in on their quarry.

Arkady crooked his arm around her throat causing her backpack to slip from her shoulder onto the sidewalk. In the commotion, none of them noticed.

Vasily got out and opened the door. Arkady shoved Sara into the back seat. As he slid in beside her she began screaming for help in Polish, and then in English. He backhanded her hard across her face. "We will hear no more of that!"

She stopped screaming. "Who are you people? Where are you taking me?"

"Shut up or we will never let you go. Keep quiet and we will not hurt you."

"What have you done with my backpack?"

Arkady checked under and behind the seat. Finding no sign of the backpack, he shoved her forward and searched her pockets.

"Vasily, stop the car! Her papers are not here."

"Idiot! What if someone has found them? You know the rules about identity papers."

"Stop mouthing at me! Just go back."

Sara was not about to tell them that her passport was in a purse that had been snatched from her shoulder an hour earlier.

Vasily wheeled the car around, sped to the spot where they had grabbed her, and then screeched to a halt beside the backpack. Arkady leaned out and scooped it up. Sara screamed for help again before Vasily could pull away from the curb. He turned to Arkady. "If the bitch does not shut up right now, tie a rag around her big mouth."

Arkady took hold of her arm. "You have one more chance to stay quiet or I will gag you and stuff you in the trunk."

She stopped screaming and resisting. Whatever her fate now, she couldn't give them cause to put her in the trunk. Within minutes they were on a highway, heading out of town. *Where are they taking me? Why?*

Headlights reflected on signs along the highway. One caught Sara's eye: Droga Ekspresowa S22. Realizing they were headed out of Poland toward the Kaliningrad Oblast, she banged on the window with both fists, screaming for help in Polish. She couldn't let them take her into Russia.

Vasily slowed and pulled over onto the shoulder of the highway. "Control the bitch before someone drives by."

Arkady pulled an OTs-38 revolver from his jacket and pointed it at her forehead. "That is enough! Silence!" He put the revolver back in his pocket and dragged her out of the car. He tied a swath of linen around her mouth and tried to shove her into the trunk. She uttered a muffled scream and kneed him.

Moaning in pain, he grabbed her by her hair and held on. It was all he could do to prevent her from escaping. "Vasily! Help me with this wildcat!"

Vasily lunged out of the car, grabbed her arm and bent it behind her back. Pressing his forearm hard around her neck, he executed a perfect hammerlock.

Arkady tied her hands behind her. They forced her into the trunk, and then as a safety measure, tied her ankles together. Arkady slammed the trunk closed.

Vasily whipped the Mercedes back onto the highway.

Sara was overcome with claustrophobia. She kicked with her bound feet, making only a clunking sound, but it was enough to alarm her captors.

Vasily took the next turnoff and pulled over to the side of the road. He looked back at Arkady. "She leaves us no alternative. Use the chloroform. Hurry!"

Arkady jumped out and raised the trunk lid. He jerked the swath away and held a chloroform-soaked cloth over her nose and mouth until she lay slumped like a rag doll. That accomplished, he closed the trunk, and then joined Vasily in the front seat. He leaned back and sighed. "Quiet never sounded so good."

When they approached the Polish checkpoint, Vasily rolled the window down and handed their identification folders to the guard. He read the information and looked at their photos before waving them on. At the Russian checkpoint, Vasily cut around the other vehicles and stopped at the front of the line. The guard recognized them and the Mercedes. He saluted. They sped through.

Mamonovo,
Kaliningrad Oblast, Russia

In exactly seven minutes after leaving the checkpoint, Vasily pulled the Mercedes up under a canopy on the side of a gray house. A white window box lent a semblance of innocence, despite its wilted geraniums. He pushed the remote button to open the double doors of the garage and entered.

Arkady flung his hat onto the front seat, exited the vehicle and opened the trunk. Sara's head was pounding and so was her heart. When he took her out of the trunk and untied her, adrenalin coursed through her. She drew her right arm back and hit him square in the mouth as hard as she could. Then she began screaming and punching him.

Arkady was relieved that she was still alive, but he had to stop her from fighting him and screeching like a banshee. He put his hands around her throat. "Make one more sound and I will choke you until you are dead. It would be my pleasure." His harsh words took the fight out of her. She trembled and became silent.

Her captors each took her by an arm, led her into the house and into the first room on the left.

A swarthy, heavyset man motioned for her to sit in the straight-backed chair opposite him.

Looking him in the eyes, she said, "Why was I brought here? I am not a criminal! I am a tourist."

"That is what they all say, Liesel."

"I am not Liesel. My name is Sara Thornburg. Let me go! You have no right to keep me here."

"We have every right to hold you for as long as we wish. Your belongings have been searched. You have no passport or identity papers. Citizens who have nothing to hide will carry proper identification with them at all times."

"My passport was stolen! I went into the cafe to eat and to ask directions to the police station. When I came out, those two stooges took me hostage. Call the police station!"

He stood and walked over to the door. "We will call no one. We know who you are, Liesel Heitbrock. You will remain in our care until we decide to release you. Furthermore, you will refrain from insulting my men. Do not say another word."

His stance and the expression on his face frightened her. She looked down at the floor, afraid to move.

After the man left the room, Arkady led her down the hall to another room. "This whole place is soundproofed. Enjoy your stay!"

Sara winced when she heard the lock click into place.

A narrow cot had been placed against a wall. A newly varnished wooden table sat beneath a steel-louvered window. She moved the table aside and opened the louvers. The window had been bricked in. Now was not the time to be brave. She cried.

Early the next morning, a woman in faded blue coveralls brought in a tray with bread, butter, cheese and a pot of tea. She set it down on the table and left without a word, locking the door behind her.

Sara consumed the breakfast as soon as the woman left. It had been a long, miserable night in complete darkness. The light bulbs had been removed from the chandelier. She banged and kicked on the door with all her might. No one came. *This place must really be soundproofed. The butter knife!* She opened the louvers and tried to pry the bricks loose. It would take days to loosen even one, but she kept scraping hard at the mortar between the bricks until she heard footsteps in the hallway. She closed the louvers and wiped the knife clean before hiding it under her mattress.

The woman who had brought in the breakfast entered, picked up the tray and shuffled out. The lock clicked. Then came the silence.

Chapter 8

Burbank, California

Amber dreaded the call to Millicent, Brian's mother. She wanted to let her know that she was in Burbank. Millicent picked up after the first ring. "Amber! I'm glad you called. When can you come over?"

"I can be there within the hour, if it's convenient for you."

"That's fine. I'll put the teakettle on."

Seeing the house Brian grew up in brought more pain to Amber. They had always been neighbors, schoolmates, best friends, and later, much more. She knocked lightly and entered. Millicent greeted her with a hug. "Come into the kitchen. I'm sorry Brian hurt you. I was shocked when I found out about that woman."

"I had quite a shock myself, when Brian said he didn't want to see me anymore." She sat down at the old maple table where she and Brian had eaten many lunches and snacks together. He would sit across from her, trying to smooth down his unruly reddish-brown cowlick. Sometimes, he'd have a wide grin on his freckled face as if hatching some mischief. The freckles faded by the time he was out of elementary school, and soon he was able to tame his cowlick.

Millicent poured their tea, untied her apron and placed it across the back of a chair. She sat down facing Amber. "I have something to tell you. You never knew my husband. He died before Brian was born. George was my first and only love. He was ill for a long time. One night, when he was in the hospital, he became worse and I thought he was about to die. I was so upset that I didn't trust myself to drive to the hospital. I would have asked a friend to take me, but she wasn't home, so her husband volunteered to drive me to the hospital. He stayed while I visited George, and then he drove me home."

"Are you sure this is something I need to know?"

"Bear with me, please. I have to give you the background so you'll understand. I was crying on the way home, so our friend came in and made coffee. He stayed, trying to comfort me. Suddenly I was in his arms. We made love."

"I don't think you should be telling me this, Millicent, or do I know the man?"

"It was your father. I don't expect you to forgive me. Please don't hate me. Your mother never knew. I always felt guilty around her after that. I was carrying her husband's child! Your parents and everyone else thought the child belonged to my husband. I'm so ashamed."

Amber sat motionless for a few seconds, her mind in a whirl. Then nausea engulfed her. *Brian is my half-brother! And he had been my husband for eleven years. Thank God, Brian was sterile. Is it incest if the parties involved don't know they are related?* She was living a nightmare.

Millicent watched as the color slowly drained from Amber's face. "Please say something. Anything."

Amber stood and held on to the chair for support. "Nothing that I could say would make it right. I don't hate you, but I do hate myself and I hate Brian. Don't worry, I won't ever tell my mother or anyone else that you bore a son by my father. You let me marry that son! Someday I may forgive you, but I can never forget what you and my father did to me and my family."

"I'll never be able to forget it either. I've had to live with it all these years. Thank God, Brian never knew. He thought George was his father. He still does."

"And I thought Brian was my husband. Not my brother! Why didn't you stop us from getting married?"

Millicent wiped away the tears that were running down her cheeks, and then looked up. "You two were always inseparable. I couldn't bear to tell either of you, back then. It would have broken Brian's heart if he knew George wasn't his father. I had told him so many stories about him. We'd sit together looking at pictures of the father he would never know."

"Don't ever try to make me feel sorry for Brian! I have no sympathy for you or my father, either. I only feel sorry for myself, my sister and my mother."

"Brian didn't know he was sterile. I told you that before you married him. You knew he had Klinefelter's Syndrome. He was

66

born with that extra X chromosome. It caused him to be sterile, so I knew there would be no children involved. I made myself believe it would be okay. That didn't make it right, I know. Until now, no one in the world knew George was not Brian's father except me. It was my dirty little secret."

"And now, Millicent, it's my dirty little secret too. I feel dirty because I slept with my half-brother. I slept beside him for eleven years! How can I even face my reflection in the mirror again?"

Amber couldn't bear to hear any more. She felt as if they were acting out a sleazy soap opera.

She moved toward the door but turned back and said, "Goodbye, Millicent. Have a nice life." She walked out, leaving the door wide open.

In the car, she sat with her hands gripping the steering wheel. *What else? What else must I bear?* She leaned her forehead on the steering wheel, causing the horn to emit a loud, steady beep. She didn't remember that it was a signal for help until a passerby knocked on the window and asked if she was okay.

She drove to the cemetery without stopping to buy red roses, as she usually did. Her thoughts were only on what she would say to her father.

A dozen fresh red roses were already there, lying across the gravestone. *Ari or Mom must have been here today, or maybe his other daughter, Barbie Sue, his little porcelain doll.*

Amber ran her hand across the embossed metal nameplate.

Roderick Allen McFarland
Loving Husband and Father

She couldn't help thinking that he was the father of too many children. He had gotten not two but three women pregnant in the same year. *Oh, Lord! Brian has married another half-sister!*

"Dad," she whispered, "You'll never know the agony you have caused your offspring." Although there was so much more she needed to say to him, she could only put her head down and sigh. She finally raised her head and said, "Goodbye for a while, Dad."

Amber couldn't tell Ari that Brian was their half-brother. She had already upset her with the news about Barbie Sue.

Ari has had enough grief in her young life. Four years ago, her husband Evan and their six-year-old son Roddy were in a bank during a robbery. One of the robbers panicked and started shooting. Evan and Roddy were killed instantly. A young woman and an elderly man were also shot. They both died in the ambulance on the way to the hospital. Ari had spent the next several months after her family's funeral in a state of depression, and the years that followed were never without the haunting memory of her loss.

Amber needed to get away. She dialed Cotter's number. "Hi, it's me. Do you want some company?"

"Yes! I'll meet you at the airport. Take the next flight out and call me with the arrival time."

She called Willoughby as she had promised. "I'm leaving for Washington today to visit a friend."

"Okay. Pack only the things you'll be taking with you to Finland. You won't have time to come back to California. We'll do the final briefing at PDI. Do I know the friend?"

"Although you know all my friends, I'm not going to tell you who I'll be with this time. This is strictly on a need-to-know basis and you don't need to know."

"That borders on insubordination, Kiddo!"

"I know, and it feels good. I've always wanted to say that to you! I'll see you at PDI in a couple of days. Bye."

Washington, D.C.

Amber worked her way through the packed aisle to deplane. In the terminal, she spotted Cotter walking toward her through the swarm of people.

When he reached her, he put his arms around her. "I'm here, for now or for always. You're welcome to stay at my place but if you'd rather, I can take you to a hotel. What do you think?"

"I'd like to go home with you. I don't want to be alone right now. I'll be going on assignment soon and this will probably be my last holiday for a long time."

"You'll make me a happy man if you spend this time with me. Just having you near is enough. For now."

He concentrated on the heavy traffic until he pulled off the exit and onto the street leading to his apartment. Then he turned his head slightly toward her. "I'm glad you came to me. How long can you stay? Or is that classified information?"

She laughed and patted his shoulder. "You could say the information is classified, but I guess you have a *need* to know. We'll have two nights together."

"I was hoping for more time … like forever."

He pulled into the parking garage. They took the elevator to his fourth-floor apartment. Cotter shut the door behind them and twisted the deadbolt to the lock position. "Make yourself comfortable. I'll take your things to the bedroom. I can sleep on the daybed."

His living room resembles an office with its light-gray carpet, black metal desk, a built-in bookcase and assorted tables. A double recliner faces a television. The daybed substitutes as a sofa. The kitchen walls were painted off-white. The sheer curtains were embroidered with blue windmills and bright-yellow tulips. Amber smiled at the slightly feminine touch. The biggest surprise was the table that was set up like an outdoor cafe, complete with a yellow umbrella. A copper windmill holding toothpicks sat in the center of the table.

Cotter joined her. "Let's go out to dinner."

"Okay. It's my treat!"

"You've got a deal. Do you like Chinese food?"

"Yes. Is there a place close by?"

"There's one right up the street."

"Why don't we walk? I could use some fresh air after that flight."

"Suits me. We'll need our jackets."

The air was cold and crisp. Amber pulled her zipper up to her neck and rubbed her upper arms briskly.

The Green Lantern restaurant was lit up like a Christmas tree. A huge red and green lantern with red tassels hung from the ceiling at the entranceway. Inside, there were strings of tiny matching lanterns hanging above each aisle. The host led them to a booth near the golden statue of Buddha. Lantern-shaped sugar bowls printed with cherry blossom sprigs and mimosa flowers graced each table. They sipped green tea while waiting to be served.

Bowls of steaming rice were placed in front of them. Their main dishes were brought to the table on platters.

After they finished the meal, the server brought another pot of tea. "Will there be anything else?"

Cotter said, "No, thank you. You may bring the check."

Amber laid her napkin on the table. "I am so stuffed. I can't even hold another drop of tea."

As they were leaving she rubbed the golden Buddha's tummy for luck.

Cotter paused at the threshold. "I'll call a taxi."

The driver let them out in front of the apartment building. Amber unpacked, showered, and then relaxed in the recliner while waiting for Cotter to join her.

He came into the room whistling. His hair was still damp from the shower and even more tousled than usual. He grinned. "I remember the traveler's hug you gave me when you first got back from your assignment. Could I get the real thing now?"

She looked up at him, stood and placed herself just inches in front of him. He took her firmly in his arms and kissed the back of her neck. Suddenly she pulled away and asked, "Does your mother have blue eyes?"

He tilted his head to one side. "Yes, her eyes are sky blue. Why do you ask? Are you planning to bear my children?"

She felt a surge of relief. *He can't be my brother with those brown eyes. Two blue-eyed people always have blue-eyed children. According to Mom, Dad's eyes were 'as blue as the sky'.*

"Not necessarily. I was just wondering. And wipe that smile off your face, Cotter!"

"My first name is Jordan. You don't have to call me Cotter when we're not around other agents."

"Hello, Jordan. Now we have been properly introduced after all those years of friendship."

"Does that mean we can share the bed? Or do I have to sleep on the daybed?"

"I'd rather lie beside you."

He didn't want to wait until the night. Without speaking, he led her to his bed. Holding her close again, desire burned through him like a fever. "You don't know how long I have hoped and waited for this moment."

After they made love, she rested her head on his chest. She knew she needed to confide in him. Even so, she couldn't look him in the face, and the words came hard. "When I found out Brian was cheating on me and wanted to marry someone else, I felt as if I had failed somehow. I felt hollow inside and insecure. You've made me feel desirable again. I needed that, and I know it's because you really care about me. Thank you."

His voice was choked with emotion when he said, "I have loved you since the day we first met. I knew then that you were the one I had dreamed of all of my life. I never let my feelings show, because you were married and I respected that."

"Thank you. That means a lot to me."

"Do you think you could ever love me, Amber?"

"I need time to get over my hurt and my anger before I move on. I have known Brian Haworth all of my life. I thought I knew him as well as I know myself, yet I never knew him at all. It makes me question my judgment. I have to be sure of myself again. I do believe if I could ever love anyone, it would be you."

"That's good enough. I can live with that." He rolled onto his side, at the same time laying her head back on the pillow to kiss her. Leaning back to look at her face again, he said, "Now, let's get up and watch a film. Not a spy movie!"

"Agreed. Do you have any popcorn?"

"Sure, and it's microwavable."

While Cotter popped the corn, Amber searched through his DVD collection looking for a comedy or a drama. "Ah! How about *National Lampoon's European Vacation?*"

"Good one! Let it roll."

Amber stirred as sunbeams peeked through the slats of the blinds. She was in Jordan Cotter's bed. *Agents are not supposed to fraternize. I should feel guilty. I don't. I feel good about myself. I feel wanted.* She touched Cotter's cheek. "Are you awake?"

"Now I am. Your touch woke me." He sat up and looked down at her. "What did you have in mind? Something wild, I hope!"

She pulled him back down and rolled on top of him. "Yes, Cotter, I want to do something *really* wild today. I want to ride a merry-go-round, so please get up."

He laughed. "I can't get up until you let me. Or, shall we just have a merry *go around* in bed?"

She tweaked his nose and rolled off. "Today I want to be a kid again."

"I wouldn't mind feeling young again. There's bound to be an amusement park open in the area. You can take your shower first. I'll check the Internet."

When she came out of the bathroom and into the living room, Cotter was still at the computer. He looked up and gasped. She was standing there wearing only a pair of red panties. He rose from the chair and put his arms around her. She felt his hardness against her and she was tempted to forget about the amusement park. Instead, she eased away from him. "I'm sorry, Cotter. I just wasn't thinking. Let's save it for tonight. Okay?"

Reluctantly, he agreed. "I'm gonna hold you to that." He smirked. "And don't you forget it."

"Oh, I won't. I promise."

"I'll be quick with my shower. I did find a fair going on in Tysons Corner, Virginia. It's only about a dozen miles or so from Washington."

Amber dressed in jeans and a flannel shirt. She hadn't worn makeup since she started training but today was different. She put on coral lip gloss and mascara.

Cotter stepped up beside her. He was wearing khakis and a turtleneck sweater. "Let's get going. We can grab breakfast somewhere."

At the fairgrounds, Amber heard the unmistakable calliope music of a merry-go-round as they entered the parking lot. Her heart rate increased with her excitement, as she hurried over to ride, while Cotter searched for breakfast fare. When she spotted the silver-colored horse with its pink and green saddle, she climbed on. The wind in her face and the carnival smells brought her back to her childhood. Memories swept over her in waves as the horse galloped in time with the music. It was magical.

Cotter was waiting when the ride was over. Amber laughed when she saw the funnel cakes. "That's breakfast? Looks good."

"They won't stay hot much longer. Where shall we eat?"

"I saw a picnic area over to the right. You go ahead. I want to get some cotton candy. Shall I bring you some?"

Cotter shook his head. "No, I'll pass this time."

He set the cakes down on the first table he came to.

Amber came over to the table holding a pink cloud of sugary fluff.

Before they finished eating, dark clouds blotted out the sun's rays. At the first thunderclap, Cotter gathered their trash and tossed it into the waste barrel. "We'd better get back to the car. That sky is getting ready to cry a river."

Everyone else seemed to have the same idea. Chaos ensued as they all tried to get to their cars at once. The rain came down hard and fast. Amber and Cotter ran to his car and got in the front seat, dripping wet.

"Amber, this rain is only going to get worse. Let's stop by a drive-through place on the way. What's your pleasure?"

"We've had Chinese. How about Italian?"

"Yes. Pizza would be good."

The parking garage saved them from another dousing.

Amber showered and put on one of Cotter's pajama tops. While she waited for him to shower, she listened to the news. The rain was expected to let up by early tomorrow.

Cotter came out of the bathroom wearing pajama bottoms.

He put the pizza in the microwave. "Amber, would you get us a couple of wineglasses from the cupboard, please?"

"Sure. Shall we have white or red?"

"I think the red goes better with Italian."

After they had finished up the pizza, Cotter asked, "Do you want to watch another movie?"

"No, thanks. I'm tired. We've had a busy day. I'd rather just rest and listen to a little music."

He put a tape of "golden oldies" on. They sat side by side on the daybed. He put one arm around her shoulder. "This has been a special day for me."

"The day was special to me too."

When "Spanish Eyes" began to play, Amber stood and pulled him up. "That's my song. Let's dance."

He held her close. She laid her head on his shoulder and clung to him, sensing that later tonight they would be making love.

After a few slow dances, Cotter said he was hungry again. He checked the freezer. "I think I've found just the right bedtime snack … butter pecan ice cream! Join me at the table while I dip it up." He served the ice cream in banana split dishes and topped each scoop with whipped cream and maraschino cherries.

Amber rinsed the dishes and stacked them on the counter. "Shall I make another pot of coffee as a nightcap?"

"Then we'd never get to sleep tonight. Or are you planning to stay awake, making love all night?"

"Tempting, but I need to get up early. Willoughby is back in Washington and I have a meeting with him before my flight."

"Let's just hit the sack."

She ran to the bedroom, laughing. "What are you waiting for?"

He followed, eased her down on the bed and kissed her. She responded with a deep kiss. He pulled her up, unbuttoned her top, slid it off and cupped his hands around her breasts. Her nipples hardened and her breathing became heavy. He put his arms around her and held her so close that she could feel his heart beating against hers. A warm flush spread across her face. She slipped her panties off. "I want you, Cotter."

He stepped out of his pajama bottoms. They made love with such passion that it was hard to catch a breath afterward. They lay in one another's arms under the sheet, listening to the sounds of rain and thunder until sleep claimed them.

Amber was awakened by the rain pinging against the windowpane. Cotter was sleeping on his side, turned away from her.

After she showered, she padded into the kitchen and put the coffee on to perk. Sitting at the table, she thought about her feelings for Cotter. *As long as I've known him, I've sensed I could trust him. There's definitely a strong chemistry between us. I don't believe he would ever hurt me willingly. Maybe someday we can be together. For now, I have a job to do.*

Cotter woke to the tantalizing aroma of freshly brewed coffee. He showered and dressed, then joined Amber. She held a cup of coffee under his nose. "I have to get over to headquarters pretty soon. Get a move on."

"I'm moving. Do we have time for a quick breakfast?"

"Sure. How about making us some toast?"

He reached up and opened the umbrella over the table. "How about something that goes better with my Parisian sidewalk cafe?" He brought out a package of croissants from the cupboard and put four in the microwave. Amber set out the paper plates and plastic knives. Cotter served the croissants with butter and blackberry jam.

When they had finished eating, Amber went to the bedroom and packed. It was time for her to get back to reality. She went back to the living room with her things and looked around again. She wanted to etch the image of the little hideaway into her mind.

Cotter came in from the kitchen. "Do you know when you'll be back in Washington?"

"No, but I'd better get started. Call a taxi for me, please."

"If you insist. I really don't mind driving you."

"I'd rather say goodbye here. I hope you understand."

He nodded, made the call, picked up her suitcase and opened the door for her. In the elevator, he was deep in thought. Finally, he turned his head to face her. "Old friend and new lover, I will see you after your mission, whenever that may be."

"Thanks for yesterday. I haven't had so much fun in ages."

"You're welcome, and thanks for the fun last night!" He gave her the sideways grin that she was becoming so fond of.

"Oh, don't thank me. I enjoyed last night too."

He walked over to the taxi with her. The rain had ceased. They said goodbye with a traveler's hug. Cotter opened the door for her, and then stood on the curb until the taxi was out of sight, wondering when he would see her again.

Amber joined Willoughby in his office for the final briefing. He motioned for her to sit down while he glanced through a file. "This is a two-fold mission. Grayson Montgomery, a Canadian freelance agent, was sent to Russia to rescue Doctor Heitbrock shortly after we learned of her disappearance. He was an opera singer in Milan, so we gave him the code name, Milano. We know he arrived at Sheremetyevo Airport, a few miles northwest of Moscow. He didn't meet his contact. Find out if he's alive and why he didn't complete the mission. Get him out if you can. Bring Doctor Heitbrock home. That's your main mission. We're racing the calendar on this one."

"Why all the cloak-and-dagger stuff? The cold war has been over for more than twenty-five years."

"Things seem to be warming up. Anyway, that has nothing to do with the doctor's abduction. The Russians are not going to send Doctor Heitbrock back. You have to go in and get her."

"Where am I flying to?"

He took an envelope from his pocket. "You're booked for tomorrow under your own name, from Dulles International to Helsinki, Finland. Ludmila is staying in her mother's apartment in Kouvola. Her address is in the envelope. Memorize it and give it back to me. Take a train from Helsinki to Kouvola."

"I got it. Will you call a taxi for me, please?"

"Don't go to a hotel, Amber. Let me drive you to the new house. You haven't seen it yet. Ari's there and you need to talk to her. She is now a redhead for her cover in Moscow."

Genevieve showed Amber around the new three-bedroom home. The living room was strictly modern, with neutral tones of beige, cream and white. Genevieve pointed to the three tall windows. "Come and look at the view."

Amber looked out on the beautiful garden. "Whoever did your landscaping did a great job, Mom."

"That garden is what sold me on the place. Let's go see the bedrooms now." She took her to the master bedroom first. It was furnished with an elegant oak set that included an armoire.

The smallest bedroom had been turned into an office for Willoughby. With no-nonsense furnishings and the lack of personal touches, it suited him. When it came to his work, he was all business. In the guest room, twin beds sat on opposite sides of the room. Genevieve said, "You and Ari can choose bedspreads for this room. I hope you'll stay with us from time to time."

"I'm sure we will. You have found the perfect place and I think the change is good for you. You seem happy."

"I am. Let me show you my fancy kitchen."

Copper-bottomed skillets and pans, hanging from hooks above a marble-topped counter caught Amber's attention. Then the rest of the place came into focus. "This room looks like it could be featured in a top decorating magazine."

Ari was sitting at the breakfast bar. When she heard Amber's voice she jumped up and held out her hand. "Look at my rings!"

Amber ogled the diamond cluster, set in gold. She was surprised to see Ari so excited over rings that were just part of her cover. *PDI went all out on those. They're a bit fancy for a wedding that's meant to be a sham.*

Genevieve went back to the living room, giving the sisters a chance to catch up on the latest developments.

Amber studied Ari's new look. "You look good with red hair. Now we don't look much like twins. You'll have to dye it dark again when you're covering for me."

"I know and don't worry. I'll do fine with this secret agent stuff. I hope this doesn't shock you. You know I've been alone for a long time. After Slaney and I got to know each other, we married for real. We love each other."

Amber was shocked, although she was glad that Ari had found someone. *So, PDI didn't pay for the rings.* "What's your new name? Real name, I mean. Are you Mrs. Arianne Slaney, or who?"

"I'm Mrs. Niall Patrick O'Bannon!"

"Congratulations, Mrs. O'Bannon. Did your husband tell you why his code name is Slaney?"

Ari nodded. "He was born in Enniscorthy, Ireland in a house near the Slaney River. He told me about his childhood and his family. I'll go to Enniscorthy and meet them someday."

"Let's go out for hot fudge sundaes to celebrate. Where is the lucky guy?"

"He's in California packing up my things. I'm going to sell my house and move into his condo in North Hollywood. I'll still be able to take care of the family graves. We have a few things to work out about the cover thing." She called out, "Mom, Amber and I are going out. We'll be back in a couple of hours."

"Have fun, you two. See you later."

Ari drove to a nearby all-night cafe. The server seated them in a corner booth near the back. Amber said, "I think we're ready to order. Two hot fudge sundaes and coffee, please."

When the server walked away, Amber said, "We need to talk about places to meet in Moscow. If I need you to cover for me, I'll have the cobbler contact Slaney at the embassy and he will tell you when and where to meet me. My first choice for our meetings is the little Turkish tea shop on the Arbat." She drew a map of the area on a napkin, marking the spot. "When I need you, Slaney will be told the time of the meeting and he'll relay the information to you. If I'm not at the first place in thirty minutes, go to the second place. From the tea shop turn east, walk two blocks and turn left. There is a church sitting back from the street. Go in wearing a scarf over your hair. Not a black one. That's a danger signal. If you see me wearing a black scarf, ignore me. Then get back to Slaney."

"What if you aren't at the second place? How long should I wait before I panic?"

"If I'm not at the church within twenty minutes after you arrive, it may mean that I've been found out. Go back to the embassy as quickly as you can and report to Slaney."

"This assignment is going to be a much bigger responsibility for me than I had imagined. It sure sounds exciting."

"Don't get too carried away. There's a chance I may not need you at all. Anyway, just being in Moscow will be exciting enough for you."

She paused when the server came to the table to refill their cups with fresh coffee.

"Did you wear Mom's wedding dress when you married Slaney? You didn't when you married Evan."

"I didn't wear Mom's dress at either wedding. You kept your promise to, so at least one of her daughters made her happy."

"Oh, a wedding dress is just a dress, whatever Mom thinks about passing it down from mother to daughter." *Oh, yeah, I wore my mother's wedding dress to marry my half-brother!*

"I have married another stranger. Evan and I were married after knowing each other for one weekend and you know Slaney was a stranger to me up until about a week ago."

"It seems to me that your strangers turn out better than my boy-next-door type." She looked at the clock. "Maybe we should get back. I need to get some sleep tonight."

Chapter 9

Helsinki, Finland

The Boeing 757 landed at Vantaa-Helsinki Airport just before two o'clock in the afternoon. Amber set her watch to the local time. She remained in her seat until most of the passengers managed to grab their luggage and file toward the exit.

A bus to Helsinki's Central Station was waiting when she walked out of the airport. She hopped on, paid her fare and took a seat just in time.

The bus stopped in front of the imposing train station. Huge stone statues holding globe-shaped lamps stand like sentinels, two abreast on either side of the arched entranceway. Amber hurried to buy a ticket to Kouvola. An InterCity train would leave in less than ten minutes. She rushed to the platform, boarded and took a seat next to the window. *Until this mission is over I am not Amber McFarland. I will be Doctor Ludmila Kirsinova. I have to live and breathe as Doctor Kirsinova.* She leaned her head against the backrest. *What in the world have I gotten myself into?*

The cadence of the wheels on the track mesmerized her as she watched the scenery rush by.

As the train neared her destination a light rain began to fall, misting her window. She placed her open hand on the glass and felt the coolness. The view changed quickly from countryside to a cityscape as they approached Kouvola.

Kouvola, Finland

Walking in the light rain was refreshing, although it was colder here than it had been in Washington. Amber searched her memory for Ludmila's address. According to the directions, she had only three more blocks to go. The apartment was on the top floor. Amber knocked on the door of number 409. A dark-haired woman opened the door and spoke in Finnish. Amber stood there holding her suitcase, not understanding.

Ludmila studied the stranger's face, and then took the suitcase from her. Not wanting to speak English or Russian in the hall, she opened the door wider and motioned for her to enter.

Amber quickly stepped in and closed the door. "PDI sent me." She took her passport from her purse and held it out to Ludmila.

After examining the passport, Ludmila was satisfied with Amber's identity. "I figured it was you, but I had to be sure. My mother is working in the sewing room. I must introduce you."

Amber followed her down the hall.

Ludmila tapped her mother on the shoulder. The whirring sound of the sewing machine stopped abruptly. The woman stood and offered her hand to Amber. "I'm Sofia. It's good to meet you."

Amber took her hand. "I'm glad to know you."

"May I offer you some refreshments?"

"No, thank you."

"Then I will continue my work and speak with you later."

Ludmila said, "Would you like to sit and talk or shall I show you to the guest room?"

"I would like to talk"

Back in the living room, Amber sat down on the sofa. Ludmila sat next to her. "I was an agent-in-place for PDI. I was not a traitor to my country. Willoughby knew from the start that I would only become involved in situations that were for the good of humanity." She paused for a moment. "After you get Doctor Heitbrock out, I won't be welcome or safe in Russia."

"What will be expected of me at the research center?"

"You will assist Doctor Heitbrock with her work."

"I'm afraid I won't be much help. I have had no medical or scientific training at all."

"I am aware of that. Your special training in other fields may be needed more." She stood and opened a drawer on the stand next to the sofa. She handed Amber a folder. "These are my certification papers and passport, with *your* picture."

Amber checked them out. "These are perfect. Can you get rid of my passport, please?"

"I will take care of it after you leave tomorrow. Try to get to Sergiev Posad soon. The cobbler's store is there, near the monastery complex. The code word is *Gudok.* Use it in a sentence as soon as you meet him. I wasn't told the name or address of the store. It's the only shoe repair shop in the area."

"Do you mean that one of our cobblers is a real cobbler, as in repairing and making shoes?"

"Yes. Clever, isn't it? He has a clean-line phone, the only one you can contact your embassy on. You won't be allowed to have a personal cell phone."

"I disposed of mine before I left Washington."

"I was accepted as Doctor Heitbrock's assistant, not only because of my qualifications but also because I have a brother who had been in the military working near the Barents Sea. His job was classified and labeled as what you would call top secret. He won't be allowed to leave Russia, so they knew I was not a risk. He is now in a school for the blind, in Dmitrov."

"What happened that caused him to lose his sight?"

"We were only told there had been an explosion involving chemicals. He was in a hospital near my home in Murmansk, so I was with him every day after work. You must visit him in my stead. I haven't told him about my acceptance at the research center yet, or that I have left Murmansk, so you will have to convince him you are taking my place. At the school, show the papers with my name and your photo to the receptionist. My brother's name is Fyodor Nikolaevich Kirsinov. We still go with the Russian way of adding an "a" at the end of certain last names for females, so you will be Ludmila Nikolaevna Kirsinova." She handed Amber a few photographs of Fyodor. "Please keep these in your purse or wallet, as I would do."

"Is there something I can say to Fyodor that only the family would know?"

"When he was little, I often read him a story called *The Snow Dacha*. It's about Kalinka, a little girl who skated on the frozen lake near the family's dacha. Fyodor liked to hear about the icicles hanging from the roof."

"That should convince him to trust me. Where is Dmitrov?"

"It's about thirty kilometers from the research center. Visit Fyodor when you can. Please promise me you will take him with you when you leave Russia."

"What do you mean? I was only told to get Doctor Heitbrock and possibly another agent out."

"I never discussed it with the agency, but I do expect you to bring my brother to us. Don't bring him here. My mother and I will be ready to leave Kouvola soon. Contact the American embassy in Helsinki after you are safely out of Russia. The top official will know of Operation Winterset and where my mother and I have been relocated. The cobbler won't be told. Bring Fyodor to us after you get him out safely. If you can't get him out, then someone else will have to. He will never be safe in Russia again."

"I can only promise you that I'll do my best. Before I forget, we need to exchange suitcases and clothing."

"I already have you packed." She took a suitcase from the hall closet. "Let me show you to the guest room."

The guest room was larger than most of the hotel rooms Amber had stayed in. The queen-size bed was against the far wall. A mahogany dresser was against the opposite wall and a chair covered in orange velour sat beneath the window. "Thank you. This is a beautiful room. I will rest well on that big bed."

"Good. Now let's go back to the living room. I need to give you more papers."

She took an envelope from the top shelf of the closet. "Here is your ticket and the papers you will need in Russia."

Amber read the information for tomorrow's flight on Finnair to Moscow: *Depart Helsinki at 9:25 a.m., arriving at 12:05 p.m. Moscow Time at Sheremetyevo Airport.* "These are fine, thanks."

"Now I'll ask Sofia to join you. I'll prepare our dinner." She stepped into the hallway and called, "Mother, come and sit in the living room."

Sofia folded the material she had cut, took an album from her desk and went to the living room. She sat beside Amber on the sofa. "I would like to show you some pictures of my family." She opened the album to an old black and white picture with ragged edges. "This is my mother by the house in Russia where my family lived." She turned the pages slowly, showing the pictures of her parents and her siblings. The rest of the album was filled with pictures of Ludmila and Fyodor at various ages, posing like little tin soldiers.

Ludmila called out, "Dinner is ready."

The table was covered with a lace tablecloth and set with fine china in a pattern of pink and yellow roses. Ludmila pointed to a chair at the head of the table. "Sit down and we will begin."

She passed the platter of sliced beef to Amber, unaware that she was a vegetarian.

Amber explained and Ludmila laughed. "I am sure you will be offered meat many times in Russia. You must refuse graciously, without mentioning that you are a vegetarian. I didn't claim that I was, on the resume."

After a dessert of spice cake, served with coffee, Amber said, "That was a very good dinner. Now, I insist on cleaning up."

Ludmila rose from the table. "No, you are our guest. I will stack the dishes."

Sofia cut in. "Allow me to straighten up the kitchen."

Considering Sofia's determined tone, there could be no argument. Amber and Ludmila went back to the living room and sat on the sofa. Ludmila leaned toward Amber and spoke softly. "Someone may, just in conversation, question you about the family. My father died not long after my brother was born. When Fyodor was old enough he joined the military. I was a doctor by then, so my mother had no more responsibilities. She moved from Russia to Finland."

Ludmila opened the photo album. "It has been a long time since I've seen these pictures. I miss Fyodor so much and I know he must be lonely without his family."

"I will visit him as soon as I can. Ludmila, I'm feeling tired. I'm ready to sleep now."

"What time shall I wake you tomorrow?"

"I'll set my alarm watch for four a.m. Good night."

Amber's alarm buzzed. After a shower, she opened the suitcase Ludmila had given her and chose a brown skirt and a beige blouse. *That ought to be suitable for my grand entrance at the Biochemical Research Center. Jeans wouldn't do, I suppose. That's why I'm leaving them with Ludmila.* She followed her nose to the kitchen. "Sofia, that coffee smells good. I didn't expect you to get up so early for me."

"I rise early every morning." She took her apron off and hung it on the back of the pantry door.

Amber sat down at the table and poured the coffee.

After Ludmila came in Sofia brought a bowl of sour cream and a platter of apple pancakes to the table. "Now we are ready to enjoy our breakfast."

When they had finished eating Amber stood. "I must get ready to go."

In the guest room, she packed her toiletries, and then went to the front door.

Ludmila shook her hand. "I believe you will accomplish what you are setting out to do. Thank you."

"You are welcome."

"It has been a pleasure knowing you. I will never forget you or what you are doing. Get used to being me. Stay safe."

"I'll try. Please call a taxi for me. I'll be waiting on the corner by the newsstand."

Sofia said, "Goodbye, and thank you."

The taxi drove up within seconds after Amber arrived at the newsstand. She climbed in. "To the rail station, please."

When they reached the front of the station she paid the driver, went directly to the ticket window and bought a ticket to Helsinki Central Station. From there, a bus would get her to the airport for her flight to Moscow.

Chapter 10

Outskirts of Mamonovo,
Kaliningrad Oblast, Russia

The hours and the minutes passed slowly for Sara. With nothing at all to occupy herself, she was left with endless anxiety. That and the questions she had no answers for.

She promised herself she wouldn't cry anymore, but she still screamed and yelled whenever she felt like it. She did it to release the stress and in the hope that someone would hear and come for her. The only thing she had to look forward to was the next meal, when someone would show up. Even though they wouldn't talk to her, it was good to know she wasn't entirely alone in her world. They had taken her watch from her, so she didn't know what time it was. She waited for daylight. Then she waited for night again. She waited for someone to free her from her prison.

In the late afternoon, she heard whispering in the hallway outside her room. She held her ear against the door, but she still couldn't make out the words. Then she heard the sound of fading footfalls. Whoever was out there was walking away. She kicked on the door and called, "Please, come back! Who's out there? What do you want?" No one answered. The house was deathly quiet for a moment. Then heavy footfalls broke the silence. A key rattled in the lock. Sara stared at the door, waiting, hoping.

Arkady came in, took her arm and led her out into the hallway. He spoke in Russian on a cell phone before taking her out to a vehicle that was parked under the canopy. It was the same Mercedes that had brought her here. *They are going to release me! Someone will take me back to Poland.*

Vasily was waiting behind the wheel. Sara was seated next to Arkady in the back. *It's over. It's finally over. They didn't put me in the trunk this time. I'm going home!*

Vasily backed the car out and headed toward the border.

Sara asked, "How far is it to the Polish side?"

Arkady glared at her. "You sit there and say nothing."

She leaned her head against the window, holding back the tears. *Why is he angry with me? Kidnapping me was their mistake, not mine.*

When Vasily turned down a narrow dirt road, Sara's eyes widened. *This couldn't be the right way!*

The road became a path. Sara sat in silence. She knew better than to scream or beg or even to ask where they were taking her. She thought it had to be better than the place she had left.

Vasily pulled the car over and parked at the edge of a thickly wooded area. A corrugated tin shack, tilting to one side, was the only building in sight. He took Sara's backpack from the trunk. He walked to the shack, opened the rusty padlock on the door, threw her backpack in a corner, and then went back to the car. "Get a move on, Arkady! This place gives me the creeps. She had better not start screaming!"

"No one will hear her screams out here." He pulled her from the car by her arm. "Here is your new home!"

"No! You can't leave me here. Please, don't leave me out here." She struggled, trying to escape his hold on her.

He held her arm tighter and yelled, "Shut your mouth and cooperate, damn you!" He grabbed her other arm and twisted it. She kicked him so hard that he released her arms.

"You asked for it, you bitch!" He dragged her over to the shack. At the entrance, he held her with both hands and shoved her in onto the floor. He closed the door and locked her in. She screamed but there was no one to hear. *They're leaving me here in the middle of nowhere, alone, trapped like a wild animal. And I'm still in Russia.*

Sitting on the cold concrete floor, her body hurting from the violent manhandling, it seemed like hours before she could stop the tears.

She got up from the floor and looked around her new prison. There were no windows, just screen-covered, narrow openings near the roof. *At least I'll be able to breathe.* The skylight brought a little sunlight in. There was no bed, just a makeshift wooden platform covered with a thin mattress. A square metal table, a tall wooden stool and a slatted bench completed the furnishings. A closet-size room contained a shower stall, toilet and a sink. She tried the spigot. Out came rusty water, the color of curry powder. She wrinkled her nose. *Whew! Not much chance of a bath.* Turning around, she eyed her backpack. *My cell phone! I can get help!* She sat on the bench and rummaged through her things, finding all of her clothes, toiletries and money. *My cell phone is missing!* Her hopes were dashed once again. They had also taken her camera.

In the side pocket, she found a bag with a cheese sandwich, an apple, a candy bar and a can of cola. Someone had packed her a lunch. She ate a few bites of the sandwich and half of the candy and wrapped the rest back up. *I have to ration this out. When will they bring me more food again? At least I still have my backpack. I can change my clothes after I wash off this dirt.*

She remembered the rusty water. It was too much. She called out for help. No one answered.

Early evening brought a deep chill that made Sara dread the night. She looked around for something to cover with, finding nothing suitable other than one woolen blanket. When she unfolded it, dust flew out, causing her to have a sneezing fit.

As night fell, the stillness was even more frightening. She would have welcomed the hooting or even the screeching of an owl. There was no sound of life. She was alone in the woods.

The moon shone faintly through the skylight. A few stars were visible. She tried the light switch. *It works! Oh, thank God. At least I won't be living in darkness this time.*

Dawn brought coral streaks across the few clouds that were visible through the skylight. Sara ate the rest of the sandwich and finished the other half of the candy bar. Then she walked back and forth around the room for exercise.

She stopped short at the sound of a motor. *Someone is coming for me!* The rattling of the door didn't frighten her. Anyone would be welcome. Before she could call out, a tall broad-shouldered man came in and set a huge cloth-covered basket down. He opened his coat to show a holstered revolver. Sara took two steps back, her heart pounding in her chest. The man snarled at her. "Do not move! I will be watching you." He went back to the car and brought in four boxes. After he unloaded a small portable heater and a hotplate, he pulled an electric coffee pot from the third box. Without another word, he went out again.

Sara stood still for a moment, listening for the dreaded sound of a lock clicking. *I'm locked in again. At least I know there is someone checking on me.* She opened the last box and found several cans of vegetables, a few dishes, a pan and some plastic tableware. The basket contained canned soup, a can of coffee, a loaf of bread, cheese, fruit, cookies, powdered milk and a twenty-four pack of bottled mineral water. *A veritable feast!*

Chapter 11

Biochemical Research Center

Pavel found Sabine in the sunroom relaxing with a cup of tea. Darya was sitting by her side, reading a book.

"Sabine, there is a package for you. I'll sit with Darya while you check."

"Thank you." She rushed to the main office, thinking the package may contain one of the medicines she had ordered. *Why would the order come here? It always comes to the post office box in Pavel's name.*

The man that had given her the news that her daughter would be taken, was waiting. He handed her a clipboard and a pen. As soon as she signed, he pointed to a package on the desk and left the building.

She puzzled over it being heavier than she had expected. *I'd better open this in private.* She went to her lab. When she opened the box, she found a metal urn. *Oh, God!* She knew without opening it that it held Alexei's ashes. Her first thought was to relay the news to Svetlana. She stopped at the doorway. *If I ever am allowed to return to my home, I'll need these ashes with me. Svetlana will ask me to share them. I can't do that.* She stepped back, closed the door and held the urn against her heart for a moment before returning it to the box it was sent in.

She hid it in the back of a cupboard in the storage closet and went back to the sunroom. "Thank you, Pavel. You can get back to your work now. Darya and I will relax here a little longer."

Moscow

The plane touched down at Sheremetyevo International Airport, which is less than twenty miles from central Moscow. Amber was taken to the terminal building. A man wearing a black leather coat and a narrow-brimmed hat searched the faces of the passengers. When he spotted Amber, he looked at a photo in the folder he was

90

holding and was convinced that she was the one he was to meet. He walked directly over to her. "Good afternoon. Are you Doctor Ludmila Kirsinova?"

"Yes, I am. Good afternoon."

He flashed his identification and asked for her papers. He scrutinized the certification papers and passport. Satisfied, he said, "I am Oleg Popov. Welcome, Doctor. Do you have checked baggage?"

"No, I have it all with me."

He took her suitcase. "I have a car waiting. Please come with me."

A black sedan was waiting in front of the airport. A man in chauffeur attire stood by, holding a German shepherd dog on a short leash. Popov set Amber's suitcase down beside the car and motioned for her to take her backpack off. She slid the straps from her shoulders and set it next to the suitcase. The dog immediately sniffed the suitcase, then the backpack.

Finding nothing suspicious, he settled back on his haunches. The driver opened the back door to let the dog into the back seat, looked at Amber and nodded. She took her place, keeping an eye on the dog next to her. He seemed to be docile, so she sat back and relaxed.

Popov set her suitcase and backpack on the floor next to her. With one swift movement, he slid into the front passenger seat and pointed forward with a flip of his wrist.

The driver eased the car into the traffic.

Amber watched from her window as they drove through the city. On the street between the Moskva River and the Kremlin, she was able to see above the fortress wall to an impressive view of the upper stories and the unbelievable roof line.

She sat back against the seat. It was as if she were living a dream. Not her own dream. The dream of a stranger ... one who was innocently thrust into the unknown. *I am a stranger. I am Ludmila Kirsinova, a Russian doctor.*

Forty-five minutes later, the driver pulled into a parking lot and stopped. Popov got out, opened the back door, lifted Amber's suitcase out and set it on the ground. He took her arm to help her from the vehicle, and then handed her the backpack. The sedan pulled out.

She stood still, waiting for Popov to say something. From the corner of her eye, she saw a black SUV approaching. Popov opened the front passenger door for her, set her suitcase in the back, and then went to one of the parked cars.

Amber sat next to the new driver. She wondered why they weren't moving. He seemed to be waiting for someone or something. She hesitated.

Finally, she said, "I am ready to continue the journey."

Without turning his head, he nodded once and pulled away.

Biochemical Research Center

After traveling for an hour, the driver came to a wooded area, then immediately turned down a side road leading to a circular driveway. He parked in front of a large brick building, which stretched into a U-shape. A flagpole was centered in a grassy area. He picked up his cell phone and pressed a number. "The passenger has arrived." After helping Amber out of the car, he set her suitcase down beside her and drove off.

She waited for something to happen. *Should I knock or call out? Ring a bell maybe?*

The front door opened and a tall auburn-haired woman in a white uniform and lab coat stepped out. "I'm Sabine Heitbrock. Welcome, Doctor Kirsinova. I will show you to your quarters."

After they passed through the lobby, she opened a glass sliding door that led to a hallway with four wooden doors. She opened the first one, revealing a small room with a single bed, a dresser, a desk and two folding chairs. "This will be your quarters. Please call me Sabine. May I call you Ludmila?"

"Yes, that will be fine."

"My room is to the left. The next one down is my private lab and the last one is an anteroom. You must be tired after your long journey."

"I'm fine. I just need to freshen up. Then I'd like to see more of the building."

"I'll come back in an hour."

Amber stretched out on the bed. Shortly, a loud knocking on the door startled her. She jumped up, slipped her shoes on and opened the door.

Sabine stood in the hall holding a carafe of water. She entered the room and set it on the desk. "The tap water here is safe but the mineral water tastes better. Would you like something to eat?"

"No, thank you. I would rather wait until dinner."

"Then I will show you around."

Amber glanced up at a mirror on the wall. "Just a second, I'd better do something with my hair." She brushed it back and fastened it with a barrette. *I'll have to test that mirror when I get back. I hope it's not a two-way.*

Sabine led her past the main lab and down a hallway to several rooms with closed doors. "These are the rooms of some of our patients. We have a different section for the critically ill. I'll take you there tomorrow. Now, I'll introduce you to Alena, one of our nurses. She is with one of my little charges."

Sabine showed Amber through the lobby and into a small sitting room. "Alena Minsky, this is Doctor Ludmila Kirsinova."

Alena stood and shook Amber's hand. "Welcome, Doctor."

"Thank you. It's good to meet you, Alena."

"I will return to my duties now."

Amber checked out the room. Bookshelves lined two of the walls, one held reference books and medical journals, the other was stocked with children's books. Crayons and pencils were scattered around on a low table. A folded easel leaned against a closet door.

Sabine moved toward a little girl who was looking out of the window, twisting one of her long brown braids.

"Darya, come and meet Doctor Kirsinova."

The child turned around and came over to them. She looked up at Amber. "Are you the new one everyone has been expecting?"

"Yes, and I am glad to meet you. You have a very pretty name."

"I am pleased to meet you. You are a very pretty doctor."

"Thank you. What did you see from the window, Darya?"

"I was watching the wind blowing the flag. The wind is magic. We cannot see it but we can feel it, and sometimes, I hear it

93

whispering. The wind makes trees seem more alive. I wish the leaves had not fallen. I like to watch them dancing in the wind."

Sabine took Darya's hand. "I like to watch the leaves dance too. Soon it will be time for dinner. I will help you put your things away later."

"Where are we going?"

"We must find Doctor Antipova. She is in the sunroom with Cassandra. Come with me."

Sabine slid the glass door open. Darya went to the chair where Svetlana sat holding the infant. "May I hold the baby?"

"Not right now, she needs to sleep." She eased Cassandra down in the portable bed, and then went over to Amber. "I'm Svetlana Antipova and I'm happy you have joined our staff."

Amber extended a hand to her. "I'm Ludmila Kirsinova."

Svetlana shook her hand. "Please excuse me. I need to get back to the lab. I'll see you later in the dining room."

Sabine got Darya comfortable on the sofa with a book, and then turned to Amber. "Come and take a peek at our little sleeping beauty."

Amber gazed down at the infant, sleeping so peacefully. "Is she a patient here?"

"Yes. We all take turns caring for her. The other doctor on our staff is Pavel Demidov. Today is his day off." She looked up at the wall clock. "I'm going to stay here with the children a little longer. I'll stop by your room in an hour and we'll go to dinner."

After her shower, Amber looked through the clothes she had brought from Finland. She decided on the blue dress.

She touched the tip of her forefinger to the wall mirror. *There's a gap between my nail and the image. It's only a normal mirror. Good. I can rest easy.*

When Sabine knocked, Amber stepped into the hall. "I'm ready for a hot meal."

"Svetlana and Darya are already there." Sabine led the way. "It's always buffet style. Let's get started."

Amber loaded her plate with hot vegetables and took a dish of rice pudding for dessert.

Darya waved as they approached the table. "Doctor Kirsinova, you have not met my doll." She held the doll up. "Her name is Anna Jelina. Do you like her?"

"Oh, I like her very much. Hello, Anna Jelina."

Svetlana scooted her chair back and touched Darya on the shoulder. "We're ready for dessert. You can come with me and choose your own."

Amber watched them walk away, and then asked, "Sabine, why is Darya here? She doesn't appear to be ill."

"She isn't. All she needs is thyroid medicine. We hide the truth from the authorities so they won't take her from us. We try to give her a lot of attention. Darya needs us. Her mother died giving birth to her." She paused. "Here they come."

Darya held up a plate. "Look at this cake! And I have some ice cream too. Wait until you see what they have tonight. It takes a long time to choose."

Svetlana laughed. "And you should take a long time to eat." She sat down and turned to Amber. "Ludmila, I heard that you have been visiting your mother in Finland. Is she well?"

"Yes, she is in good health. We had a nice visit."

"Were you in Helsinki?"

"No, my mother lives in Kouvola. It's a little more than a hundred kilometers from Helsinki." *I need to change the subject before she asks me something I don't know about Kouvola.* "What time do our duties begin?"

"We usually start at five o'clock but tomorrow is my day off." She looked over at Darya. "I think you are getting tired. Would you like to go to your room now?"

"Yes, please. My doll is getting sleepy."

Sabine stood and hugged her. "Sleep well."

Amber said, "Good night, Darya. I will see you tomorrow."

Sabine stacked their dishes on a tray. "I'll bring uniforms and lab coats to your room at five o'clock. We'll go from there."

The alarm sounded. Amber sat up, stretched, and then opened the blind. The sky was still pitch-black. *Here goes the first day of my nightmare job. Someone is bound to see through me within the hour. Maybe not until after breakfast.* She showered quickly and put on a skirt and blouse. *It's after five o'clock. Do I wait for the uniforms? Or do I go to the dining room now?* She opened the door and waited in the hallway.

Sabine walked toward her with a package. "Here you go. Change into one of these and come to the lobby. I'll meet you there." She took a cell phone from her pocket. "You'll need this to contact me. The black numbers work only within the complex. If we need outside help, we push the red button and an operator will be on the line immediately."

The uniform fit perfectly. Amber draped a lab coat across her arm and went to the lobby.

Sabine gave her a stethoscope and a packet of forms. "When you need more of these forms you can get them from the supply closet."

Amber hung the stethoscope around her neck. *Now I look professional. Ha! I probably have it on backward.* She took it from her neck and stuffed it in her pocket.

They walked into the dining room, the only ones there so early. Sabine put a full pot of coffee and two cups on a tray. "Bring me a sweet roll, please." She poured their coffee and sat down.

Amber brought a plate of assorted pastries to the table and sat across from Sabine. "Where will I be working today?"

"There is no set plan. At times, you will be with Svetlana in the main lab. Soon I will need you in my private lab. We got an early start with breakfast today, so there is nothing urgent. We can talk in my room when we finish our coffee."

Sabine's bedroom was a tad larger than Amber's, enough so a baby crib could fit next to her bed. A rocking chair sat in a corner. Otherwise, it was the same utilitarian style as Amber's.

Sabine pointed to the rocker. "Have a seat while I give you the basics. I keep Cassandra with me at night. I feel more comfortable having her close by." She sat down on the bed. "Cassandra was abandoned in a waiting room in Moscow's Kievsky train station soon after her birth, most likely by her mother. She was taken to a hospital and diagnosed as suffering from congenital cretinism. She was brought here the next day and she has been here ever since."

"Will she ever be completely cured?"

"I'm sure she will. I watch her progress constantly. Svetlana and Pavel often take over for me. Alena is a big help, too."

She lowered her voice. "I hope you will understand this. Most of our patients are terminal before they are sent to us, so they don't object to our use of controversial methods. We give them some hope." She filled Amber in on the way things were operated, and then said, "Very few individuals know this place exists and even fewer are aware of what goes on here. We'd better get started. I'll show you the main lab."

From the entranceway, Amber could see several long tables.

Sabine walked in ahead of her. "Svetlana does most of her own research here. Each table has been set up for different experiments. That way, the chemicals, enzymes, bacteria or whatever we are working with will be ready for the next step."

Amber checked out the array of instruments and containers. *The only things I even recognize are the beakers and the Petrie dishes. I may not last through the day as Doctor Kirsinova.*

Sabine said, "I need to work in an anteroom for a few minutes. Pavel will be here soon, and I'll introduce you. You'll work with me in my private lab most of the time. Please don't go in unless I'm either with you or send you there. Does that bother you?"

"Not at all. You're the boss, I'm the assistant."

"I'm pretty easy to get along with."

She looked up as Pavel came in. "Pavel, this is Doctor Ludmila Kirsinova. Ludmila, meet our Doctor Demidov. I'm sorry to leave so soon, but I have to get back to something. Ludmila, you can catch up with me in the sunroom."

Amber held her hand out to Pavel. "I'm glad to be working with all of you."

His grip was firm as he shook her hand. "Welcome. It's good to have you aboard." He pointed to the first table. "Svetlana has set up this table for working on one of our newest experiments. I don't know if anyone has told you that many of the patients who are sent to us have been afflicted with cancers or thyroid problems that were caused by nuclear accidents. Our research is aimed at finding a cure for such cases." He pulled a chair out for her. "I didn't mean to keep you standing." He sat down next to her and continued. "Thyroid and other cancers developed in many within a few years after the Chernobyl disaster. For some, it has taken more than twenty-five years to develop. Others suffer with congenital cretinism, passed to the fetus by the mother." He paused to check the time. "Sabine may be wondering what's keeping you."

Amber stood and said, "Thank you, Doctor Demidov."

Sabine was waiting. "You need to see a couple of our special patients." She led her through the lobby and down a long hall to a room with swinging doors.

Two elderly women were lying in beds with the rails pulled up. Sabine spoke to the nurse who was sitting by one of the beds. "We will only be here for a few minutes, but you will have time for a quick break."

When the nurse left, Sabine said, "We call this our critical care ward. Some have progressed from here to the medical ward and some have gone into remission, thanks to all of the new medicines we have developed. Others die, no matter how hard we try to save them. We are blessed to have only these two in here now. At times, we have had many more."

She checked the charts and using her clipboard, made her notes for the nurse, and then placed her filled-out forms in the rack next to the door.

When the nurse returned, Sabine said, "Ludmila, I want to show you something back in the sunroom."

Amber followed her down the hall. Just inside the glass door, Sabine pointed to a device on an end table and switched it on. "The warning light blinks if someone is approaching, even before we can see them through the glass door. Although we hear their voices, they don't hear us. Each time we enter the room we switch the monitor on, making the room soundproof. We turn it off before leaving the room."

"That smacks of intrigue, Sabine."

"You never know who is listening. We may need to discuss our work after hours. If someone enters we change the subject, or say we have to get back to work. We can never be too careful around here. Some of our work is top secret. The grounds are patrolled every hour through the night by a security guard. So far, we have had only one incident. Darya spotted a man peering in the sunroom window a few days ago. As far as I know, he has not returned."

"How did the guard miss him?"

"It happened in the daytime. We only have a guard at night, but some of our workers are armed and so is Pavel. Anyway, we have a great alarm system." She sat down on the sofa and motioned for Amber to join her. "Monday, the day you arrived was Pavel's day off and Svetlana has today off. On Wednesdays, starting tomorrow, you will drive to Sergiev Posad for the shopping and mail pick up. The authorities prefer not to have anything delivered here, unless one of their own brings special notices or packages. On Mondays and Fridays, you will only pick up the mail."

Amber frowned. "I was expecting a day off to visit my brother in Dmitrov. Do you know about him?"

"Yes, I know of Fyodor. Your day off will be on Thursdays."

"What about you? Don't you get some free time?"

"I'll be off every Friday, unless there is an emergency, which could happen at any time." She checked her watch. "I must get back to an experiment. You may familiarize yourself with the rest of the research area, and then you are free for the day. You'll need time to prepare for tomorrow."

Amber rose early and went to the dining room. Sabine was already there, a cup of tea in her hand. "Are you ready for Sergiev Posad?"

"Yes. I'm looking forward to the drive." She poured a cup of coffee, put two rolls on her tray and sat down.

Sabine slid a sheet of paper across the table to her. She pressed a finger on the paper. "This circle shows the monastery complex and the square indicates the street where you'll find the post office." She pulled a key from her pocket. "This is to box number 892." Holding up a large canvas pouch, she said, "Put the mail in this." She handed Amber an envelope. "This is the money for the supplies. The van is in the driveway, warmed up and the keys are in the switch."

Chapter 12

Sergiev Posad

Captivated by the onion-shaped domes of the monastery complex, Amber pulled over to the side of the road. *Those blue domes are amazing, and the golden ones ... they are almost blinding.*

An Opel passed by, moving at a snail's pace. *What was that about?* She drove into the city and parked the van close to the door of the post office. She took the mail from the box and stuffed it in the pouch.

A young man loaded the packages onto a cart.

Amber read the address label on each package. They were all from medical supply companies, addressed to Pavel Demidov. She led the way to the van, unlocked the back door, and then helped the man load the packages.

The job completed, she looked over the grocery list. *This is gonna take a while.*

After the groceries were purchased and loaded, she drove the van to a parking lot near the monastery complex and walked on to a row of small stores. A shiver made its way down her back as she sensed something was amiss. She continued on, constantly eyeing her surroundings.

She passed by a bakery, a clothing store and a cafe before crossing a narrow alley. Then she saw the shoe repair shop. Drapes were drawn back from the window. *No customers in sight. I guess this is as good a time as any to meet the cobbler.* Chimes sounded as she opened the door.

A white-haired man sat behind a table mending a leather valise. He stood and stepped up behind the counter. "Welcome to my shop. What can I do for you?"

She pulled a pair of shoes from her bag and set them on the counter. "The heels need replacing." She moved closer to him and whispered, "Is Gudok here today?"

"Yes, he is here. He has been expecting you. Let's go over to my worktable." He took a chair from a corner and placed it opposite a stool. "Please have a seat. I'm Gudok."

"I knew you were really a cobbler. That's amusing."

"It's safe. No one would suspect me of the double duties. My father was a cobbler, so I learned the trade as a child. After all these years, I still use a few of the tools he always used."

"Can you tell me why the name Gudok was chosen?"

"I chose it because it is the whistle of a train. When I was a child, I loved to hear the train as it chugged by. We lived in Gorky. It's called Nizhny Novgorod now and it's different from the town I once knew. There is a Metro, a mall and even a McDonald's!"

"Yes, that's what we call progress. It is inevitable."

"I'm afraid so. I will help you with whatever I can."

"At the moment, I'm just checking in with you. Later I will need several documents, most likely passports and a visa or two."

"I can have them ready at any time. Bring photos, dates and places of births that you wish to be documented. I will give you a camera if you like. I usually keep several extra ones around."

"Thank you. I don't have access to one. Do you know about the operation?"

"Yes, I have been informed. You are a brave woman. I would be proud to have a daughter or a granddaughter like you."

"Thank you. Do you have a daughter?"

"No, I have no children. No family left, either." With his head slightly bent forward, he ran his hands through his thinning hair, lost in reverie. Then he looked up. "I'm alone in the world now. When I'm no longer needed here, I may go to visit some of the places that I dreamed about in my youth."

"Where would you begin?"

"Perhaps I would go first to Greece to see the ancient ruins. Then I would go to Paris to see the sights, and then sometimes I'd just sit with a cup of coffee at a sidewalk cafe along the Seine."

"Perhaps you and I will meet in Paris one day. Who knows?"

"I would like that. I'm Konstantin Rudenko. It will be better for us if I don't know your name."

"I understand. It's time for me to go."

"Wait a moment." He opened a folding door and took a camera from a desk drawer. "Please use this. I will develop them here."

She put the camera in her bag. "Thank you."

The chimes sounded as she walked out. She stopped in front of the clothing store and transferred the keys from her bag to her pocket. She looked in the window at the display. *Maybe next time I'll do some shopping for myself.*

She slowed down as she approached the parking lot. A discreet surveillance assured her that no one was about. She moved to the van and looked around again.

As she turned the key in the lock, heavy footfalls sounded behind her. She twirled around and moved into a defensive stance. She looked into the face of a tall man with a shock of pale-blond hair. He held up both hands. "I beg your pardon. I didn't mean to startle you."

"Why are you following me?"

He lowered his hands. "You came from the Biochemical Research Center, correct?"

"Who wants to know?"

"I am a driver for a medical company."

Not the right answer, Amber thought and held her position.

"You'll have to explain that."

"I was in the area and I saw you leaving. I followed you here because I thought I knew you."

"You don't, so excuse me."

"Wait! Please. Do you know Winterset?"

She surveyed the area again, wondered where he could have appeared from, and then nodded. "Do you?"

"Yes. It's the name of an operation I was to be part of. I had a mission, but it failed. Things went bust from the start."

"Which agency do you work for?"

He looked around before answering. "I'm a freelancer. I do special work for different agencies."

"Do you speak Italian?"

"Yes. And in addition to Russian, I speak English, German, French and Spanish. Why did you ask about Italian?"

Amber held up one hand. "Let me ask the questions, please. You give the answers. What was your profession before you became an agent?"

"I was an opera singer in Milan."

"Sing something from an opera. Softly."

After he sang a few lines from *Aida*, Amber put her finger to her lips. "That's enough. If you are telling the truth, you must trust me with your name."

"I'm Grayson Montgomery."

"What is your home country?"

"Canada. I have been in Russia for only a short time, but I need to get out of here."

"How did you know where the research center is?"

"I was only told that it was about sixty kilometers outside of Moscow. It took a lot of searching to find it the first time. I was in the woods watching the building through binoculars this morning. When you left, I followed."

"All right, I believe you. Tell me what you want from me."

"It will take some time. Can we talk somewhere?"

"We do need to talk. Not today. I know who you are and what you were supposed to be doing. We'll meet early on Friday morning, in the cafe that's just before the alley by the shoe repair shop. I'll order coffee to go. You wait a few minutes, and then come to the shoe repair shop. If you don't show, we'll try again on Monday."

He nodded. "I'll be there."

"Don't approach if I'm wearing a scarf over my hair. If I'm wearing a black one, leave the area at once."

"Understood. Bye."

Amber noticed the slight limp as he walked away. She waited until he got in his car before she pulled out. *So, he was the driver of that Opel that slowed, and then passed me just as I stopped outside of town to admire the domes.*

Biochemical Research Center

Svetlana entered the main lab, poured two cups of coffee, set a cup on the table in front of Sabine and sat down across from her. "It looks as if we could both use a pick-me-up. It's been a crazy morning so far. How is the new doctor working out?"

"She is settling in, becoming familiar with the lab work and with our patients. I'm sure she will do fine."

"That is good to know. Where is she now?"

"She's in Sergiev Posad, picking up supplies and mail. She should be back soon."

"I'm glad she isn't here. I need to talk with you alone. Alexei told me that he had sperm frozen. I promised him I would bear his child if something happened to him."

"I knew about his sperm. It is still safely stored here. Keep track of your times of ovulation. Then I will let you know when we can perform the transfer. We can get together later. Now, I must go to my lab to continue my work."

The discussion about Alexei reminded Sabine that his ashes might not always be safe. *What if Svetlana has occasion to go through the closet and removes the urn? I need to disguise my son's ashes.* She opened the storage closet, took the urn down from the cupboard and went to her room. Looking through her closet, she came across her special blend of herbal tea. *The perfect cover.* The tea leaves had been ground to about the same size and texture of ashes. She emptied the tea into a jar and opened the urn. Seeing the cold ashes that her beloved son had been reduced to caused her more pain. With trembling hands, she transferred them to the oblong tea can that was printed with colorful fruit trees in bloom, pagodas and a bridge over a winding stream. She went back to her lab, placed the urn and the tea can in the cupboard in the storage closet, and then continued her work.

Amber parked the van in front of the building and started unloading packages. Sabine came out to help. "How was your trip?"

"Great. Sergiev Posad is a beautiful old city."

"I'm glad you enjoyed your morning. You may still have the rest of the day free."

"I would like to learn more about the work. Can you spare some time today?"

"I'll make time. I'll be with Cassandra for about an hour. Then I can meet you in your room."

Sabine tapped on Amber's door. "Are you ready for the show?"

Amber nodded. "I'm anxious to get started."

"Would you like to see the grounds first?"

"Yes, I'd like to get some fresh air."

"Let's go out the front door. I'll explain things as we walk." A blast of cold wintry wind greeted them. Sabine pointed to a row of cottages. "That's where some of our staff lives." The four cottages were white brick with green shutters and doors. "This first one is where Svetlana lives now. She recently moved from her room in the main building." They walked on to the next one. "The guard occupies this one. The two larger ones are for the nurses and each has four beds, two in each bedroom. At present, only one of the two is occupied, the one with the open shutters." She pointed to a separate building. "That's where the cooks and the office workers live."

"Is that a garage behind the cottages?"

"Yes. I'll show you what's inside." She unlocked the double doors, revealing an ambulance and an old truck. "If needed, the security guard or Pavel will drive the ambulance. Patients are usually brought in by the authorities in vans or ambulances."

"Which authorities?"

"I was speaking of what you might call headquarters or top brass. Let's just say they are brought in from other facilities."

"I understand and I apologize. I didn't mean to pry."

"I know." She shut the doors and locked up. "It's time for you to see my private lab. After all, you are to be my assistant."

The lab was next to Sabine's room. "This is where you will be working most of the time. What do you think?"

"It seems to be well-equipped and it's bigger than I had imagined." She pointed to the double doors in the back. "What do they lead to, Sabine?"

"After your day off you may begin working with me on the experiments behind those doors. I think you are in for a big surprise! Now I'm going back to my work. You can check on the critical care patients."

Amber changed into a uniform, and then went to the ward. The woman in the bed by the window was whimpering softly. She looked up at Amber. "Is that you, Natalya? Have you really come back to me?"

Amber touched her on the arm lightly. "Yes, I am here. Rest, now. I will be right back." She went to the lab and knocked. Sabine opened the door. "What's wrong?"

"One of the women asked if I was Natalya and I let her think I was. I didn't know what else to do. Who is Natalya?"

"Natalya is the woman's daughter. She never calls to check on her, although we have a special number for relatives to call."

"I didn't check the woman's vitals. She was whimpering when I came in."

"I'd better go back with you." She went to a cupboard and took out a vial and a package of needles. "Let's go."

The woman was crying and flailing her arms. Before Sabine could restrain her to give her the sedative, the patient put her arms down by her side, looked up at Amber and calmly said, "I'm so happy to see you, Natalya. Are you taking care of my house?"

Sabine glanced at Amber. "Natalya, I will leave you with your mother. Have a nice visit."

Amber pulled up a chair, sat next to the bed and propped the woman up on the pillows. She took her hand. "Yes, I'm taking good care of the house and of all of your things. Don't worry. I will be here with you." She stayed, holding the cold, wrinkled hand until the woman closed her eyes. Thinking she had fallen asleep, Amber let go of her hand, stood and walked to the doorway.

The woman called out, "Natalya! Natalya!"

Amber rushed back to her side. "I'm still here, Mother." She held both of her hands, rubbing them to bring back the circulation.

The woman smiled. "Thank you for coming back to me, Natalya. I love you."

Amber patted the woman on the shoulder. "I have always loved you, Mother." *What a depressing job.* She called Sabine on her cell phone. "Can you come to the ward? I think she is fading."

"I'm on my way. Don't give her the sedative."

Amber sat stroking the woman's arm, but it grew colder. The pulse had stopped. *Why didn't I come here earlier? She needed someone. I should have cared. Her daughter should have cared!*

Sabine came in and checked the woman's vitals. She felt for a pulse but there was none. There was definitely no heartbeat. "I'm sorry, Ludmila. She is dead. Thank goodness you were here to substitute for that selfish daughter. You can go back to your room now. I'll take care of things. You're free for the rest of the night."

Amber woke before the alarm sounded. *My day off! I hope Fyodor will accept my explanation. This gets more and more complicated.*

Sabine was waiting at their usual table. "Get yourself some breakfast and join me."

Amber took a bowl of cereal and a cup of coffee back to the table. "I'll be seeing my little brother today." *Oh, boy, another hurdle to get over and another lie under my belt!*

"How are you planning to get to Dmitrov? We have no vehicles here for our private use. Pavel, Svetlana and the guard each have their own."

"I planned to catch a local train. What is the name of this town? I didn't see any signs along the route."

"This complex is not in any town. It's a facility in a rural area and virtually unknown. I suppose it's just another of those secrecy things. I never bothered to inquire and neither should you."

"Understood and accepted." She nodded. "I still need to know where the trains leave from. I'll get a map and figure it out."

Sabine took a folder from the chair next to her. "I brought you one. I've marked all of the roads between here and Dmitrov. You'll need a car to get anywhere near a railway line. Forget the trains, Ludmila."

"Are you saying that I won't be able to see my brother?" Her voice rose. "He's one of the reasons I applied for this job."

"Calm down, please. I'll have to think about this. Let's finish up here and meet in ten minutes in the sunroom."

Amber went to her room and sat on the edge of her bed, trying to get a grip on her feelings. She couldn't stop the fear that invaded her being. *How can I get Fyodor out of Russia if I can't get to his school?* She went back to the sunroom.

Sabine held out a set of keys. "I asked Pavel to claim that he is expecting some important mail today. You can take the van. Go first to the post office, just in case there really is mail. Then drive on to Dmitrov."

"Thank you. A vehicle must be provided for me on all of my days off."

"You are right. I'll ask Pavel to forward your request. He has been working here for a long time and has a lot of pull."

"Are you sure he is okay with the mail idea?"

"Trust me. Pavel will go along with it." Sabine whispered, "He loves me." She grinned and walked out.

Amber raised her eyebrows. *Wow! It just gets more and more interesting around here.*

She unlocked the van and headed for Sergiev Posad.

On arrival, she parked on the street outside the post office. The mail box was empty, as expected. She checked the fuel before driving on to Dmitrov. *Now to meet my little brother!*

Chapter 13

Dmitrov, Russia

As Amber was pulling into town, she could see the famous old earthen ramparts that look much like an elongated, flat-topped hill. She passed by the Dmitrov Kremlin, with its monastery and cathedrals. The domes were almost as beautiful as those in Sergiev Posad. She spotted Fyodor's school, Nikolskie School for the Blind. *Named for the nearby Nikolskie gate, I suppose.*

The parking lot was small, compared to the building itself. She went to the administration office and approached the woman at the desk. "Good day. I am Ludmila Kirsinova, the sister of Fyodor. Would you direct me to his room, please?"

The woman smiled and asked for her identification. Amber put her passport and papers on the desk.

After checking out Amber's identification and going over the information on the papers, she made a call on a cell phone.

A man entered and said, "You may come with me. Mr. Kirsinov is in his room."

She followed him down a long hallway, past a dozen doors. He stopped at the last one on the left and knocked lightly. Amber was shaking inside. *What if Fyodor says the wrong thing in front of this man?*

When Fyodor opened the door, she recognized him from his photos. She nodded to her escort. "Thank you."

"You are welcome." He went back toward the office.

Amber whispered, "Fyodor, may I come in and explain?"

He opened the door wider. "Come in."

She entered, closed the door and started to speak. Before she could get a word out, Fyodor spoke softly. "You are a stranger and a foreigner. What do you want of me?"

She moved closer to him and whispered, "Ludmila sends greetings from Kalinka at the snow dacha. I'm here in her place."

Fyodor pulled back. "I am so glad to see you, Ludmila. Let's go out for a walk." He led her out a side door, tapping his cane on the path as he walked. He stopped by a small pond. "Let's sit down on the bench."

Amber sat beside him and glanced over at his wide-open blue eyes. She had pictured him with closed eyelids. It was hard to believe that he was blind. His straight red hair was streaked with blond and combed to one side.

"Fyodor, how did you know that I was not Russian? No one else has been able to tell."

"Blindness has its compensations. We without sight gain an extra sense or two. I couldn't see you, yet somehow, I saw you in my mind. I felt your presence and knew you as a foreigner, although you speak Russian perfectly. Please tell me why you are pretending to be my sister. Who are you?"

"At this time, I cannot tell you my name. Your mother and your sister are planning to leave Finland soon. Ludmila sent me to work at the Biochemical Research Center in her stead, so I could bring you out of Russia."

"Why would I want to leave Russia? What is going on?"

"I'm sorry, Fyodor. I'm not authorized to tell you. I can only say it is imperative that you and your family relocate as soon as possible. Be prepared to leave at any time."

"I'm not to question your reasons?"

She put her hand on his arm. "It will be safer for your family and for all of us if you can be patient until I contact you again."

"I can. Now please tell me about my family. Are they okay?"

"Yes, don't worry." She took her hand from his arm. "They are safe and in good health. They miss you very much and have asked that I tell you they love you and hope to see you in the near future."

"Where will they see me? I know that my mother is in Finland. My sister usually returns to Murmansk after her visits to her. Has something happened that I know nothing of?"

"Things have changed, Fyodor. Your sister no longer lives in Murmansk. She is with your mother in Finland for the time being. Please do not try to contact them or ask questions about them. That is all I can tell you at this time. I will come to visit you whenever I can, although this could be the only time we can get together until I come back to take you to your family."

"I have no choice but to trust you. I would like to go back to my room now. There is something I want to show you."

It was good to get back to the warmth of the room. Amber sat down on the sofa.

Fyodor hung his jacket in the closet, and then brought out a balalaika. "This is my most prized possession. Do you play?"

"No, I wish I could. I would love to hear you play."

He sat down beside her, tuned the instrument, and then began to play a beautiful, haunting classical piece. He paused for a moment. Then he played "The Song of the Volga Boatmen." He sang in a deep, rich voice.

When he stopped singing, he held the balalaika out to her. "This was passed on to me from my grandfather. Look inside and you will see the date it was crafted."

She checked the inscription. "Oh, it's from the year eighteen ninety. Such a fine old instrument could never be replaced."

"I'm glad you understand that. I will expect to take it with me when you come for me."

"Do you have a case for it?"

"Yes, and I have a padded cloth covering for the case. I will keep it ready at all times, along with a few items of clothing. I am grateful for all that you are doing to get me back to my family. You need to understand that I have never thought about leaving my homeland. I have always been a faithful servant of Russia but if leaving my country is the only way to be with my family, then it is worth the sacrifice."

"I understand your feelings for your country. I can assure you that it is the only way."

She took the camera from her pocket. "I will need photos in order to have new identification papers and a passport made for you. May I take a few of you now?"

"Yes, please do."

She snapped six pictures of him and put the camera back in her pocket. Speaking in her normal tone, she said, "Please walk with me to your door. I must leave you now."

Standing at the threshold, he said, "Goodbye, Ludmila."

Chapter 14

Biochemical Research Center

Amber sat up and stretched. *It's Friday, another post office day and a day to escape my duties. Thankfully, Sabine has directed my every move so far. I've got to get us out of here before someone realizes I don't know what the heck I'm doing!*

After a quick shower, she put on a black skirt and a white blouse. *My town outfit. Oh, for a pair of jeans and no need for pantyhose.*

Sergiev Posad

After picking up the mail from the post office, Amber parked the van in the lot near the shops and walked to the cafe. Glancing in the window, she saw Milano sitting at a table, drinking coffee.

At the counter, she ordered two cups of coffee to go, and then went to the repair shop, expecting Milano to arrive shortly.

The chimes made their usual tinkling sound as she entered. Konstantin was standing behind the counter working on his logbook. "It is good to see you again."

"I brought coffee. I hope you will join me."

"I'm glad to have your company. Let's go to my little home beyond the curtains." He pulled a cord and the curtains parted. He pointed to a wooden table with four chairs.

She stepped through, set the coffee on the table and sat down. "I know an agent in the area who needs our help. I have asked him to meet me here today. He has been hiding out but now he wants to get back home to Canada. He will need a new passport and a visa showing an entrance date into Russia."

"Are you sure he is trustworthy?"

"I have tested him and I know without a doubt that he is the man who was to be part of my mission. I'm to get him safely out of Russia. I told him your last name but not your code name."

He set his cup aside, reached across the table and patted her hand. "If you believe him, then I accept the job."

"It would mean a great deal to the agency and to me."

Konstantin put a finger to his lips and shook his head as the chimes sounded. Amber nodded and moved away from the table. As she leaned against a wall, he went quickly through the curtains to the counter. "Good morning. May I help you?"

Smiling, Milano took off a shoe and held it up. "Do you have the proper heels to fit these shoes?"

"Yes, I do. When will you need them?"

"There is no hurry." He put the shoe back on.

Amber peeked through the curtains to be sure it was Milano. "I'm glad you made it." She introduced them.

Konstantin said, "I understand you need documents. Do you have photos you can leave with me?"

"No, I don't."

"I have a camera. Let me know when you need documents of any kind."

"Thank you. I hope to leave soon, now that I have help."

Amber said, "Konstantin, it's time for me to go. I'll see you in a couple of days." She turned to Milano. "I'll leave first and wait for you in the parking lot. You know the one. We need to clarify a few things."

"I will be there."

Konstantin looked up at the clock then motioned for them to follow him to the back room. "A customer is due any minute. Wait here a few minutes, please." He hurried to the front of the store.

The chimes sounded. Amber drew Milano to the wall and whispered, "It's probably just his customer."

Konstantin said, "Good morning. The valise is ready to go." He lifted a package from the shelf under the counter. "I hope your husband will be pleased with my work."

"Oh, I'm sure he will be satisfied. How much do I owe you, Mr. Rudenko?"

"Please indulge an old cobbler. The tiny rip in the valise took only minutes to repair. Just tell your friends and family about my shop. I will not accept payment today."

"Well, just this one time. The next time I bring something to be repaired, I will insist on giving fair payment."

He chuckled. "I am in agreement. Good day."

When the chimes announced the customer's departure, Amber joined Konstantin and motioned for Milano to come through the curtains. "I'll meet you in the parking lot."

She turned to Konstantin and took his hand in hers. "Thank you. I'll be seeing you."

On her way to the van, she paused in front of the clothing store. After a moment of consideration, she pursed her lips. *I have seen many women wearing jeans here in the city. Why not me, on my days off?*

The saleswoman smiled as Amber entered the store. "May I be of service?"

"Do you have blue jeans in stock?"

"We do. You will find your size on the second counter. I will assist you."

Amber took two different styles to the dressing room and quickly tried them on. *These will do. I have to beat Milano to the parking lot.* She thanked the saleswoman and paid the cashier. According to her watch, she would have to get a move on. She walked on to the parking lot.

Milano arrived within five minutes. Amber scanned the area, and then led him to the front of a nearby car. More out of sight there, she looked up at him. "Helping you seems to be part of my mission. I'd like to know what happened to you after you arrived in Russia."

He took a deep breath. "The agent who assigned me to the mission met me at the airport in Moscow. He said the mission had been aborted, so I was to catch the first flight back out the next morning. He gave me a plane ticket and some false documents. Then he handed me a wad of cash and told me to go to a hotel for the night. The next day when I got to the airport to catch the flight, I saw a couple of men who seemed to be watching me closely. Security was extremely tight at the airport and I didn't have an authentic passport or visa. When I had the chance, I left Moscow."

"I'm glad you're alive. Where are you hiding out?"

He lowered his voice. "I'm living with a Russian woman, in a town nearby. I have plenty of money and I pay my own way, but it's her house and I feel somewhat like a kept man. It's safer for me than staying in a hotel. Meeting her was a stroke of luck." He paused and cautiously looked around. "I have no family, so I don't mind being here. It's just that I'm suspicious of everyone who even glances my way. And now, I think it's time for me to get out of here and get back to the life I used to have."

"I can't help wondering why you never contacted the agency. Someone would have come for you."

"At the time, the agent made me feel as if I had been the cause of the problem and that I was in danger. He told me not to mention anything about the assignment to anyone, ever. He made it clear that I should not report back to PDI. I was to just disappear."

"That doesn't make sense. The agency doesn't work that way, Milano. It sounds to me like a conspiracy."

"Because of my background, Russia is not a place to be stranded in. I knew I'd have to figure a way to get out eventually. Now seems to be the time."

"I'll do my best to help you get home. I'll be back here Monday morning and we can meet again. When you are sure it's safe, follow me into the shop."

"Okay. Thanks for your help. I don't even know your name." He grinned. "Shall I call you Mrs. Smith?"

She shook her head. "That's tempting, and it's ordinary enough but what about a Russian name?"

"What about Pavlova?"

Amber laughed. "That will do for now. I'll see you next time."

Biochemical Research Center

Amber had just stepped out of the shower when she heard a light knocking on her door. She wrapped a towel around her torso, went to the door and leaned against it. "Who's there?"

"It's Sabine."

"Give me a couple of seconds to put on my robe."

She opened the door. Sabine was standing there dressed for work. "Good morning, Ludmila. We work weekends around here, you know."

"I do know and I have no idea why I didn't remember to set my alarm last night."

"You only overslept a little. I stopped to ask if you'd already eaten, but I see by your outfit you haven't."

"Do you mind starting without me? I will be ready in ten minutes."

"No, I don't mind. I'll see you there."

Amber dressed in her uniform and went to the dining room. *It's probably a lab day. What if Sabine expects me to mix something in one of those beakers? I hope I don't blow up the place. Maybe I should just tell her who I am.*

She spotted Svetlana at the buffet table with Sabine. "Good morning, Svetlana. How are you?"

"I'm fine and I'm looking forward to spending some time with the little girls today."

"I see you have your tray ready. I'll get my breakfast and meet you at the table." She chose a pastry, poured a cup of coffee and joined them.

As soon as Svetlana left the room Sabine said, "Ludmila, I'd like for you to work with me in my private lab today."

"I'm ready to go with you now."

Sabine led the way, unlocked the door, closed it behind them, then reached back and locked it again. "There is something I need to show you."

Amber followed her to the double doors at the back of the lab. Inside there was a wide cupboard. Sabine unlocked it and pointed to the tanks of liquid nitrogen. "Those hold embryos that Pavel and I have cloned."

Amber gasped and put her hand to her forehead.

Sabine said, "Don't tell me you are shocked, Ludmila."

"I am utterly stunned!" She gathered her composure. "How can I assist you with that?"

"I'm not asking for your assistance." She put her hand on the tank that was marked only as *Ivan*. "Inside this one is a very special clone." She turned to look intently at Amber. "Ludmila

116

Nikolaevna Kirsinova, you have been chosen by Russia's highest powers to give birth to this human being. You will have the honor of being the surrogate."

Amber was dumbfounded. "Are you crazy, Sabine? I won't risk my life for an embryo. Especially for one of a person I don't even know!"

"Oh, you know him. Everyone does. The whole world knows of him. Let's go to the sunroom."

Amber started to tremble but managed to follow her. *Have these people gone stark, raving mad? Or am I just having another nightmare?*

Sabine switched on the monitor, and then stood face to face with Amber. "The top people want you for the surrogate because you are young and healthy. And because they know you will never try to leave Russia as long as your brother is alive and within their reach." She shook her head. "Do you think you were chosen to be my assistant because you are such a fine doctor? You don't even know what you are doing half the time! I have to coach you every step of the way. Anyway, I'm afraid you have no choice." With her eyes blazing, she said, "Your real duty here is to be the mother of the *new* Nikolas Romanov and *he* will be the new Czar of Russia." She grabbed her by the shoulders and squeezed hard. Amber tried to pull away. "Stop it! You're hurting me!"

Sabine eased her hands away and drew a breath. "You must accept your destiny, Ludmila, as I have accepted mine. I didn't ask to come to this place, be a virtual prisoner and be forced to apply my expertise to this project. You have no right to refuse the honor."

"I have no idea what knowledge you possess that gives you the right to re-create a human being. If you and your cohorts are inclined to create life by bringing back the dead, fine. I will not be any part of it!"

"You will cooperate or they will never allow you to see your brother again. Never! I know, because I have experienced their anger and their retaliation."

Amber hesitated for only a moment. "Sabine, there is something you need to know. I'm not Ludmila Kirsinova. I'm here in her stead to help you escape this place and get back home. I'm an agent from PDI in Washington."

Sabine put her hand to her heart and collapsed onto the sofa.

"Oh, my God!"

Suddenly, she broke into laughter. "Can you imagine the furor at top level over an American woman bearing a Russian czar? Especially an American agent! Ludmila or whoever you are, I'm sorry I hurt you. Please forgive me."

"You are forgiven. I know that you have only done what you had to do. Now it's time for me to get you safely away from here, as soon as possible."

"I certainly do want to go home but there is another problem that keeps me here." She looked over at the door. "One of the nurses will be coming here soon with a patient."

"Can we speak in your lab?"

"We'll talk outside, later. I need to go back to my room and think about my next step. We won't utter a word about this to *anyone*. I'll meet you this afternoon."

Amber and Sabine cleared the table after lunch, and then walked down the hall to the front entrance. Sabine closed the door behind them. "Svetlana is in the sunroom with Darya and Alena is caring for Cassandra, so we have about an hour." She pointed toward a wooded area. "Let's get out of sight."

They reached the end of the driveway and walked down the road. Amber said, "We have to get away from here. How soon can you be ready to go?"

"First, hear the problem that I mentioned earlier. I can never leave the complex as Pavel and Svetlana do. They are trusted, as long as their families are in Russia. You have been allowed to visit other towns, because the brother of Ludmila Kirsinova is in Russia. They used my son to control me until he died and now they have taken Liesel, my daughter, for security. She is only nineteen years old!"

"Where was she taken from?"

"Gdansk, Poland. I was told she would be taken to Russian territory. I figure she is being kept somewhere in the Kaliningrad Oblast, because of its proximity to Gdansk and because the man had said she would be *taken* into Russian *territory*. Otherwise, he would have said she would be *brought* into *Russia.*" She stopped near the edge of the woods. "Step in here for a moment. You must understand that I won't go back with you until my daughter is taken to a safe place and given a new identity. When and if that happens, I will be ready to leave with you."

"Surely you don't expect me to find Liesel without knowing exactly where they are keeping her. Isn't it enough that I 'm risking my life to rescue you?"

Sabine pointed a finger in Amber's face. "If you or another agent can't get Liesel to safety, I will stay right here with all my secrets until she is safe. PDI has many contacts. I'm sure that if you report this they will arrange for others to help. You are in danger yourself, and so is the brother of Doctor Kirsinova since you refuse to bear the Czar."

"If the wrong agency finds out that your daughter has been taken, it could turn into an international incident. I will not ask another agent to step in." *This is a new twist, but it seems to be part of my mission. If she refuses to go, I will have failed. Ari, you are about to be activated.* Amber turned to Sabine. "I will try to find your daughter. You must tell me her address in Gdansk. This may be just a ruse to keep you under their control."

"The man who gave me the information was very convincing and frightening. I think we'd better finish this conversation later. Svetlana may be ready for me to sit with Darya and wondering where I am. Cassandra will be missing me too."

"Could we get together in your room later?"

Sabine motioned for her to head back. "Yes, after Svetlana has retired to her cottage for the night."

Amber stole down the hall to Sabine's room. The halls were empty, the silence disturbing. She had barely tapped on the door before it opened. She entered and closed the door. "Everything is so quiet. It's eerie."

"Yes, it's spooky working in my lab late at night, but it's fine other times. Make yourself comfortable." She turned the radio on and fiddled with the dial until she found a station playing classical music. She drew closer to Amber. "How soon can you go to Gdansk? Time is of the essence now."

119

"I know. There is someone who will cover for me, beginning in a few days."

"We can't have another doctor show up in your place! How could I explain that?"

"My sister is already in Moscow waiting to cover for me. She is my identical twin."

"That's a twist on double agents! Can you contact her without arousing suspicion?"

"Trust me. I'll work out the details. I need a photo of Liesel."

"They took all my pictures from me as soon as I arrived here. Her hair is long and dark blond with a few lighter streaks."

"How tall is she?"

"About your height, I think. She has a light complexion and she weighs about a hundred and twenty pounds. Do you know the Kaliningrad Oblast?"

"I know that it's an exclave, not connected by land to the rest of Russia. I have often been up to the border in Poland, but I have never crossed over into the Oblast. I have several contacts in Poland and in Germany that I can count on for assistance."

"I'm asking an awful lot of you, I know. I'm at my wit's end. Darya and Cassandra have to come with us too." She put her head down, silent in thought for a moment, and then looked up. "I can't, and I won't leave without them."

"I have been meeting with someone that can help us. I'll speak to him on Monday."

"Earlier, I mentioned that Darya had seen a man peering in the sunroom window. Could he have been looking for you?"

"He was looking for me or any agent to help him get out of Russia, but he is not the one I was speaking of." She took the camera from her pocket. "I'll have to take a few photos of you for the visas and passport. Change your hairstyle to one you have never worn here."

Sabine took a few hairpins from a drawer, brushed her hair back, twisted it into a bun at the nape of her neck and pinned it securely.

"How's that?"

"Good. Now change to a dark or a bright-colored blouse. I'll put a sheet on one wall as a backdrop."

Sabine came back and posed. Amber took the shots. "After you snap pictures of the girls, I'll take the camera back to my source. When he develops them, I'll bring half of the photos to you. You'll need them with you in case something goes wrong in Gdansk. Without a photo of Liesel, I won't be able to get a passport for her now, but we have ways to get her out of Russian territory and back into Poland where she can get the proper documents."

"Thank you, Ludmila ... I mean ... who the hell are you, anyway? I don't know what else to call you."

"My name is not important at this time. I'll tell you when we are safely out of Russia. You'll just have to go on calling me Ludmila or Doctor, for now. I did okay with the deception, until you forced my hand by telling me I was chosen to be the mother of the Czar!"

Sabine muffled a laugh with her hand. "You'll probably never have an offer like that again."

"That's a once in a lifetime thing, I'm sure." She looked up at the clock. "What's on for tomorrow?"

"We'll work in my lab."

"Okay. I'll see you tomorrow."

"Good night, *Doctor*."

Svetlana was finishing her breakfast when Sabine entered the dining room.

As soon as Sabine sat down with her tray, Svetlana said, "Please forgive me for being so abrupt, but we must speak before Ludmila arrives." She looked down at the table, then into Sabine's eyes. "From the sunroom window, I saw you two speaking in front of the building yesterday. Then you both walked toward the woods and disappeared. I think you have chosen her to be the mother of Alexei's child."

"I would never ask her to bear my grandchild. I hardly know her. You were supposed to keep track of your times of ovulation. If you had, I would have done the transfer immediately."

"I have been checking faithfully and the time is right! I had to wait until Ludmila was not around to let you know. She makes me uncomfortable. I don't know why. Anyway, you should ask her to assist during the procedure. I would be embarrassed for Pavel to be present. When can you arrange it? It must be done very soon."

"We can do it today, if you like. First, I must check your chart. It may be too late for this month."

"I know that I have counted the days properly, and I checked my temperature this morning. Today will be fine."

"Okay, Svetlana. I will ask Ludmila to assist. She is with Darya in the sitting room. They had breakfast early this morning. As soon as I finish here, I'll go speak to Ludmila. Meet me in the sunroom in two hours."

Svetlana touched her on the shoulder as she walked past to take the tray away. "Thank you. I'm happy that the time has finally come."

Sabine waited a few minutes, and then went to the sitting room. "Good morning, Darya. I see that you are busy." She patted the child's cheek. "I will see you later this afternoon. Now, I would like for Alena to come and sit with you. Okay?"

"Oh, yes. I want to stay here. I'm going to paint a beautiful picture after I am finished coloring. Then Alena might take me outside to play."

"Please save your painting to show me later."

Darya looked up and smiled. "I will."

Sabine leaned close to Amber. "We need to speak privately. Meet me in my room after Alena gets here, please."

As soon as Amber greeted Alena she rushed to Sabine's room. The door was wide open. Sabine was sitting on the bed, staring into space.

Amber closed the door. "I think we need a little music."

Sabine switched the radio on. "Things are piling up."

She motioned for Amber to sit in the rocking chair. "I don't usually come apart like this. The last couple of days have been very difficult for me. Now, there is another problem that needs fixing. Svetlana was engaged to my son. We have vials of his sperm frozen and stored here. Svetlana had promised him she would bear his child by artificial insemination if something should happen to him." She put her head in her hands.

"Take your time, Sabine. I know this is difficult for you."

122

Sabine raised her head and looked up at her. "I'm sorry. It just hurts so much to think back about his death. This morning Svetlana reminded me about the sperm again. I don't want her to bear my grandchild, because she will never leave Russia. I would never see the child if I do get back to the States. Svetlana advised me this morning that she is ovulating and she expects me to do the transfer. We have planned to do it today and I want you to assist. It's a simple procedure that only requires one person to complete, but as a safety measure, it's good to have someone standing by."

"Standing by is one thing that's easy for me to do."

"I am going to fake it. I just hope she doesn't realize what I'm doing … or not doing. Anyway, she is resting now."

"I don't understand why you think it's permissible to do the transfer without authorization."

"We have the freedom to perform any operation, on anyone we choose. You might say we are the *Black Ops* of research."

Amber grimaced. "Then why can't you choose someone else to bear *Ivan?*"

"You've got me there. I wouldn't want to take the chance. I've done enough against the big guys and that would put me higher on the hit list when we leave here."

"Shall we go to the dining room for a snack and something hot to drink?"

"You go on ahead. I'm supposed to get back with Darya."

"Why don't you bring her to me in the dining room? She can stay with me while you and Svetlana talk."

"Good idea. I'm sure Darya is ready for a snack by now."

Amber made a fresh pot of coffee. *I'm gonna need a lot of this to keep my sanity. Things can sure get crazy around here.*

Sabine brought Darya in. "Ludmila, I'll come back later. If you aren't here, I'll check the sitting room. Wish me luck!"

"Good luck. You may need it."

Darya sat beside Amber. "I brought the painting with me!" She unrolled a paper and held it up. "Do you like it?"

"Yes, I do. It is really beautiful, Darya."

"I made a bunch of trees. See the little baby ones beside the mama tree?"

"Yes, I see them. And you made a rainbow behind the trees! You are a very clever girl and a good artist. Give me a hug!"

Darya reached over and put her arms around her. "Can I have a dish of ice cream?"

"You sure can. I will go with you to choose."

Sabine came back in a few minutes and stood behind Darya's chair. "Ludmila, the transfer has been arranged. It's to be done today. Now I'm going to take over for the nurse who has been with Cassandra most of the day. Meet me in the main lab about five o'clock." She patted Darya on the head. "Let me have a look at that painting."

Darya unrolled her masterpiece and held it up.

Sabine smiled. "Oh, that is a wonderful painting. Would you like to come with me? You can play with the baby."

"Yes! Goodbye, Doctor Kirsinova."

"Goodbye, Darya. I will see you later."

Amber changed to a clean uniform and went to the main lab. It was time to assist with the transfer procedure.

Sabine handed her a cap to cover her hair. "Svetlana will be here any minute. I put a sheet on that table by the ultrasound machine, and the sperm is ready for transfer to the catheter. It's just water. I hope she doesn't notice. I'll scrub up again when she gets here. Are you nervous about this?"

"Yes, I am. I hope I don't faint."

Sabine laughed. "You won't. *Doctors* don't faint!"

Svetlana opened the door and looked around. "I see you are ready for me." She went behind the screen and changed into a gown. Then she sat on the end of the table, slipped her feet into the stirrups and laid back.

Sabine scrubbed up and put on sterile gloves. "Svetlana, I'm going to give you a shot to relax you."

"I was expecting it. Even doctors want something to lessen the pain."

Amber scrubbed, put on gloves, and then stood beside the table, waiting to be asked for assistance. Sabine put a sheet over Svetlana's torso and rolled it up to just past her waist. She turned away as she transferred the "sperm" to the catheter. She inserted it into Svetlana's vagina, pretending to guide the catheter through the cervix and into her uterus.

It was all over in a few minutes. Sabine leaned down and said, "It is done. You are going to be a mother. How do you feel?"

"I'm okay ... maybe weak and groggy from the shot."

"That's to be expected. When you feel up to it, I'll go with you to your cottage where you can rest longer." She removed her gloves and cap. "Ludmila, I'll see you later."

Amber threw her cap and gloves in the waste basket and went to the door. "Congratulations, Svetlana." She turned to Sabine. "I'll see you at dinner."

When the sound of Amber's footsteps died away, Svetlana sat up. "I don't want to go back to my place. I'm too excited to rest now. I'm hungry! Walk with me to the dining room, please." She put her hand on her stomach. "I have to be careful. I'm carrying precious cargo!"

Amber came in as the others were finishing their desserts. She fixed a salad plate of fresh greens and tomatoes, and then joined them at the table. "I'm sorry I'm so late. I was reading and I fell asleep."

When Svetlana was ready to go to her cottage Sabine said, "I insist that you allow me to escort you home."

"Okay, but I'm feeling fine."

Sabine turned to Darya. "I will be right back."

When Sabine returned, she said, "Ludmila, I'll take Darya to her room now. Then I'll have to get Cassandra. She's with one of the nurses. Please come to my room in about half an hour."

Amber nodded and said good night to Darya. After they left, she lingered over her coffee for a few minutes, then stopped by the sunroom. She switched on the light, opened the drapes and looked out at the starry night. The moon hovered above the dark woods, dispelling a few of the shadows.

She looked up at the clock. *Oh, no! I'm supposed to be with Sabine now.* She switched off the light, walked down the silent hall and knocked lightly on the door.

Sabine opened it and motioned for her to enter. "We'll have to talk quietly. Cassandra is asleep."

125

Amber looked down at the baby. *This is not a place to raise children. We've got to get them away from here.*

Sabine took the camera from a dresser drawer. "I just wanted to return this. I snapped several photos of each of our little ones. You can take the camera back to your contact."

"Okay. I'm sure they'll be fine. Now I think I'd better get myself to bed. I'll be leaving early for Sergiev Posad."

Sergiev Posad

As usual, the post office was Amber's first stop. She stuffed the mail in the pouch. *Lucky for me there were no packages today.* She drove to the parking lot. At the bakery, she bought six cinnamon buns, and then stopped by the cafe to pick up three cups of coffee.

When she arrived at the repair shop, Konstantin was already at his worktable. He put his work aside. "You are here early this morning. I sense there may have been trouble, but let's have that fresh brew while we talk. You know I could have coffee waiting if we had a certain time to meet. You wouldn't have to stop at the cafe."

"I don't mind. Anyway, I can never be sure of an exact time that I would be here. Uncertainty is part of the job."

He opened the curtains for her. After she was seated he took the chair across from her.

She leaned forward. "You were right. There has been trouble. I'll need to call the embassy. Things have changed."

The chimes rang. *It had better be Milano!*

Konstantin stepped through the curtains. "Please come in." Milano followed him to the kitchen.

Amber was relieved. "I expected you earlier."

He shrugged. "I saw someone in the parking lot that looked familiar, so I sat in the car pretending to study a map until he left. I waited a couple of minutes before I went to the cafe. You were nowhere in sight so I figured you'd already been there."

"If you see him again, let me know and we'll use a different parking lot."

Konstantin pulled a chair out for Milano. "I'll heat up a couple of the cinnamon buns for you."

Milano moved the chair next to Amber. "Do you have any idea when you will be leaving? I'm thinking I should wait and help you get the others out."

"I was hoping you would. We can leave soon but something has come up, and I need to make a solo trip first. I'll be leaving in a couple of days. It will be at least a week, maybe two, before I get back and ready to roll."

"No problem. I'm prepared to leave anytime."

Konstantin set the buns and coffee in front of Milano, and then he turned to Amber. "You mentioned a phone call?"

"Yes. We should get that done before a customer comes in." She looked over at Milano. "Listen for the chimes, please. If anyone comes in, signal us." She looked back at Konstantin and nodded. "Lead on."

In his private room, he dialed the special number. "I need to speak to Mr. O'Bannon." He was asked for his code name. "I'm Gudok. I have Mrs. Winter waiting." When O'Bannon came on the line, Konstantin handed the phone to Amber.

"Greetings, O'Bannon. If I suddenly hang up, stay around. I'll call back when it's clear. The mission has come close to a standstill but not yet gone Humpty Dumpty. There has been a change of plans. Tell Ari to forget about the Arbat meetings for now. I need her here. Is she still a redhead?"

"Yes. Will that work?"

"No. Take a few shots of her first and use them on a passport for me, made out in the name of Cynthia Blackwell. The visas will be done here. Then ask Ari to dye her hair back to dark. If you have any qualms about her carrying the passport, send the photos with her and I'll have it done here. I'll be the redhead when I leave here for the next piece of the game." She paused. "Ari needs to be wearing a dark-colored jacket with a hood and a light-colored scarf, or a black one if she needs to signal. She is to bring a backpack with two sets of casual clothing, including shoes. Please add a red wig for me. Ari absolutely *has* to leave her rings with you. I'll need about two hundred thousand Russian Rubles, ten thousand Polish Zlotys, one thousand Euro and one thousand United States Dollars. Okay?"

"That's a big request. Will you be able to account for it?"

"As well as I can. That's only equal to about eight thousand dollars. I may not use all of the money, but I'd feel a lot safer having it to fall back on. Will it play, or not?"

"Yes, if you give me a hint about where the money is going."

"Sorry. I can't. Please trust me on this one, unless you know something about the operation that I don't."

Slaney stayed quiet for a moment. Then he said, "I'm sure you know more about it than I do, and I need to know what you're planning. Don't forget I'm *control* on this operation."

"This is one of those things that shouldn't be *controlled* from Moscow. I can't tell you more. Get it?"

"Got it. When is D-Day?"

"If all goes as planned, it will be the day after tomorrow. Tell Ari to catch the suburban train from Moscow's Yaroslavl station that leaves just before seven a.m. I'll be waiting at the station in Sergiev Posad. If she doesn't make it, I'll wait for the next train to arrive. If she's not on that one, I'll call you."

"Anything else?"

"The rest can wait until she arrives. Bye now." Amber hung up the phone. She looked at Konstantin and grinned. "So, I am Mrs. Winter now."

"That is an alternate code for those of us who have not been informed of your personal code name."

She nodded and handed him the camera. "I took several photos each of a woman, a man, a little girl and an infant. Hold on to them until things clear up."

"Let me know when you need the documents. Will you be back here on Wednesday morning?"

"I'll be here very early. Is that okay?"

"Yes. I'm an early bird. I'll make a pot of coffee when you arrive. You won't need to stop by the cafe."

"Good. I'll see you on Wednesday."

Milano was still waiting at the table in the kitchen.

Amber came over and threw the paper cups and napkins in the waste basket. "It's time for us to leave. Konstantin is expecting people. You go out first. I'll meet you in the parking lot."

Milano was sitting in his car when she arrived. She scanned the area. Finding nothing out of the ordinary, she walked on toward his car. After another look around, she stood by his open window as if asking directions. "Has anyone tried to contact you?"

"No. It's as if the agent that brought me here has abandoned me. How did you first hear of my plight?"

"At one of my briefings for the operation, I was told that a Canadian agent had been sent, but he failed to meet his contact in Moscow. I was to find you and get you out, if possible. You were not my first priority. Sorry about that."

"That's okay. I'm glad I found you."

"It's a good thing you did. I wouldn't have had any idea where to look for you. I will see you again in a week or two. Come to the shop only on a Tuesday or a Thursday. Konstantin will tell you when it's safe to come on the other days. I can't say why."

"So, it's one of those need-to-know things. I get that a lot."

Amber laughed. "Don't feel bad, that's a way of life for me. It won't be long before we have to find a way out, so be ready to leave at any time. Let me pull away first. I'm running a little late."

Chapter 15

Outskirts of Mamonovo, Kaliningrad Oblast, Russia

Rain pelted against the roof in a steady cadence. Sara looked up toward the skylight and shook her head. *At least I don't have to bear the silence.* She opened a can of soup and heated it in the only pan the man had left for her. She wasn't hungry. It was something to do and it would keep her strength up. *I have lost all track of time. How many days have I been here? They can't keep me here forever.*

She looked around the bleak room. Sometimes she recited poetry or sang to pass the time but not today. Her throat was sore from screaming for help.

Looking up at the skylight, she noticed that the sky had darkened, although it was only late afternoon.

Thunder rumbled in the distance. Then she heard the deafening sound of a thunderclap. She counted ... *one, one thousand, two, one thousand, three, one thousand ... four, one thousand ... five ...* lightning struck. She spoke aloud. "That's not far away!"

By late evening the sky was as black as midnight. Sara couldn't see the glimmer from a single star as she stared up toward the skylight.

She took the blanket from the cot, clutched the warm wool around her shoulders, and then sat down on the bench to wait out the storm. Thunder and lightning were still wreaking havoc and the rain had become a torrent.

Feeling hungry, she laid the blanket aside and checked the food box. There wasn't much left other than a can of soup, yet there was still bread and enough marmalade to make a sandwich. She poured a cup of water. Before she got back to the bench, thunder roared. As soon as she began counting again, she heard a loud cracking sound. *That was close. One of the trees in the grove must have been struck.* The light flickered and died. In the darkness, she fell over the bench onto the floor, spilling the cup of water. After screaming her frustration, she yelled out, "What more can happen on this wretched day?"

She sat on the bench and ate her sandwich in the dark. Then she made her way to her bed.

Sara woke to dead silence. The storm was finally over. She threw the blanket off. *I must have fallen asleep during the storm.*

She flipped the light switch. *It works! Now I can make coffee.* Daylight was already peeking through the skylight. She took the coffee pot to the sink. *What the heck?* Water was streaming through a slit in the wall and into the sink. *The storm was a blessing! I might never have noticed that slit if the storm hadn't brought so much rain.* She looked for something sharp to enlarge the opening with. Finding nothing, she checked the bathroom. *The hook!* She twisted the metal hook on the back of the door until it came loose, and then took it to the sink. She forced the hook deep into the slit and twisted it back and forth. It was slow work on the tough metal, but she finally made it a little wider. After she worked on it for a couple of hours her hands couldn't bear it anymore.

I'll work on it again this afternoon and every day. Now, it's breakfast time!

She started a pot of coffee, sliced the last of the bread with the plastic knife and sat down to wait for the coffee to perk.

Chapter 16

Biochemical Research Center

Svetlana overtook Sabine as she entered the dining room. "I'll join you for coffee before I leave. Shall I bring a cup for you?"

"Yes, please do. I'm just going to grab a pastry this morning. I'll catch up with you." She studied the selection of goodies. *They all look tempting, but I'm going to resist them today.*

She sat down across from Svetlana. "Will you be seeing your family today?"

"Yes, as I usually do on my days off." She glanced toward the entrance. "I see Ludmila will be joining us." She set her cup down and waited until Amber came to the table with her breakfast. "Good morning, Ludmila. I have to be going now. I got off to a late start today."

"Oh, it's your day off. Have a good time." *Svetlana always hurries away when I arrive.*

Svetlana stood and took her coat from the back of the chair. "Thanks. I have a busy day planned. I'd better get started. Goodbye."

Amber asked, "What is on the agenda for us stay-at-homes today, Sabine?"

"I hate to admit that when Svetlana is away, I tend to slack off on my work. I can afford to, now that I've already accomplished the most important task. My *Ivan* is the prize, the triumph. For Russia, that is. And if I had succeeded in transferring that prize into your womb, Doctor Kirsinova, I might even have been canonized."

Amber laughed loudly. "Whoops! I hope no one heard me."

"Don't worry, Ludmila. No one would begrudge us a little fun and laughter. It's a pretty rare happening around here. I see that you are finished with breakfast. Let's go to my lab."

Sabine unlocked the wide cupboard at the back of the room. She pointed to the liquid nitrogen tanks. "When I first arrived, I believed that I had been brought here only to care for Alexei, my son, but I was assigned to clone *Ivan*, our *John Doe*. Some of the other embryos were cloned by Pavel before I began working here."

"Who were the others?"

"I wasn't told. Their identities are to be kept secret. I do know that a couple of them are clones of family members of top officials. I suspect that at least one of the others may be royalty. I have no way of knowing for sure, although rumors are still flying around about the missing remains of two of the Czar's family members."

"What will happen to the Czar's clone after you leave?"

"I don't know. I imagine Pavel will take over. Then a new surrogate must be chosen."

"I'm certain that many Russian women would be honored. By the way, I've been wondering how you were able to clone the Czar, as he and his family were cremated."

Sabine closed the cupboard. "They were not cremated until much later. Anyway, they had been buried for many years before their remains were positively identified. The ground where they were interred stayed frozen for much of each year, and the DNA proved that the remains were those of the Czar. Samples had been taken from his bones, hair and from wherever else possible. Later, some were secretly brought here. They were enough for me to complete the process."

"I wonder what God thinks about cloning. Worse, what will He do about it?"

"We'll just have to wait and see. Maybe He lets us do whatever we want. It looks as though He's going to let us destroy humanity, and the planet, too. A few other things are still being experimented with, such as somatids, also called bions, that were discovered long ago. They are able to withstand up to fifty thousand REMs of nuclear radiation, and carbonization temperatures of 392 degrees Fahrenheit. They can return to the soil and live for millions of years longer after the death of the host. I think that the bions assemble as the spirit after we die."

A chill stole down Amber's back. "That's creepy, Sabine."

"To you, maybe. It's all in a day's work for me. And that would prove, once and for all, that those who claim to have seen a ghost were not imagining it." She shrugged her shoulders. "It is believed by some scientists that bions were the first cosmic manifestations of life, the precursors of DNA and I tend to agree with the theory. Scientists have discovered other things that would cause widespread panic if the public knew about them. If I hadn't managed to speed up the cloning of *Ivan*, someone else would have. Lately there has been talk of a group that is planning to take Russia back to the old ways. I assumed it was back to communism. Now, I'm wondering if they want to go back to being ruled by a czar." She closed the cupboard. "Come with me. I want to show you something in one of the anterooms."

Amber looked around the room. "What is this place? It looks empty, and it's so cold."

"It's an extra room that's used for storage. There's nothing in here that will shock or even surprise you." She unlocked a small closet and showed Amber the liquid nitrogen tank on the lower shelf. "This contains what is left of my Alexei. At his request, his sperm was frozen and stored in vials in that tank."

"For Svetlana, but you didn't use it."

"Right. I still have the sperm. I need to take it with me when I leave. I'll choose someone to bear my grandchild, whatever it costs. I'm really sorry I had to deceive Svetlana. She had been with Alexei for several years before he became ill. They were very much in love. One of them should have told me about his illness, but I'm sure they believed he would recuperate, and they wanted to spare me the worry. As soon as I got here I began caring for Alexei. His cancerous thyroid had been removed but not before it had spread to his lymph nodes, bones and lungs. It was in his larynx. He had been in a coma for a week before I arrived, so there were no last words for me to treasure. I can only hope that somehow, he knew that I was with him. I tried every treatment and medication we knew about, to no avail. Alexei was the only reason I agreed to come here."

"What do you mean? You were abducted, weren't you?"

"Not exactly. A man came to the research center in Maryland. He told me my son was critically ill in Russia and that I could come and take care of him, but I could tell no one. I was to simply disappear. So, I went with him willingly."

"Who was the man?"

"I don't know his name. I think he was CIA. He told me to bring all of my records, notes and any other information I could find. Then I was forced to steal all of our newly discovered drugs and some of the smaller equipment. A different man, a Russian, showed up when we got to the airport in Washington. He sat next to me on the flight to Moscow. When we arrived, he had a van waiting to bring me here. As soon as I arrived, Svetlana briefed me on Alexei's condition. I spent as much time with him as possible."

"Did you ever see the agent again?"

"No. He left as soon as the Russian met us in Washington. Anyway, I didn't question anyone. I only wanted to be with my son." She put her head in her hands. "Give me a few minutes to compose myself. We can talk later in my room."

As soon as Amber entered, Sabine turned the music on and sat down on her bed. "Sit wherever you like."

Amber sat in the rocking chair. "My cover will meet me tomorrow. I'll fill her in on the details about the mail and groceries. Then I'll have her drive here. She should be arriving close to the time I would have."

"What about a code word or sentence?"

"Let me think a moment."

"Tell her to pull up out front. I'll be watching for her from the sunroom window, and then I'll help her unload the van."

"Good. Rather than using a code word, I'll have her bring something for you to give to Darya."

"I like that idea. I'm sure Darya would love to have a teddy bear."

"I'll stop by the department store and get one. Ask my cover for the bear as soon as she arrives. That will be the code."

"Okay. I believe that you will get my daughter to a safe place. When you come back we can prepare to leave."

"We still have a long way to go before we get out of Russia. I'll leave for Gdansk from Sergiev Posad tomorrow."

"Liesel rents a room on Zimozielony Street and she works in the spa at the Hotel Baltika." Sabine wrote the address and the name of the woman who owns the house on a piece of paper. "Burn this after you memorize it."

"Is Liesel's last name Heitbrock also?"

"Yes. She is not married."

"Does she speak English?"

"Yes. She also speaks Russian, Polish and German. She was born in Berlin. Alexei was born in Moscow. I had moved there from the town in Siberia where I was born. I studied in Moscow to become a doctor and was working in a hospital in 1986 when the nuclear disaster happened in Chernobyl. I treated the injured that were brought to us. I worked with Doctor Evgeny Borodin and we fell in love. After we married, I moved into his apartment. Alexei was born two years later. My husband became ill soon after. He lived for only nine months after the onset of the disease."

Sabine grew silent. She seemed to be lost in thought for a moment. "When Alexi was three years old, I received a grant to study biochemistry, genetics and a few other subjects in Berlin. My cousin lived nearby and she took care of Alexei while I trained. After two years, I married one of the instructors, a widower, Werner Heitbrock. He adopted Alexei and we changed his name to Heitbrock."

"Was Mr. Heitbrock Liesel's father?"

"Yes. She was born three years after I married him. He died when Liesel was six years old. I stayed in Berlin until she finished her education. Then, after she took the job in Gdansk, I applied for the position at a research center in Maryland and soon became an American citizen." She jumped up. "Oh, I forgot!" She opened a drawer and took out the keys to the van and the mail pouch. "I've been babbling about my life, keeping you from sleep."

"I'm glad you confided in me. Your life has been unusual." She grinned. "And it may be about to get way past unusual!" She rose and walked toward the door. "You're right, I do need to sleep."

Amber woke with a start. Tension prickled under her skin. *This is it. No mistakes!* She quickly made her bed, showered and dressed. Then she made her way down the halls to the front door and out to the van.

Sergiev Posad

She arrived at the post office just as a worker was unlocking the door. She put the mail inside the pouch and loaded the packages in the back of the van.

After parking four blocks from the train station, she tore off a sheet of paper from her notepad and jotted down a note for Ari. She put a scarf over her hair, took a look around, and then walked on to the station.

With a few minutes to spare before Ari's train was due, Amber checked the schedule for trains to Poland. *It looks as if I'll have to risk taking a train to Moscow first. Or take the long way around. Neither is a good choice. Tomorrow I'll leave from Moscow on the Polonez, although it passes through Belarus. That means having Konstantin forge a transit visa for me.*

She watched as Ari stepped off the train. Without making eye contact, she walked past her, turned back, passed her again, and then bent down as if retrieving something. Approaching her, she held the note up. "Excuse me, I think you dropped this."

Ari read the message: *Wait a couple of minutes. Then walk four blocks south. Then just follow my lead.* She tied her scarf a little tighter and walked on.

Amber waited by the van until she saw Ari, and then walked to the shopping center. She slowed at the entrance to a department store, glancing back over her shoulder to make sure Ari was still with her before going in. She went to the restroom with Ari right behind her. Amber pointed to the backpack. "Quick, give me the wig." She went into a booth, put the wig on and the scarf over it. Then she joined Ari at the sink. "Let's exchange jackets and get out of here. We can walk together now."

"Hey, Sis, did I do okay?"

"You were perfect. Did you have any problems?"

"No, it went just like clockwork."

"Great. Please tell me that you have at least one pair of jeans for me."

"I do. I figured you'd need them for whatever you do next. And I added a skirt."

"Good girl. Now, I have to buy a teddy bear."

Ari shook her head. "I won't even ask why."

"That's not one of those need-to-know things. You can help me choose one."

They stopped by a display of stuffed animals, which were mostly bears. Ari picked up a brown bear with a bright-green ribbon tied around its neck. "What about this cute little fella?"

"He's perfect. Let's pay and move out."

Ari's curiosity got the best of her. "Who's getting the bear?"

"I'll explain when we get to the shop."

They started toward the exit. Amber stopped. "Wait, I should get the hair dye now." She chose a shade of red that was close to the color that Ari's had been, and bought four bottles of it, and two of the darkest brown. They left the store together and walked the four blocks to the street where Amber had left the van. She drove to the regular parking lot and stopped. "This is where you'll leave the car after you have picked up the mail. Then you walk to the shoe repair shop. This time, let me leave first. Walk on the other side of the street, staying a few feet behind me. When I go into the shop, you pause and look in the window of one of the stores. Give it a minute or two before you cross over and walk on. I'll let the cobbler know you're on your way."

Konstantin was sitting at his worktable when Amber entered. She quickly took off her scarf and the wig. "It's only me. My cover should be here momentarily."

"I have started a fresh pot of coffee. Let's go into the kitchen."

The chimes sounded as soon as they had stepped through the curtains. Konstantin went back to greet Ari. "I am Konstantin. Welcome to my world."

"Thank you. It's good to be here."

"Please come with me." He pulled the curtains back and motioned for her to follow.

Amber said, "Konstantin, meet my cover."

"You've found the perfect one. She looks exactly like you."

Ari looked at Amber. In a hushed voice, she said, "I may have been followed. A man was standing across the street watching me when I had paused to look in a store window. I saw his reflection in the glass, but when I turned to look at him, he had disappeared."

Konstantin said, "Allow me to have a look. It is not unusual for me to step out for a breath of air."

Amber said, "You may have an early customer. I'll go out the back way and check around." *It was probably Milano.*

In a few minutes, Amber returned. Looking at Ari, she said, "I didn't see anyone. Was the man tall and blond?"

"He was tall, but I couldn't see his hair. He was wearing a hat."

"You must be extremely observant when you leave here. Try not to appear nervous. Don't give anyone a reason to suspect you."

The aroma of the freshly brewed coffee wafted through the room. Konstantin brought over a tray with three cups of coffee.

With a half-smile on her face, Amber said, "I cannot tell you my sister's name. You know how it is."

He leaned toward Ari. "You may know my name, though. My last name is Rudenko." He pushed his chair back. "Pastries are in the breadbox. I must get to work now. I will check with you soon, in case I'm needed." He reached back for his coffee. "I'll finish this while I work."

Amber brought the goodies to the table. "Keep your hair dark until you hear from me. As soon as you leave, I'll dye mine red. Every Monday, Wednesday and Friday you will drive to Sergiev Posad to pick up the mail." She gave Ari the key to the box, the mail and the pouch. "Here's the mail for today. On Wednesdays, you will be given a shopping list." She held out two slips of paper. "This is the list for today, and this is a map that shows how to get to the grocery store from the research center and the best way to get back." She took an envelope from her purse. "Here's money to pay for today's supplies. When I come back to take over, I'll be sure to arrive at Konstantin's shop on one of the mail days so we can switch. Any questions, so far?"

"May I know where and why you are going?"

"I'm afraid not. No one at the embassy knows. Willoughby doesn't even know. Remember that you are Ludmila Nikolaevna Kirsinova. The doctors call one another by their first names. The nurses, the patients and the security guard will call you Doctor Kirsinova."

"Who shall I ask for when I first arrive?"

"Sabine will meet you outside the building. Just pull up in the driveway in front of the door. She will ask you for the teddy bear. Then you'll know for sure she's Doctor Heitbrock. It's for her special charge, a little girl named Darya. Sabine will help you unload the van and show you to *your* room. She will explain, in private, about the meals, patients and whatever. She knows that I'm not Ludmila, but she will always call you that. You will be working closely with her. You can trust her. I didn't tell her my name, so don't tell her yours or anything else personal. Doctor Svetlana Antipova is in her late twenties. She is suspicious of me, so don't get too friendly. Doctor Pavel Demidov is the only male doctor there." She paused and leaned back. "Thursdays will be your days off. Ordinarily you would go to Dmitrov to visit *your* blind brother, Fyodor. He knows I won't be there for a week or two, so you'll have to figure out something else to do on those days."

"How long will you be gone?"

"I can only tell you that I expect to be back in less than two weeks, maybe in one week, if all goes as planned. So, you should only have a couple of Thursdays to worry about, at the most. You could go to that shopping center where we were today or just hang out somewhere for a few hours. Don't come to Konstantin's shop on a Tuesday or a Thursday unless your cover is blown and your life is in danger. Then, use Konstantin's phone to call the embassy. Clear?"

"Yes, clear." *Good grief! That's a heck of a lot to absorb.*

Konstantin came in and spoke to Amber. "Will you be leaving from here today?"

"That's the plan. While I'm away, my cover will be coming here in my stead, always on the same days and about the same times."

"Okay, I'll be looking for her."

"May we use one of the rooms to change our clothing?"

"Yes, come with me." He showed them to his bedroom. "Just go back to the kitchen area when you are finished."

They disrobed and each put on the other's outer clothing and shoes. Amber reached for the backpack. "I'll take this with me. The clothes you will wear, including my jeans, are in the closet and dresser drawers in my room. You'll be wearing a uniform most of the time. I guess that's about all. Sabine will answer any questions you might have."

Amber gave her passport and ID papers to Ari. "Give me the Cynthia passport."

"It's in the backpack."

Amber took the passport out and looked at the photo. "It looks good. Now I need the money Slaney sent."

Ari took an envelope from her purse. "I hope that's enough."

"It's more than enough. I'll leave about a third of the rubles with you. Give them to Sabine to use in case things go wrong."

Ari frowned. "What do you mean, wrong?"

"It's just an expression. Sabine will understand. Now, we need to exchange purses." She removed the few cosmetics and gave her the purse. Reaching for Ari's purse, she deliberately gazed into the eyes that were so like her own. "You're on duty. Be vigilant."

"I will. I'm just going to pretend to be a doctor, while you're off to do who knows what or where."

Amber took her by the shoulders. "Please look at me. It takes all of us to complete an operation, but you are the only person in the world who can cover for me. I could not do this without you!"

"Could you let go of me so I can fulfill my duty?"

Amber released her shoulders. "I guess I got carried away. I'm sorry. Let's go back to the kitchen now."

Konstantin was already there. "How are things going?"

"We're finished. My cover will leave as soon as it's clear."

"There is no one here. Come on out to the front."

They stepped through the curtains. Amber gave Ari the keys to the van. "Go now. Be very careful!"

"I will. You too." She shook Konstantin's hand. "Goodbye and thank you." She hurried out the door and walked back to the van. She checked the directions again and started off. *My life as a spy is about to begin.*

Amber turned to Konstantin. "I need to mess up your bathroom sink. I'll have to dye my hair red and it will take two applications. Is it safe for you if I'm here that long?"

"You are welcome to stay as long as you want. Customers will presume you are either family or a friend if they should hear you moving around. Just keep away from the front."

"Okay." She took seventy thousand rubles from the purse Ari had given her. "I want to leave this with you. Use it if needed. Some of our people may have to leave in a hurry. I have more than enough with me."

He accepted the money. "I'll keep it in my safe."

"I may need to stay in town overnight. My train leaves very early tomorrow morning."

"I have a sofa in the living room that opens to a bed. You are welcome to sleep there. No one comes here after my working hours."

"Thank you. I feel safe here. I'll go color my hair now."

Amber checked the color of her hair after it dried. *It's a muddy red. I may have to do it over.* She relaxed at the kitchen table until Konstantin came in to join her.

She showed him the passport Slaney had sent. "Do you think my hair color will pass inspection?"

He studied the photo. "It's a little different, but you may get away with it. I don't mind taking more photos."

"I think the dull red would attract less attention. Let's take the photos. I'll need an exit visa for Russia, a transit visa for Belarus and a visa for the Kaliningrad Oblast."

Konstantin looked up at the wall clock. "I close the shop in about three hours. Fix your hair the way you want it for the photos. Later tonight I will begin work on the documents."

"No one at PDI or the embassy knows where I'm going. You know, because of the visas I need. The doctor I'm to get out of Russia has asked me to find her daughter, who was taken from Poland into Russian territory. We have reason to believe that she is somewhere in the Kaliningrad Oblast. Do you know of a place in the area where they would have taken her?"

"I would need to think about it. I do know the area. I'll get the camera. Come back here after you style your hair and we will discuss the matter."

Amber joined Konstantin in the kitchen. He took several extra shots of her, and then sat down at the table. "That should do it. Sit, please, while I tell you what I know about the Kaliningrad Oblast."

She sat across from him. "Have you been there?"

"Yes, many times in the past but only once last year. The authorities would want as few people as possible to know about her. So, she would be taken somewhere temporarily. Somewhere secluded. If she was taken to the Kaliningrad Oblast, it would not be to the city of Kaliningrad. It would be to a place very near the border so she could be transported quickly. Which border have you chosen to check first?"

"I thought maybe Mamonovo would be best. The border can be crossed by train or taxi from Gdansk, Elblag or Braniewo. Any of the three would be convenient for me."

"She could be just over the border into the Oblast. If you do get to Mamonovo, nose around … talk to people. Just don't ask or tell too much. Offer money if necessary. Finding her may be more difficult than getting her to safety."

"I'll do my best."

"I believe you will. Good luck. Perhaps you should rest until I'm finished for the day. You have some difficult times ahead of you." He sighed. "It has been a long time since I've had company after business hours. Perhaps we could go out for dinner. With your new look, you certainly won't be recognized."

"That would be great. I haven't been out for the evening in a long time. I'll take a rest now. I want to be ready for tonight."

She looked through the clothes that Ari had packed for her, and then stretched out on the sofa.

Konstantin stood at the entrance to the living room and called out, "Hello in there. Are you awake?"

Startled out of a deep sleep, Amber raised her head from the pillow. "Come in. I'm awake."

"Wait in the kitchen for a few minutes while I dress for our special dinner."

"Okay. I'll see you there."

In a few minutes, Konstantin came into the kitchen wearing a navy-blue suit, a light-blue shirt and a yellow tie. "Is this proper attire for our date?"

"Perfect! Now, I must get ready."

She dressed in the black A-line skirt and the long-sleeved lavender blouse that Ari had brought. Reaching into the backpack, she pulled out a pair of black flats with silver buckles. She styled her hair, put her jacket on and went back to the kitchen. "I'm ready. Where shall we go for dinner?"

"I think we should drive to a place on the outskirts of the city." He took his overcoat from the coatrack. "Come, I'll show you to my car." He stepped out the back door, checked the area, and then led her to a maroon sedan.

After driving for fifteen minutes, he pulled up and parked in front of the Golden Samovar restaurant.

The host met them at the entrance. "Please allow me to take your wraps before I show you to your table."

Amber looked around the dining room. The servers and the host were wearing black tuxedos, white ruffled shirts and red cummerbunds. The violinist, also wearing a tuxedo, played classical music as the band accompanied him. Amber hadn't expected anything more than an ordinary restaurant. *I feel like I'm in a dream or a fairy tale, not in the middle of an assignment.*

The server brought two wineglasses and a bottle of red wine to their table. He poured a little of it in Konstantin's glass. "Compliments of the house." Konstantin took a sip. "It is perfect. Thank you."

After the man poured their wine and moved on, Konstantin held his glass up. "To my lovely companion!"

Amber lifted her glass. "To a terrific evening!"

The band struck up a waltz. Konstantin stood and held out his hand to Amber. "Would you like to dance?"

She took his hand, and he led her to the dance floor. She managed to keep in step as they twirled around. *It has been forever since I've danced a waltz. And I haven't stepped on his toes!*

When they returned to their seats, the server came to the table. Amber ordered cheese blintzes and a salad. Konstantin chose the Beef Stroganoff. They dined by candlelight.

The meal ended with goblets of raspberry sorbet.

"This really has been a special evening, Konstantin. I haven't had so much fun in a long time."

"I haven't had this much fun in many years."

The band began playing "My Lonely Heart." Amber asked Konstantin to dance with her.

When the song ended, he pulled her chair out for her. "How about topping off the night with some Irish coffee?"

"Yes! That's something I haven't had since New Year's Eve. It will be a grand finale to a grand evening."

Back in the shop, Amber laid out her clothes for the next day and went to the kitchen to wait for Konstantin. He was in the back room working on her documents. When he finished, he joined her at the table. "Please see if these are satisfactory. I didn't use that American passport O'Bannon sent you. As a citizen of the United Kingdom, you can have a special seventy-two-hour visa for the Oblast. So, you are English! I added a hotel reservation, which may still be mandatory."

She checked the passport and visas. They were as perfect as forged documents could be. "Everything looks authentic. Now, I am Cynthia Blackwell, a tourist from England. Thank you." She stood and started toward the doorway but turned, sat back down and said, "You told me that you had no children. Did you ever marry?"

"No, but I was in love when I was very young. A family from Perm, in the Urals, moved into my neighborhood. I became friends with the son who was my age. One summer, a beautiful young girl from a village near Perm came to visit that family. I was introduced to her and it was love at first sight for both of us. That is something that doesn't happen for many people. She stayed until the beginning of autumn." He reached across the table and took Amber's hand. "I worked hard and saved my money so we could be married when she finished her education. I visited her and her family in their village whenever I could." He paused, then let go of her hand. "I was shocked when I heard she had married another. The family moved away from that village and I never saw her again. I was heartbroken."

"Did you ever fall in love again?"

"No, but there were a couple of others that I was involved with over the years. No one could make me forget my first and only love. Would you like to see a picture of her?"

"Yes, I would."

He went to the special room, opened the bottom drawer of his worktable and took a photo album out. Then he came back and sat down. He took one of the photos out and handed it to her. "This is my love."

Amber stared at the photo. Chills ran up and down her spine. Her hands felt so cold that it was all she could do to hold on to the photo. She trembled. He didn't speak at first. His mouth hung open. Finally, he stood. "What has come over you, child?"

She stood up and faced him. "A photo exactly like this has a place of honor on my mother's mantel." She put one hand on his shoulder and held the photograph in front of his face. "Konstantin, this woman is my grandmother, Lilia Sokolovskaya!"

"But … her name was Lilia Avdeeva."

"That was my grandmother's maiden name!"

He put his arms around her. "So, I have a part of Lilia right here with me. You should have been my granddaughter, you know." He pulled back to study her face. "I think you look a little like her. You have her expressions and her eyes. No wonder I've been dreaming about her lately."

"You should see my mother. She looks very much like Lilia."

"I would love to meet your mother. Perhaps I will someday. Tell me about Lilia. Is she in good health?"

"I'm sorry, Konstantin. She died a few years ago."

He sat back down, put his head in his hands and wept.

Amber stood behind his chair. "Lilia had a good life and my grandfather was a good husband to her. Before she died, she told my mother that her marriage had been arranged. Her parents had betrothed her to a man who had been assigned to a diplomatic post in the United States. My grandmother also said that she had never forgotten her first love, her true love from her youth in Russia."

With tears still in his eyes, Konstantin stood and pushed the chair back. "You must get your rest. You need to steel yourself for what lies ahead. And I, an old man, need to rest and to grieve."

Amber touched his hand. "Good night, my dear friend."

"I will cook breakfast for us tomorrow. Good night."

After Amber went out, Konstantin held the photo and traced the outline of Lilia's face. *So, you didn't forget me. You loved me for the rest of your life, as I have loved you. Good night, my love.* With heavy steps and thoughts of what might have been, he made his way to his room.

Konstantin was preparing breakfast when he heard Amber stirring in the next room.

She pulled her jeans on, put on a blouse, brushed her hair back and fastened it into a ponytail. *Now, I really look like a tourist!* She joined him in the kitchen.

He carried their coffee and a pitcher of milk to the table, and then brought in a tray with a platter of waffles and a bottle of syrup. He sat down across from her, put three waffles on a plate and handed it to her. She cut a piece off with her fork. "Delicious!"

When they were finished eating, Konstantin said, "I hope you are up to all of this."

She scooted her chair back and stood. "I have to be."

"I can drive you to the train station."

"Thanks, but it's not far and it's safer that way."

He nodded and looked through the curtains. "It's clear. Take care of yourself."

"I'll be okay." She hurried out the door and headed to the train station for the short train ride to Moscow.

When the train arrived in Moscow, Amber reserved a place in a three-berth sleeper on the *Polonez* to Warsaw.

She found a kiosk and bought bottled water, bread, cheese, cookies, chips and a couple of apples. Her eyes took a thorough sweep of the area. Seeing nothing suspicious, she walked to the platform and boarded the train.

In her compartment, she reached up and laid her jacket at the foot of the top bunk, and then stepped back into the corridor to look out the window.

As soon as the conductor checked her ticket, she hoisted her backpack up onto her bunk, climbed up and relaxed.

Amber woke just before the train stopped at Brest, Belarus. She stood in the corridor to wait for the customs agents. The Polish border at Terespol was less than ten kilometers away.

The agents at both borders stamped her passport and examined the contents of her backpack. No problems. In just three more hours she would be in Warsaw, waiting for a train to Gdansk.

Chapter 17

Outskirts of Mamonovo,
Kaliningrad Oblast, Russia

Sara listened to the soft soughing of the wind from her prison. It only added to her melancholy.

She looked through the slit in the wall, which was just wide enough to see a few trees now. It brought in more light and a bit of hope.

The humming of an engine startled her. She quickly placed the coffee pot in front of the slit.

The man that had brought the food before entered with two bags and set them down on the floor.

She mumbled, "Thank you."

"Don't bother to thank me! If it were up to me, you would starve and save us all a lot of trouble." He turned and went out the door. The padlock snapped shut.

Sara opened a bag and found two cans of soup, a can of mixed vegetables and a carton of powdered milk. The second bag held a couple of packages of cookies, a loaf of bread, a block of cheese and a box of crackers.

She moved the coffee pot away and started working at the opening with the hook. *I have to keep going!* Her blistered hands bled again. Cold water from the spigot barely eased the pain.

At twilight, she heated a can of soup and made a sandwich.

Soon the darkness took over. She switched on the light and tried singing to pass the time. It only made her feel worse.

Later, when she glimpsed a few stars shining faintly through the skylight, she turned in for the night. She found temporary peace in her dreams of home and family.

Chapter 18

Gdansk, Poland

In Gdansk, Amber took a local bus to Zimozielony Street. She remembered the number of the house where Liesel had been living and walked the few blocks to her destination.

She pushed the buzzer. An elderly woman opened the door.

Amber smiled. "Excuse me, do you speak English?"

"I speak a little of the English. May I help you?"

"Yes, please. I am looking for Liesel Heitbrock. I understand she rents a room in your house."

"She is away now. How you say, *wakacje?*"

Not surprised but disappointed, Amber said, "Vacation. I am sorry that I missed her. When she gets back, would you tell her that Cynthia stopped by?" The woman nodded her head. "Yes, I will tell her."

"Thank you." Amber walked back to the bus stop and caught the next bus back to the train station. She made a call to the Hotel Baltika and asked for Liesel Heitbrock. The receptionist said that Liesel had been scheduled to begin her vacation but so far, she had not picked up her vacation check. *That doesn't mean she was taken. Maybe she didn't need that check right away. It does seem suspicious though. I'll have to look for her.* She bought a one-way ticket to Elblag and went to the platform to board the next train. *A train goes on across the border, but I'm not sure I want to chance crossing by train.*

Elblag, Poland

Amber spotted a taxi parked in front of the station. *That may be the best bet.* She opened the door and leaned in. "Will you drive me to Braniewo, please?"

"Will you pay in Euro or dollars?"

"I have both and also zlotys. Which do you prefer?"

He took only a couple of seconds to decide. "One hundred and eighty-five dollars."

"Will you stop and let me out when I ask?"

He shrugged. "Give me the money."

She got in the back seat, counted out the money and handed it over the seat to him. "Can we go now?"

He nodded, put the money in his pocket and drove away.

Amber leaned back against the seat. The ride would take less than an hour.

Braniewo, Poland

When they arrived in Braniewo the driver said, "We are here. Where do you want me to stop?"

"Please just drive through the town. Then I will tell you when I want out."

"Okay, but do not wait much longer or we will be too close to the Russian border."

"I understand. Please warn me when we are getting close and I will get out. Is that okay?"

He pulled over to the side of the road. "This conversation does not sit right with me. First, you wanted to come to Braniewo. Now you want to get close to the Russian border. What are you up to?"

"Nothing illegal. I have a friend who lives on the outskirts of town near the border. I want to surprise her by just walking up to her house. She has no idea I am in Poland now."

"If you want to go any closer to the border, it will cost you another fifty dollars. Is your surprise worth it?"

"Yes." *As Konstantin suggested, offer money if necessary.*

She took a one-hundred-dollar bill from her neck pouch. "Here. Please take this and drive on." She reached over the seat and pressed the money into his hand.

"Thank you. I refuse to go closer than two kilometers from the border."

"That will be close enough for me. Carry on."

Soon, he pulled over. "Okay. Now we are a little less than two kilometers this side of the Kaliningrad Oblast. This is the end of your ride. Are you sure you can find your friend's place?"

"Yes, I am very sure. Thank you. Goodbye."

She looked behind them, and then forward again. There were no vehicles in sight. She stepped out and waved him on. When he was out of sight, she crossed to the other side of the road and ducked into the wooded area. As she walked toward the border, she stayed within the cover of the trees.

Although she couldn't see the vehicles, she could hear the sound of the engines. She had made her move just in time.

The going was slow without a path to follow. She zigzagged through the woods, tripping often over fallen branches. Breaking a new trail put her training to the test. The sun shone overhead, bringing a little warmth and light in between the trees. She continued on her way, wondering if she had passed into Russian territory yet. *I've come almost two kilometers, I'm sure.*

Without warning, voices came from nearby. Amber froze in place for a moment. She stepped behind a tree. *They're speaking Polish. This can't be a checkpoint so far from the road. It's got to be a guard post. A Polish one!*

Soon she heard one of the men say goodbye. Dry leaves rustled as he walked away. She waited a couple of minutes before calling out, "Hello! I am an English tourist. May I approach?"

A soldier pointed his rifle in her direction. "Come out with your hands high!" He took one step forward.

She slipped her backpack off, dropped it to the ground and came out from behind the tree with her hands up. "I was on my way to Mamonovo and somehow I got lost. My backpack is behind that tree. I have proper documents."

The soldier came closer, stepped behind her, cuffed her hands behind her back and searched her pockets. Then he looked behind the tree, picked the backpack up and searched it. He led her to the foot of a lookout tower. "Where are your papers?"

"My passport is in a neck pouch, inside my blouse. If you will take these cuffs off, I will get it for you."

He glared at her. "I will get it!" He unzipped her jacket, unbuttoned the top button of her blouse, reached for the straps of the pouch and pulled it out. He studied the photo, and then checked her passport and visa. "You could have entered the Kaliningrad

Oblast legally. You have no reason to be skulking through these woods. You had better tell me the truth, young woman. Now!"

"I am desperate. A friend of mine was taken from Gdansk to somewhere in Russian territory. I'm not sure if she is in this area or elsewhere in Russia. She is being held captive. Have you seen anything unusual near the border in the last week or so?"

He scoffed. "Every day and every night I see something unusual. Your trespassing through my post is the first unusual thing today." He slung the strap of his rifle over his shoulder, unlocked the handcuffs and removed them. Handing her things back to her, he said, "I am on duty. My replacement will arrive in a few hours. You cannot remain here, and you are not safe hiding in these woods. You are in grave danger!"

"I know, but I will not walk back to Braniewo. I will take a chance and go through the woods into Russian territory."

"You cannot do such a thing! Do you think the Russians are stupid? They also have soldiers guarding their borders, and not only at the checkpoints. They have guard posts scattered at places along the border, as we do on this side." He pointed straight ahead. "There! That is the Russian side. You will find no houses or buildings in this area. If there were any close I would have seen them. I stand on that lookout tower with binoculars many times during the day, scanning the area. My replacement does the same at night. You are wasting your time searching. Leave the area. Go back the way you came. I cannot help you. Do you know the Russians are bringing men and equipment into the Oblast now?"

"No. I have been traveling, so I have not heard. I will go back." She held out her nearly empty water bottle to him. "Could you spare a little water, please?"

"Yes, that is one thing I can do for you. Come with me." He led her to a small lean-to, took out a jug of water and filled her bottle. "Walking makes one very thirsty. Do you need food?"

"Yes, I do. Thank you."

He gave her another bottle of water, half a loaf of bread, a few slices of cheese and a chocolate bar. "This will keep you going for a few kilometers."

"Thank you."

"I am sorry that I cannot help you find your friend."

Amber reached for his hand and shook it. "I understand your reasons. Now I will go through the checkpoint legally. Thank you."

When she was sure she was out of his view, she sat down and leaned against a tree. *At least I know about the soldiers and these woods. I may have to bring Liesel this way.* She rested for a couple of minutes, and then struggled on through the wooded area, keeping away from the road, although she was still in Polish territory.

Tired and hungry, she sat down on the gnarled trunk of a fallen tree and ate some of the bread and cheese. Then she drank the rest of a bottle of water. *I'm almost back to the point where I entered the woods. It's time to move on.*

She walked to the edge of the road and turned back toward Braniewo to catch a train to Mamonovo. The traffic was moving faster now. She was startled when a taxi pulled off the road. The driver beeped the horn. Amber walked over.

He leaned across the seat, rolled the window on the passenger side down and asked, "Are you going into Braniewo?"

She answered in English. "That depends. May I get in?"

He nodded and pointed to the seat beside him. "I speak English."

"I was going back to the town of Braniewo but if you have time, I would like to go into Mamonovo instead."

"I will take you."

"How much to Mamonovo?"

"Sixty Euro."

"Fine. I will go."

As soon as there was a break in traffic he turned the car around, and then headed for Mamonovo. "Do you have a visa?"

"Yes, I do."

After clearing the checkpoint, they drove into town. The driver slowed and looked over at her. "Where do you want to go from here?"

"Just let me out as soon as it is convenient for you."

He drove a few blocks and pulled over by a park.

"Will this be okay?"

"Yes, it will be a good starting point to explore the town."

She paid him, adding an extra ten Euro.

Chapter 19

<u>*Mamonovo,*</u>
<u>*Kaliningrad Oblast, Russia*</u>

Amber went into the park. Children were playing on the swings and the ponies that bounce on springs. Mothers and grandmothers watched from the benches. She thought of Darya, living in that hospital environment with doctors and nurses her only companions. *We are going to get that child to a place where she can play like these children are. Whatever it takes!*

In the restroom, Amber took more money from her neck pouch, slipped it into her pocket and walked on. *I don't know what I'm looking for, but I have to keep looking. At least I'm on the Russian side. I need to find a secluded area, closer to the border.* She came to a grocery store. A bicycle with a tiny Canadian flag attached to the handlebars was leaning against the wall, near the entrance. She spotted a young man wearing a helmet, sitting on a wooden crate near the frozen food section, drinking a soda. She stopped and asked, "It's a bit cold for bike riding, isn't it?"

"I'm dressed warm enough. I rented the bike in Poland to get a good look at the countryside. I left my gear in a locker at a train station. When I get back there, I'll take a train. What are you doing here this late in the season?"

"I'm just traveling around Europe for a few weeks. I need to talk to you outside. Okay?"

"Yes. I'll meet you out front by the bike."

She bought a chocolate-covered ice cream bar and joined the Canadian outside. "What I tell you is confidential."

He frowned and put up his hand. "Wait a minute! You're not going to ask me to smuggle something across the border, I hope. Several people have approached me for that kind of favor."

She shook her head. "Of course, not! I just wanted to say that I've been traveling with a friend, but she went missing. Have you seen or heard anything suspicious at or near the border checkpoint while you were waiting to cross over?"

"No, I haven't. Things are changing around here and most of the tourists have already left the area. Maybe your friend just decided to wait for you back on the Polish side. I may not stay until my visa is up. I'm surprised that you even got a visa. Have you spoken to the police about your friend?"

She shook her head. "No, I haven't. I'm sure she'll turn up. Is there somewhere I could rent a bicycle in town?"

"I have no idea. There is a thrift store at the end of the street that has a couple of used bikes in the window."

"It's worth a look. Thanks."

"Good luck and take care. Watch your step!"

She turned and waved. "Have a nice ride." *Why didn't I think of a bike? I can always ditch it later.* She walked to the end of the street and peered in the shop window at the bikes. One of them looked promising.

Amber entered the shop. A young woman approached and asked in Russian, "May I be of assistance?"

"Do you speak English?"

"Yes, I do."

"I'm interested in the bicycles." She pointed at the one with a basket on the back. "May I see that one, please?"

The woman took it down from the window. "This is in good condition. You may try it if you like."

Amber checked the tires first, then the handlebars. *A little too loose, but they'll do.* "How much is this one?"

"Will you be paying in rubles?"

"Are dollars okay?"

The woman hesitated. She tilted her head slightly, mentally converting the rubles to dollars. "You would pay … seventy-five dollars."

"I will take it. I would like to buy a few tools."

The woman smiled. "Come with me. You can choose from my stock." She pointed to a bin at the end of the aisle.

Amber took out a couple of screwdrivers, a pair of pliers and a crescent wrench. "Please take these to the counter. I want to check out a few more things."

"They will be waiting for you."

156

Amber picked up one of the hammers. *This looks like a roofing hammer. It feels heavy too.* She spotted a wooden crate, rummaged through it and discovered ... *binoculars!* She looked through them and adjusted the different levels. *They work! I can always claim to be a birdwatcher.*

Back at the counter she asked, "How much for all of these?"

The woman picked up the tools, one by one. Then she checked out the binoculars. "That will be one hundred and fifty dollars, including the bicycle."

Amber put the money on the counter.

The woman said, "Thank you. I will open the door for you."

Amber nodded, put her purchases in the basket and rolled the bike out the open door. She turned back, thanked the woman, straddled the bike and pedaled it down the street.

The bike wobbled considerably. She wheeled it back to the park, sat on a bench and tightened the handlebars. Then she leaned the bike against the side of the restroom building. Inside, she took all the rubles from her neck pouch and put them in her backpack.

Out on the street again, she hopped on the bike and turned back toward the store where she had seen the Canadian.

He had moved on. Amber leaned her bike against the wall and entered the store. She bought two bottles of water and a candy bar, and then continued on toward the border. She rode slowly past the business district to a residential area. Pedaling on, she passed only a few houses. Just past the last house in view, she saw the beginning of a wooded area. *Those woods are close to the Polish border. It's a good place to start the search for Liesel.*

The handlebars had loosened again. Amber slowed down and eased the bike over to the side of the road.

A Doberman in the yard across the road ran to the fence, barked and bared his teeth. A man came from the back of the house, shushed the dog and patted it on the head. Then he came across to Amber. "Do you need help?"

She answered him in English. "The handlebars keep getting loose. I have tools. I can manage."

"I speak English. May I help you?"

She took the wrench from the basket. "Yes, please."

He tightened the handlebars and handed the wrench back to her.

157

"May I ask where you are going?"

"I am looking around for my friend. We had planned to meet in Mamonovo. Somehow, we failed to connect."

"I have seen a few tourists in town. Describe her, please."

"She is about as tall as I am and she has long, dark-blond hair. She would not be on a bicycle."

"No, I haven't seen her. By the way, I'm familiar with the American and English way of using contractions."

"That will make it much easier for me!"

He pointed back toward the houses she had passed. "If you plan to approach any of those houses to ask for information about your friend, do not approach the gray house that has a canopy and a window box. I will only say that certain types of officials and vehicles have been coming and going at odd times. If you were to ask about your missing friend, you could be in serious trouble."

"What do you mean? Have you heard something?"

He shook his head. "No, but if you don't find her soon, you must contact your embassy or consulate. This close to a border is not a place you want to be lost in. Do you get my meaning?"

Amber shuddered. "Clearly. Since you are being so honest with me, I must admit that I know my friend is in trouble. I have reason to believe that she is very near the border between the Oblast and Poland. Will you allow me to walk through to the back of your property?"

"Yes, of course. Would you like to discuss this over tea?"

She remembered what Konstantin had said. *Nose around. Talk to people.* She nodded and followed the man across the road to his gate. The Doberman wagged his tail. Amber left the bike at the side of the house.

A stone fireplace sent heat through the living room into a dining area. Amber sat down at the oak table while the man made their tea. He turned toward her. "Where are my manners? I should introduce myself. My name is Luka Kalinow."

"We did get off to an unusual start. Pleased to meet you, Mr. Kalinow. I'm Cynthia Blackwell, from England."

"Please call me Luka. Mr. Kalinow sounds too formal."

"I agree." She held out her hand to shake on it. He took her hand in a firm grasp and gave it a squeeze. "Lucky for us, I bought a fresh cheesecake this morning."

He cut several slices and put a piece on each plate. Then he poured their tea and took a seat across from her. "These dishes were passed down from my wife's family. She died last year and I'm glad to have a reason to use the dishes. My Marta had been ill for a long time. Lately, I've been thinking of selling the house and moving away, but I imagine that I feel her presence here. We were together for more than fifty years. She would have been seventy-five years old had she lived until this past October." He became quiet for a moment, then spoke softly, "This house is filled with happy memories of my years with her."

Amber reached across the table and took his hand but didn't speak. He patted her hand and smiled. "I didn't mean to make you sad. Our tea is getting cold. Let's drink up."

When they finished the cake and tea, Luka asked, "How long will you be staying in the area?"

"I just arrived today. I have a seventy-two-hour visa. When I find my friend, we may have to leave in a hurry."

He pushed his chair back and stood. "You must be anxious to begin your search for her. The checkpoint is a little more than one kilometer from here, although the border is closer at some points. I have often walked from the back of my property to the wooded area. If you like, I'll walk with you to the spot where I usually stop."

"Please do. Thank you for the tea and the delicious cake. I'm ready to go when you are. By the way, I speak fluent Russian. Maybe we shouldn't speak English when we leave the house."

"You are right. Anyway, it was good to practice my English! We can leave straightaway."

She followed him out the back door and switched to Russian. "I want to take my bike in case I find a path in the woods. I'll look for my friend between here and the border."

"Bring the bike with you."

Amber rolled the bike along, pulling it or dragging it over the rough places, until they came to the edge of the woods.

Luka stopped. "You'll see a few clearings and one path just ahead. After we reach the path I'll leave you. I have never gone further toward the border in this area, although I have often crossed the checkpoint in my truck to visit Poland."

They walked on until they came to the path. She leaned the bike against a tree, took the binoculars from her backpack and hung them around her neck. There wasn't much to see other than more trees and an occasional clearing.

"I'll leave the bike wherever the path ends and walk deeper into the woods. Later I'll walk back for it. Thank you so much for your help."

"You are welcome. If you don't find your friend soon, come back and I will drive you to wherever you need to go next."

"Thank you for the offer. I know you must wonder why a tourist would take such a chance and search these woods." She pulled her passport from her neck pouch. "I'm a tourist with a legal passport and visa. I'll be okay." She took another look through the binoculars. "I should get started."

"I hope you find her soon. Be careful. Things have become different in the border area lately. You can always come back to my house if you need help or a safe place to hide."

"Thank you! It's good to have a friend in the Oblast."

She got on the bike and started down the bumpy path, stopping often to search with the binoculars.

When she reached the end of the path she took her tools from the basket, put them in her backpack, wheeled the bicycle into the bushes and walked on.

After winding through the woods and crossing clearings, Amber looked through the binoculars toward the border. She saw only tall, thick trees. She walked on to another clearing and sat down on a mossy mound of dirt. She drank some of the water and ate the rest of the bread and cheese.

Still hungry, she nibbled on the chocolate bar as she explored. *If I don't find Liesel closer to the border, I'll come back and check out that gray house.*

After crossing the next clearing, she spotted a tree with a few branches that were low enough to reach. She climbed as high as she could and scanned the woods ahead. In the distance, she saw a hint of silver between the trees. *It could be a tree with a lighter trunk ... or maybe fog or mist.*

Back on the ground again, she walked on until she found another tree with low branches. She climbed up and surveyed the area. The trees were closer together here, so she saw even less of the silver. *At least I get to rest when I'm up here. Down again. Travel on.* Hearing a rustling nearby, she stood still by the tree and listened hard. Seeing or hearing nothing more, she stepped away from the tree to look around.

Subtle movement disturbed a bush to her left. She trembled, her leg muscles tightened, ready to run. Then she heard a louder rustling. A fox dashed past her. *I'm getting jittery out here!*

When her heart slowed back to normal she finished up a bottle of water and started out again. Most of the trees ahead were evergreens, making the way more difficult.

She heard a faint sound coming from behind the trees ahead. It sounded like someone crying. *That's no animal!* She looked straight ahead and saw more of the silver. She stepped a few feet closer and scanned the area. *It's a building of some kind!* Whatever the sound had been, she no longer heard it. She gripped the hammer in her right hand, as a weapon. One careful step at a time, she moved toward the building.

Almost there, her heart skipped a beat and fluttered. She stopped and listened. Not even the sound of a tree limb falling or a bird twittering broke the silence. She stayed still, not moving an inch for several seconds before she approached. *It could be used as a warehouse for storage of some kind. Liesel might be in there!* Amber edged her way around the building, checking for an entrance. *A door! It's padlocked. To keep someone in or out?* She jiggled the lock.

Sara cringed and stepped back. *Who could be fooling with the padlock? I didn't hear a vehicle pull up.*

Amber checked around the building again, looking closely for an opening. She tripped over a large root as she stepped back to get a wider view.

Sara heard twigs snapping. She peeked through the slit over the sink. She saw no one. *Someone is really out there! I have to get a grip! I have to keep looking.* She put one eye in front of the slit. *Where did they go? Should I scream for help?*

Amber spotted the opening in the metal. She took the pliers from her backpack, twisted the metal back a little wider and looked through. An eye looked back at her. Her body jumped, involuntarily. Her heart pounded. Her hand flew to her chest as she stepped backward. *Someone's in there!* She stood near the edge of the opening, bent down next to it and whispered in Russian, "Hello! Who is in there?" No answer. She tried Polish. "Do you want out of there?" In desperation, she spoke English. "Are you Liesel? I'm here to help you."

"Yes! Please get me out of here!"

"I will. Just hang on. What's down the path in the front?"

"It turns into a narrow road that leads to a wider one with a couple of old buildings along the edge of the road, farther up. That's the way they brought me here."

"I'm going to walk down and check it out, so stay quiet. Do not answer anyone except me. Do you understand?"

"Yes. Please hurry!"

Amber followed the electric wires from the path to the narrow road and on to the next one. She looked in all directions with the binoculars, but she didn't spot any buildings. She went back and whispered through the opening. "Liesel, it's me. There was no one on the road. How often does someone come to check on you?"

"A man brings supplies every few days. He brought a lot more this morning."

"We have some time then. I'll get you out of there as soon as I can. I'm going to try hammering on the padlock. If I hear a vehicle, I'll have to disappear for a few minutes. Don't worry. I'll come back, so hang tight. Gather your things quickly and be ready to go."

Amber went back around to the door and began pounding the rusty padlock. *There's probably a lot of noise near the checkpoint, with all the activity. They can't hear me.* She hit the lock with all her might. It broke. *I did it!* She pulled the lock off, opened the door and cried out, "It worked! I'm coming in."

"Oh, thank God!" Tears streamed down Sara's face.

"No time for tears, Liesel. Do you have a coat?"

"I have a warm jacket. They didn't take that from me."

"Hurry up! Let's get the heck out of here!"

"Okay." She grabbed her things. "I'm ready! I put some water and food in my backpack." She zipped up her jacket, stepped out into the fresh air and took a deep breath. She looked up at the sky. *Thank you, God!*

Amber closed the door behind them. "Don't speak unless it's necessary. Walk behind me and tread softly when possible. We're going back the same way I came."

They walked along in silence through the trees and across the clearings until they drew close to the road.

Amber looked back. "Let's stop for a minute." She sat down on the ground and leaned against a tree. "Rest while you can." She took a scarf from her pack and handed it to her. "Put this over your hair. Tell me what happened to you."

"Two men kidnapped me in Gdansk and took me to a house not far from the checkpoint. A couple of days later, they brought me out here."

"What did the house look like?"

"It was gray and white with a window box and it had a canopy over the driveway."

"I think I know where it is." *That sounds like the house Luka warned me about.* "How long did it take the vehicle to get to the shack from the house?"

"It was quick. Not more than ten minutes, I'm sure."

They walked on until they came to the place where Amber had left the bike. "I know where we are now."

Sara took two bottles of water from her backpack. She put one in her jacket pocket and handed the other to Amber.

After taking a few sips of the water, Amber put the bottle in her pocket. She pulled the bike out and rolled it into the thick bushes where it was better hidden. "We won't have any use for this. The road that I came down on is just ahead. Let's go."

When they got to the edge of the road, she motioned for Sara to stop. A truck went by, and then one car. They ran across the road and into the woods on the other side.

The going was rough and slow. Sara kept glancing back the way they had come. "And I thought I was safe!"

163

"You're half-safe."

"Half-safe is a lot better than no-safe. Thank you. Just tell me what to do and I'll do it."

"For now, just stay with me. I know the way. My passport says I'm Cynthia Blackwell, an English tourist. Do you have your identification with you?"

"None whatsoever. My passport was stolen in Gdansk."

"We'll figure something out, don't worry about it. I've told someone that you are a friend and that we got separated while traveling. So, let's say you're … uh … Marie Conroy, but you've lost your ID. Is that okay?"

"Yes. That's fine." *Any name except Liesel.*

Amber slowed and turned back to her. "Soon comes the scary part. We'll have to sneak across the border."

"Whatever I do or wherever I go, I won't be half as scared as I was back in that old shack!"

Amber led the way. *We're nearing the checkpoint. I can tell by the lack of traffic noise. They're backed up and waiting to be cleared. We just might make it before it gets completely black out here.* She took out the binoculars. "Marie, I can see the checkpoint. We're almost free." *Just a few more minutes. Then we'll make our move.* She looked back over her right shoulder. "Don't stop, Marie, just listen. We can't risk the slightest noise. We're close."

Chapter 20

The Border of Kaliningrad Oblast, Russia and Poland

When Amber was sure they had gone far enough, she searched for a tower or a guard post. *Nothing but trees. We must be past the towers. That means we can get through.* She looked back at Sara and whispered, "Come on!"

They ran for it, sometimes stumbling over rocks, fallen tree trunks or branches. They kept moving until Amber was sure they were in Polish territory. She stopped and faced Sara. "We can get out of these woods now. It's safe. We've finally made it!"

"Are you sure we're out of Russia?"

"Yes. I recognize the area. I came this way. We are really on the Polish side now."

The traffic was still heavy. They walked as close to the edge of the road as they could. Amber stopped and turned to Sara. "Marie, I have a notion to hitch a ride. Should we?"

"Yes! Let's stick out a thumb or an arm. Or a whatever."

"Since I'm not sure which it should be, you stick out your thumb and I'll hold out my arm."

It was close to fifteen minutes before a pickup truck slowed, passed them and pulled over to the side of the road. A woman sitting in the passenger seat opened the door as they approached. She asked in Polish, "Where are you going?"

Amber answered in English. "We would like to get back to Braniewo to catch a train."

The man in the driver's seat leaned across. "I speak English. We are going to Braniewo. You may ride in the back of the truck."

They climbed in. Amber said, "Marie, we are really safe."

"Just thinking about freedom stirs my emotions."

"It's almost over. Let's eat that food you brought from the shack!"

"Good idea. I'm famished."

The driver slowed as they drove into Braniewo. He pulled up near the train station, parked, and then went around to the back of the truck. "Are you ready to exit your limousine?"

They grabbed their packs. Amber said, "Thank you for the lift. You are a lifesaver." She shook his hand, pressing two twenty-dollar bills into his palm.

He started to protest. She put her hand up and shook her head slowly. "I insist. Thank you!"

"You are welcome. We were happy to help you."

Sara pulled the scarf off and stuck it in her pocket.

"Leave it on, Marie. You can't afford to be recognized. Hair or the lack of it is usually the first thing about a person given as a description. Come on, let's get some hot coffee. I saw a restaurant back there."

"Do we have time before the train leaves?"

"What train? I only *said* we were going to take a train. We don't want strangers to know our plans. You don't have a passport, so we need to get further away from the border area before we catch a train to anywhere. They're more likely to ask for identity papers this close to border towns. Besides, the Russians are sure to check all the trains, buses, trams and taxis as soon as they realize you have escaped. You have no way to prove your identity."

"Maybe we should forget the coffee for now and get going. What do you think?"

"I think you're right. Let's go."

"I'm right behind you."

A cold, brisk wind blew hard against them. Shivering, they walked single file down the highway, each holding an arm out or a thumb up whenever they heard a truck approaching. Amber shined her flashlight on the edge of the road as they walked. *We did make it out of the woods before nightfall.*

Several trucks passed them before a driver slowed, blinked the lights, and then eased to a stop. Amber glanced in at the driver. He seemed safe. She got in first and Sara hopped in beside her.

The driver pulled back onto the highway. In Polish, he asked, "Where are you headed?"

Amber said, "To Elblag."

He switched to English. "I will be going past Elblag on my way to Orzysz."

"How long will it take to get to Orzysz?"

"It is about a three-hour drive."

"Could we ride there with you?"

"Sure. No problem. You must be tourists."

Amber nodded. "Yes, we are."

"It gets very cold this time of the year. Most tourists come to Europe in the spring or the summer."

"We had to come when we could get time off from our work. We'll be going back soon." *One lie after the other!*

Miles down the road, Amber whispered, "Wake up, Marie. You were snoring."

Sara sat up straight. "How embarrassing!"

"Stay awake. We'll be coming into Orzysz in a few minutes. I see the lights ahead."

The driver eased up on the pedal, took the exit and pulled into the edge of Orzysz. "My delivery is not in town and I am on a very tight schedule. I need to turn. Would you mind walking from here?"

Amber said, "No, we don't mind at all. Thanks a lot for the ride. Would you please accept payment?"

He shook his head. "No, thank you. It has been my pleasure."

"Thank you. Have a safe trip."

Sara said, "Thank you for the ride."

They got out and walked on. Amber said, "We're only about thirty kilometers from Elk now."

"Where are we going after we get there?"

"That's as far as we need to go. There's a safe house in Elk. Someone there will do a passport for you and see that you get to safety."

Sara's jaw dropped. "Do you mean my nightmare is almost over?"

"Yes! And you can sleep in a real bed tonight. We're going to stay in a hotel."

"I can't believe it."

"It's true. Let's look for a place to lay our heads."

Orzysz, Poland

After walking a few more blocks, they came to several hotels and restaurants. In between the streetlights and the neon signs, Amber flicked the flashlight on to light their way.

"Marie, look for a hotel with balconies. We have to show identification to check in, so you'll have to sneak into the room."

"You mean climb up to the balcony?"

"Yes, if necessary. Do you have a better idea?"

"No. I'll do whatever it takes."

"Okay. You check the hotels on this side and I'll check on the other. Signal if you find something."

Just as Amber was about to give up, Sara raised her arm, beckoned and pointed.

Amber crossed back over. The *Ciemne Rzeki Hotel* is a small three-story building with private balconies that overlook the street. *That means the back rooms will have balconies too.* "Wait here for me. I'll be back in a minute."

She spoke English to the receptionist. "Do you have a single room for one night?"

"Yes, we do. It's one floor up, at the back of the building."

"I will take the room." She put her passport on the counter.

The woman opened it, checked the photo page, glanced up at Amber and handed it back to her.

Amber signed the register and paid. *I'm glad she didn't insist on keeping my passport until I check out, like some do. There's no way I could let that happen.* "I will be back later. Will you be here all night, or do I need a lobby key?"

The woman gave her the room key, reached under the counter, pulled out another key and handed it to her. "We always give our guests a key for the front door. It locks automatically after you exit. You have rented the last room, so I will close soon. You may leave the keys on the desk if you leave early tomorrow."

"Thank you." She nodded and hurried back to Sara.

"Quick, let's get away from here and find a restaurant. I'll explain later. We do have a room and it's on the back, so no one will spot you climbing up to the balcony."

They walked back to a restaurant they had noticed earlier.

When the host greeted them in Polish, Amber asked, "Do you speak English?"

"Yes, all our workers do and we have international menus. You will find English on the second page." She showed them to a booth and gave them each a menu. "Your server will be with you in a moment. Would you like coffee? Wine?"

Amber and Sara answered in unison. "Coffee, please."

Soon a young woman came to the table carrying a large tray laden with a pot of coffee, a pitcher of cream, a saucer of butter pats and a basket of bread. "Good evening." She poured their coffee. "I will be your server tonight. I will be back for your order in a moment."

Sara checked the menu. Her mouth watered at the choices. *Wow! I dreamed of food like this!*

The server came back. "Are you ready to order?"

Amber ordered a vegetable plate and a baked potato. Sara said, "I would like a steak and a Caesar salad."

The server nodded and went to place the order.

They were content to sit without conversing until the server came back and placed their meals on the table.

Sara started on her steak. "This is the best steak I have ever tasted. Maybe it's because I haven't had one in so long. I ate a lot of steaks in my imagination, back in that prison."

When the server brought the check, Sara said, "Cynthia, I want to pay for this. They didn't take my money and I have the equivalent of almost a thousand dollars in my backpack."

"No, Marie. I have enough money with me. You may need yours later. Anyway, I need to use more of my Polish Zlotys."

She paid the check. "Let's get back to the hotel."

The night had turned much colder. They zipped up their jackets and hustled back. Sara stayed away from the entrance while Amber checked the hotel. The lobby lights had been dimmed and there was a no vacancy sign on the door. She came back to Sara. "You're in luck, Marie. You won't have to climb up to the balcony. The receptionist has gone for the night and I've got a key to the lobby." She unlocked the door and checked the stairs. "It's okay."

They walked quietly up the stairs and down the hall to their room. Amber motioned for Sara to wait in the hall. She eased the key into the lock, opened the door, glanced around and stepped inside. She checked the closet, under the bed and behind the shower curtain, and then turned and whispered, "Come in, quick."

Sara came in and put her backpack down on the floor. She took out a pair of jeans and hung them across a hanger. "That's the last clean pair I have."

"I'll sleep on the bed nearest the balcony. We're lucky we have two beds, since I only paid for a single room. You can take a shower first. I need to do some more planning before I crash." She sat down and pondered the situation. *Things have worked out okay so far. We should be at the safe house tomorrow. Then, I'll have to figure a way to get Sabine and the others to safety before the big guys discover the empty shack.*

Sara came out of the bathroom and said, "The water is still hot. I'm finished in there and I'm going to bed."

"As soon as I shower, I am too."

It took a few seconds for Amber to remember where she was. She shook Sara gently and whispered, "Wake up! You've got to get out before the receptionist arrives."

Sara flung the covers back, slipped her jeans and blouse on, brushed her teeth and combed her hair, all in short order. "I'm ready. Shall I climb down from the balcony?"

"You won't have to if you're downstairs and out the lobby door in the next few minutes!"

Sara put her jacket on, grabbed her backpack and darted to the door. "Where shall I meet you?"

"It's still dark. Go back to the closest restaurant on this side of the street but wait until I check things here." Amber stepped out and scanned the hallway. *All clear.* She motioned for Sara to come out, and then locked their door.

Sara followed close behind her. At the stairway, Amber held a hand up to stop her. She crept down the stairs and checked the area. Seeing no one, she unlocked the lobby door and beckoned Sara down. "It's clear. Go quickly."

Amber went up to the room, packed her things, and then went back down to the lobby.

The receptionist was just coming in. "You are leaving without your breakfast?"

"Yes. I have a busy day planned. I left the keys on your desk. Goodbye."

"I hope you will visit us again. Goodbye."

Amber turned back. "What does Ciemne Rzeki mean?"

"It means Dark Rivers."

"Thank you. I will remember that." She walked back toward the restaurant and soon spotted the sign: *Kawiarnia Czarny Róża. Ah, that one I know. I'll have breakfast in the Cafe Black Rose.*

Sara was sitting in a booth near the center of the room, eating pancakes. Amber sat down across from her. "Those pancakes sure do look good."

The server came over with coffee and a menu. She touched her name tag. "My name is Magda. Would you like coffee?"

"Yes, and I would like an order of pancakes, please."

"I will return with your order shortly."

Amber looked over at Sara. "We shouldn't stay in *any* one place too long. We need to keep moving."

"That's fine with me, after you-know-where." She leaned forward and whispered, "I was hoping we could just go to an American embassy and ask them to send me home."

"That's where the people who took you would expect you to go. When they find that shack empty, they will search all of the routes to the embassies and consulates." She paused as Magda brought the pancakes to the table. After she walked away, Amber continued. "The safe house in Elk is our best bet and it's closer to us than an embassy or a consulate. Please be patient a little longer. This isn't exactly a walk in the park for me, either."

"I'm sorry. Don't think that I don't appreciate what you're doing for me. You are a fantastic, brave person. If you hadn't come for me, I might have spent the rest of my life in that place."

"It's just part of my job. You're pretty brave yourself!" She looked at the wall clock. "By the time we've finished eating, it will be almost daylight."

Magda refilled their cups. "Would you like anything more?"

Sara looked up. "Could we have some sandwiches and a couple of packages of potato chips to go?"

"Yes. What would you like on the sandwiches?"

"I will have one bacon and tomato sandwich, and one cheese. Add mayonnaise to both of them, please."

Amber ordered a cheese sandwich, and one with lettuce and tomato.

The server nodded. "You can pick up your order at the cashier's counter."

Sara insisted on paying and leaving the tip. Amber held the door open for her. "We're ready to head for Elk. Let's get a ride."

They walked along the street until they reached the spot where the trucker had let them out. Amber said, "We'll just walk until we hear a truck coming."

Cars and delivery vans passed. The few trucks that came by couldn't or wouldn't stop.

Sara asked, "How far do you think we've walked?"

"A couple of kilometers, I guess." She looked back over her shoulder. "Do you hear that droning? Motorcycles! As soon as they get closer, stick out your thumb. I'll wave my arm. Maybe we've got our ride."

The first two riders spotted them and signaled for the others to stop. They slowed and pulled over. One of the men asked, in Polish, "What is the trouble?"

"No trouble, we just need a ride." Amber stepped closer while she mentally counted the bikes. *A dozen. All Urals.*

"You can ride with us. I'm Marek." He motioned for her to get on behind him. She climbed on. "Do you speak English?"

"Yes, we all do." He pointed to his buddy. "This big guy is Ro."

Ro tipped his head toward Sara. "Hop on."

They rumbled along for about thirty minutes, slowed and turned into a dirt driveway in front of a bar. The other riders put their kickstands down and entered the bar.

Sara said, "Thanks for the fun ride, but I need help getting off this thing."

Ro grinned and helped her off. "You are very welcome."

Amber dismounted and faced Marek. "It looks like this place is in the middle of nowhere. Where are we?"

"You are just outside the village of Rekusy. This is as far as we go. How about a drink?"

"Thank you, but we really need to move on."

He grinned. "Too bad. By the way, thumbing is the right way to hitch in Poland."

Amber laughed and put her thumb up. "I'll do that the next time I need a ride. Thanks for the tip."

She turned toward Sara. "That was short and sweet. Let's walk down this road until we see a sign or get another ride, whichever comes first."

"We'll get a ride. We always do."

"Yes, so far. The rest of the way will be easier."

"I hope so. I'm hungry again. Are you?"

"Yes. Dig out a sandwich for me, please."

Sara took two sandwiches from the food package and gave one to Amber.

They traveled on, without a single vehicle passing by. Sara said, "We haven't seen a soul. This place must be a ghost town!"

"Not quite. I hear dogs barking. I hope they're fenced in."

"We'll soon find out. Let's brave it."

They walked on toward the sound of the barking. Two dogs were behind a fence at the first house. They wagged their tails as Amber and Sara came near.

The village turned into farmland. Finally, they saw a woman sitting on the porch of a yellow wooden house. Amber waved and called out, "Hello! Can we speak with you, please?"

The woman walked over to the fence and said, "I speak not much English."

Amber spoke in Polish, "Where are we? Is this still Rekusy?"

"No. You have come through the village."

"Thank you." Amber looked at Sara. "Shall we hoof it some more?"

"There's not much else we can do."

After about fifteen minutes they heard rattling behind them. A tractor pulling a cart filled with straw stopped beside them. The driver called out, "Where are you going?"

In her limited Polish, Amber said, "To the next village and as far as possible on down the road."

"Come, get in the cart."

They climbed in and eased down into the soft straw.

Amber said, "Why are you letting me do all the talking when it's necessary to speak Polish?"

Sara wasn't sure how to answer that. She shrugged. "I think you speak more of it than I do."

"I just figured that living in Gdansk, you would have picked up more of the language." She paused and sniffed the air. "Ugh. Something stinks around here. It must be fertilizer."

Sara's eyes watered. "It's awful!" She reached down and moved the straw that was sticking to her jeans. She brought her hand back up in a hurry. "We're in deep shit!"

"Are you just figuring that out? We have been for two days."

"I mean this straw is mixed with manure! We really are in shit. And I do mean deep! It's all over my jeans."

Amber yelled, "Hey, let us out!"

The man drove a few feet farther and stopped in front of a gate. "This is as far as I go, ladies."

They got out, pulled off some twigs from a bush and scraped the straw from their jeans.

Sara laughed until tears ran down her cheeks. "We got our ride! What else can happen to us?"

"No more surprises, I hope. We're almost to the safe house. Did you notice the Gypsy wagons parked behind that old church we passed?"

"Yes, I spotted them. Do you think they'll help us?"

"What have we got to lose? They won't have showers. They might let us wash off, though. Let's go back."

Not sure what to expect, Amber walked up to the first wagon and called out in Polish, "*Jest tu ktos?*"

No one answered although the remains of a fire still smoldered. Amber managed a shrill whistle.

"Behind you!" Sara yelled.

Amber turned quickly and faced a young dark-skinned Gypsy. He spoke in Polish, "*Dzien dobry.*"

"Do you speak English?"

He shook his head and spoke in Russian. "Are you hungry?"

"Yes, we are. And we need to bathe."

"I will send someone to fetch water for a bath."

A little dark-eyed girl led them to a clearing in a wooded area and gave them each a bar of soap and a towel. Several teenage girls carried buckets of water and poured it into two wooden barrels, which were taller than they were wide, then hurried away for more water.

A ladder leaned against each tub. Amber and Sara set their backpacks on the ground and checked them out. Only the bottoms were dirty. Amber picked up a stick and scraped the straw away. "After we bathe, we can wash the backpacks off. I hope we can rescue some clean clothes." She disrobed, keeping only her neck pouch on. She dropped her dirty clothes on the grass, climbed the ladder to one of the barrels and eased down into the water.

Sara climbed up and stepped into the other barrel. "Oh, this water feels good, even if it's not very warm."

"Sometimes, good things happen. They're even going to feed us. We can't eat our leftover food after the manure incident!"

"Darn! And I was looking forward to that other sandwich."

"The fire was smoldering when we got here. I wonder why they let the fire go out."

They heard fast-paced music playing on a violin and an accordion. The sounds were coming from behind the trees on the other side of the wagons, but they couldn't see the women dancing, their long full skirts swinging back and forth, or the men stamping their feet as they sang.

Sara clapped her hands to the music. "It's pretty neat to be entertained while we bathe."

Amber stood up to wash. She felt for her neck pouch. It was soaking wet. *Oh, no! What was I thinking?* She took it off and hung it on the top rung of the ladder where she could keep an eye on it. For added safety, she hung the towel over it. She soaped up and started scrubbing herself.

The music stopped abruptly. An old Gypsy woman came over to them and offered them drinking water in glass jars. She spoke in Romany, smiled a toothless smile and walked away.

Amber didn't understand a word the woman had said. *Maybe she was saying that someone will bring us some fresh water for rinsing. Or that the food is almost ready.*

Two young women ran up to the barrels. They each pulled a ladder away, along with the towels and Amber's neck pouch. One of them reached down and took Amber's dirty clothes, shoes and backpack. The other one grabbed Sara's things and both jackets.

Amber yelled, in Russian, "What the hell are you doing?"

Both of the Gypsies ran back toward the wagons.

Amber tried to climb out of the water and over the barrel. Being naked, it was almost impossible without the ladder.

The sound of wheels turning and the clip-clop of horse's hooves were sure signs that the Gypsies were absconding with Amber's and Sara's belongings.

"We have to get out of these tubs, naked or not, Marie. Let's rock and roll!"

They rocked the barrels back and forth until they fell over, then they crawled out onto the wet grass. The wagons were long gone. They sat there soapy, naked and laughing helplessly.

"Fun time is over, Marie. We'll freeze to death unless we get to shelter. We'll have to run back to the church. Maybe we can find a couple of choir robes."

An old dried-up fountain sat in the middle of the courtyard. Narrow windows, reaching almost to the gabled roof of the church were glazed with multicolored stained glass. The paint had peeled off in spots from the double doors, and long thin strips of it were hanging down, moving in the wind, like wriggling worms. One door was slightly ajar and it squeaked as Amber pulled it open. She peered in and looked around. "It's okay, Marie. We can rest and hide here while we think of a way to get some clothes."

Sara paused as she stepped into the dank room. "This is creepy. It's like something out of a Gothic novel." There were no pews. The afternoon sun shone through the stained-glass windows, making a kaleidoscope of colors cascading down the plastered walls to the floor.

Red velvet curtains, streaked with various shades of red from years of fading, hung across a stage-like platform. Amber peeked behind them and discovered an old reed organ sitting against the back wall. The foot pedals were covered in red velvet, a match for the curtains. The musty curtains were nearly stiff from the dust and grime, accumulated over the years. She called to Sara to help pull the curtains down. The odor was overpowering as they shook them, but they each wrapped one around themselves, sari style.

Amber spotted a stone basin of what must have been "holy water." She picked out the dead moths and dropped them onto the floor. "This water isn't safe to drink but we can use it to rinse the soap residue from our feet." She scooped a little of the stagnant water from the basin onto her bare feet, saving the rest for Sara, and then went back to the organ. *I wonder if the bellows still work.* She imagined music filling the church. "Marie! Come back and check out this organ."

Sara went to the stage. "Can we play it?"

"We can try."

"I can't play anything except Chopsticks."

"That's the only thing I can play!" She sat on the red velvet bench and motioned for Sara to sit down beside her. Amber worked the foot pedals and played on the top keys, while Sara played the lower ones.

Amber stopped suddenly. "Wait! No one is supposed to be in this old place. Someone might call the police. We'd better not play it anymore."

"Okay. It sure was fun though!"

They left the stage and sat down on the floor next to the wall, away from the windows. Amber said, "We'll send a message to your mother when we get to the safe house."

"You know my mother? Where is she?"

"Your mother is at a research center in Russia, working on her medical experiments. She sent me to find you and get you to safety."

"What are you talking about? My mother is a school teacher in West Conshohocken, Pennsylvania!"

Amber burst out laughing. "I can't believe this! You mean I've rescued the wrong Liesel?"

"I'm not Liesel. I'm Sara Thornburg, an American tourist."

Amber spoke calmly. "Then why did you answer 'Yes' back at the shack when I asked if you were Liesel?"

"I figured Liesel was a secret spy code, because the creeps in dark suits tried to make me admit I was Liesel. It could have been a code for a traitor or an assassin for all I knew. Then, when you finally spoke in English, I assumed that you had come for Liesel, whoever or whatever Liesel was. Besides, I didn't *care* who or what you thought I was. I would have answered to anything if it would get me out of that hellhole!"

"Okay, Sara, we'll get you home somehow."

"Who are you, Cynthia? Is that your real name?"

"I'm your guardian angel. Keep on calling me Cynthia. What were you doing in Gdansk?"

"I went there to see the *Zuraw*, the famous old crane above the river. My father is a crane operator and he had asked me to have someone photograph me in front of it, but my camera was taken by the two Russians after they kidnapped me in Gdansk."

"How long were you in Europe before they took you?"

"Almost two weeks. I took a cruise on one of the Rhine ships just before the last trip of the season. Then I had planned to visit a few Christmas markets. My vacation was completely ruined. I ought to sue whoever's fault it was that I was kidnapped!"

"You won't have to. The company has funds for that."

"The company? You're a spy, aren't you?"

"Not exactly. I just work for a company that solves problems sometimes." She rose from the floor. "We'd better go now."

Sara stood and adjusted her curtain. "We must look like a couple of Hare Krishnas! I hope no one sees us."

"There's no one around to see us. When we get to the main road, we can hitch a ride if a truck comes by. But if we hear automobiles coming we should hide, if possible. The people we need to worry about would not be driving a truck."

"Why am I still hiding? I'm not guilty of anything!"

"I know that. I also know the type of people who may be looking for you. They are the reason you are still hiding. You don't know what those people are capable of."

"I think I do! I have been beaten, gagged and dragged. Not to mention knocked out and stuffed in the trunk of a Mercedes. You can't even imagine the thoughts that tormented me day after day and night after night, trapped in that windowless metal prison. Sometimes, I thought the man who brought my food had forgotten about me and I'd starve to death. Sometimes, I screamed, hoping someone, anyone, would hear me. At other times, I stifled my screams, afraid of whoever might hear me."

Amber put her arms around Sara. "We're almost to Elk. Let's get out of here." She eased the door open. "Come on. As soon as we get to the safe house you'll be issued a passport in your own name. Then you can go home. Whoever kidnapped you has no idea that Sara Thornburg, American tourist, really exists."

"Then why am I still running?"

"You're not running *from* anything, you're running *to* safety." She looked out the door. "It's clear."

After passing a few houses they came to an old brick church with a cemetery in the yard. Statues of angels and cherubs had been placed at intervals. The whole area was deathly quiet.

Amber whispered, "My bare feet are killing me and I feel like I'm about to get frostbite. We'd better walk faster. The next village can't be much farther." Automatically, she glanced at her wrist. "Oh, I forgot. The Gypsies stole my watch."

Sara stopped and took hold of Amber's arm. "Listen! I'm sure I hear vehicles!"

"I hear them. Let's go."

They ran to the edge of the road, staying near the tree line, in case they needed to hide.

Sara frowned. "Where the heck are all the trucks? Let's just keep walking. Maybe we don't need a ride."

"Yes, we do need a ride. It's not safe to walk along the road with all the traffic. Especially dressed like this."

"Right. Can we at least put our thumbs up?"

"Only if we hear a truck."

The driver of the second truck that came by slowed, pulled over to the side and waited for them to catch up. Amber got in first, with Sara scrambling in after. The driver looked at Amber and spoke in Polish. "Where are you ladies headed?"

"We just need a ride into Elk, please."

"You speak good Polish, but we can speak in English. That is Elk right in front of you!"

"Sir, we didn't want to walk into town dressed like this. We would have held up traffic."

He grinned. "I don't usually drive into town with this rig, but I will make an exception this time. Hold on!" He eased into the traffic. "Let me know when you want to get out. Why are you wearing those cloths wrapped around you?"

"We are actors on our way to a rehearsal."

"Dressed like that? What kind of a play?"

"A biblical play." *Oh, this job makes such liars of us. My code name should have been Pinocchio!*

"What part could you play with outfits like that?"

"Harlots."

The driver broke into laughter and slapped the heel of his hand against the dashboard. "Wait until I tell my buddies I picked up a couple of harlots! I will get a lot of free beer out of that one."

Sara poked Amber with her elbow and snickered.

Chapter 21

Elk, Poland

The driver pulled into Elk and asked Amber, "Where would you like to go?"

"If you take us to Michala Kajki Street, we can walk the rest of the way."

"Sure. No problem."

Within a few blocks he eased the truck to a stop and looked over at Amber. "This is your street. Are you sure you can find your way from here?"

"Yes, I'm sure. Thanks for the ride. I want to pay you for your trouble."

"Absolutely not! Meeting you two was priceless. Take care of yourselves. Goodbye."

Sara said, "Thank you. We will be fine now."

They stepped out and waved as the truck drove away. Amber said, "I think we made his day!"

"I'm sure of it. It's hard to believe we've come this far safely."

"It hasn't been easy up until now. I know we're only a couple of blocks from the safe house." She pictured the apartment in her mind. *I remember the photo that I studied before one particular trip. It's a four-story building, painted beige, with dark wood trim and shutters.* They passed two streets and then turned left. Amber touched Sara's arm. "Now we turn to the right."

She spotted the building in the middle of the block. "We're here. It's on the other side of the street. At last, we've made it!"

Amber pushed the buzzer for apartment 3, knowing that the other apartments in the building were either empty or occupied by agents and equipment. Within seconds, the door opened. They stepped into a narrow hallway and the door closed behind them, automatically. A masculine voice came over the speaker. "State your ID numbers."

"Neither of us have numbers or identity papers. I know that the chief agent in charge is Argyle Phillips, nickname Phipps and I can give you an emergency, coded message."

"Let's hear the message. I'll relay it."

"Winterset, party of one is arriving and bringing one guest. We'll be the ones wrapped in red velvet."

"Hold on, please." He went to Phillips in the office. "Two young women are in the hallway. One of them gave an emergency, coded message." He repeated it.

Phillips shook his head. *What the hell is that for a code? Red velvet what?* "I'll handle this." He went to the inner door of the hallway and looked through a viewer. "Please step back and wait for the buzzer. Then push the door open. Someone will meet you." He went back to the office.

Amber pushed the door open the second the buzzer sounded. A young woman was waiting in the foyer and a man was standing by, watching as they entered.

The woman patted them down, and then led them to a back room. She pointed to a table with three chairs. "An agent will speak with you shortly." She left the room.

Amber shook her head. *This is going to be rough.* She glanced at Sara. "Let's sit, this could take a while."

"At least we're okay. We needed to rest anyway."

A man came in and sat down. "I'm Argyle Phillips. Please, will the *Winterset party of one* explain to me why you are here?"

Amber sat up straight. "I'm an agent on a mission for PDI. Things became complicated and I had to change plans without informing the agency." She nodded toward Sara. "I have someone with me that needs to get back to the United States. She has become part of the operation."

"First, tell me your code name."

"I'm not at liberty to tell you that."

He glowered at her. "You come waltzing in wearing nothing but a musty curtain, and you neglect to tell me your code name. I don't need a ragtag agent."

"Remember the procedure, please. I gave you the name of the operation immediately, in code and I can give you a priority number to call. As far as these musty curtains are concerned, they

182

are all we have to wear and we are lucky to have them. We stole them off the stage in a church and they are all that stands between us and complete nudity. Maybe you can scrounge up a couple of pairs of trousers for us. Underwear would be nice."

"I know the number and the code for Operation Winterset. I asked for your personal code name."

"Since you asked … my personal code name is personal and on an Eyes-Only level!"

"I had to test you. If you had told me your code name, I'd have known something was up."

"May we have a clean line? Ms. Thornburg would like to call her mother in Pennsylvania."

"Of course, she would. You females always call Mommy when things go wrong."

"Who do you call, your mistress?"

"That will be all the static I'm going to take from you."

"Then treat us with a little respect. We have had a very long, dangerous journey to reach freedom. I may be a ragtag agent and I'm AWOL from my mission, but Sara Thornburg is an innocent American tourist who has suffered because of a mistaken identity. She has been held captive in a secluded area in the Kaliningrad Oblast under primitive conditions."

"Do you have documents to prove your identity?"

She pretended to look beneath her curtain. "Nope! No place for ID. Call the priority number for the operation and you will get the proof."

"I'll just do that."

"Please let them know that I intend to complete the mission."

He made the call on his cell phone. Shaking his head, he cut off the connection and turned back to face Amber. "You're cleared. You are going to have a lot of explaining to do at PDI when you return."

"I expected that and I'm prepared to do so."

Phillips left the room.

A woman came in and set a box of clothing down beside the table. "My name is Harriet." She pointed to a door at the back of the room. "That's a bathroom with a tub and shower. You'll find towels, washcloths and assorted toiletries in the cupboard. Let me know if you need anything else."

Amber rummaged through the box of clothing and found jeans, socks and underwear. Blouses, skirts and dresses were hanging in the closet. A dozen pairs of shoes in different sizes had been placed in rows on the closet floor. Amber placed a hand on Sara's shoulder. "You should choose and shower first. You'll be flying back to the States."

"That still seems like a dream. I'll be quick with my shower."

When she came out, she said, "Everything fit, even the shoes, but my feet are too sore to wear them. I left the curtain on the floor. It was way too big for the trash can."

Amber chose a few pieces of the clothing and went in to take her shower.

Harriet brought Sara a phone. "You may call home now. I'll come back in a few minutes."

"Thank you." Sara dialed her mother's cell phone number. "Mom, it's me. I'll be home soon. Are you guys okay?"

"Sure, we're fine. We were worried when you didn't call. I can hardly wait to see you and hear all about your wonderful trip. Your father has been telling all of his buddies at work that his daughter has seen the old Zuraw. I hope you took a lot of pictures!"

Sara's throat constricted. "Mom, I have to hang up. Give my love to Dad."

"I will. We'll see you soon. Love ya!"

"I love you too. Bye now." *How will I ever tell my folks about my 'wonderful' trip? And that I have no pictures to show?*

Amber came out of the bathroom wearing jeans and a green blouse. "It sure feels good to be clean again."

"I called my mom and told her I was coming home. I didn't tell her about my trouble."

"That was smart."

Harriet came back for the phone and hurried away.

Sara said, "It's almost over. It feels great to be free. I hope to hear that you made it back home."

"I may not be allowed to contact you, but I will never forget you, or the things we went through together."

The photographer came in and set up for the photos. He looked at Amber. "You first, please."

She stood in front of the white background and looked straight ahead. The man took six photos then asked Sara to pose. After taking the shots of her, he gathered his equipment and went to the door. "Mr. Phillips will be right in."

Amber thanked him, then turned to Sara. "I hope they give us something to eat soon. We didn't think to mention that we were hungry."

"I guess getting clean was our first thought."

"Yeah, but my stomach is making all kinds of noises now."

Phillips came in. "I've brought passport forms for you."

Amber wrote her name as Rhonda Claiborne, her place of birth as Florida, USA and her birth date as 13 February 1987.

Sara filled out the form with her name and information.

Phillips took the forms. "I'll be back shortly."

Sara clasped her hands together in her lap and looked down at them. "I'm sorry I wasn't always a happy traveling companion."

"Under the circumstances, you were great. Maybe you could come and work for us."

Sara raised her head and unclasped her hands. "Not on your life! I don't do spy stuff."

"Yes, you do! You were abducted from the street in Poland and taken into Russian territory. You have escaped from your captors and now you're sitting in a safe house, waiting to get back home. That's spy stuff."

"I do feel like I'm starring in a James Bond movie. Back at the old church when I asked who you were, you said you were my guardian angel. Then you said I should still call you *Cynthia*. I guess I couldn't know your real name. I'm going to consider *Guardian Angel* as your code name. I want a code name too. Not just *Marie*, either. I read a book where one of the characters used *Rosebud* as a code name. You can call me Rosebud."

"I like that idea. You can be Rosebud and I'll still be your guardian angel."

Phillips came back in and handed Sara a passport. "Check it over and see if it's correct. If so, sign it."

He turned to Amber. "I'll have dinner brought to you. We can talk while Ms. Thornburg is having dinner in the dining room."

"Thank you. I don't eat meat or fish. Is that a problem?"

"No. We cater to all kinds of diets here."

Harriet came back in. "Ms. Thornburg, would you allow me to escort you to the dining room?"

Sara stood and nodded. "Yes. Thank you."

A woman brought Amber a plate of vegetables, two hot rolls and a cup of coffee.

Phillips came back as she was finishing her meal. "What do you need for whatever it is you're going to do?"

"For starters, I'll need money, a passport and a visa."

"Those things are being arranged. What else?"

"Liesel Heitbrock, the woman who had been marked for abduction must be warned of the attempt and convinced that she will never be safe until she has been given a new name and moved to a new location. I have her address in Gdansk. She is employed at the spa in the Hotel Baltika."

"That's a big order, but I'll have it taken care of."

"Thank you. May I use a computer? I need to check the train schedules."

He nodded. "Right down the hall. Come with me."

Computer desks were lined up along two of the walls. Phillips said, "I'll leave you to it."

Amber checked the schedules. The quickest route was from Warsaw to Belarus, then to Moscow.

Phillips came back in and sat at the computer desk next to her. "I apologize for my rudeness. You came to us, desperate for help and I insulted you. Please forgive me."

"I do forgive you. We must have given you quite a surprise, showing up dressed like that. I shouldn't have made the red velvet part of the code. Sorry."

"It was confusing but I see the humor in it now. We can get you to wherever you need to go. You'll have to tell me exactly where that is."

"I can't tell you *exactly*. If you can get me as far as Sergiev Posad, I can go from there."

"You could go by train to Vilnius, Lithuania and on to wherever. There's a U.S. embassy in Vilnius. They can help."

"I just checked. There is no way to get back to my mission in time from Lithuania. The rail route after Vilnius would take too long with all of the necessary train changes."

"How did you get to Poland from Russia?"

"I went to Moscow, took an overnight train to Warsaw and more trains and other conveyances to get the job done. I can't risk going back to Moscow on the same route."

"Why not? You'll have the proper documents."

"The customs officials or a conductor might recognize me. I was on that train about a week ago, using a different passport."

"You've been busy! We can alter your appearance and take photos. Someone will drive you to Warsaw to catch a different train to Moscow."

"What do you mean by alter?" She touched her hair.

Phillips chuckled. "We won't cut your hair." He stood and motioned for her to follow him back down the hall.

He opened the door to a small room and ushered her in. The closet was filled with clothing. He took a backpack from a shelf. "You'll need this to look like a real train traveler." He stepped aside. "You can choose clothes and anything else you need. I'll send a beautician in right away. She will suggest the changes." He left the room.

Amber checked out the clothes. *I need to wear something very different from the things I started out with.* She picked out a sweater, a pair of slacks and a jacket, and then tried on a pair of shoes. They fit. She added a blouse, two pairs of socks and more underwear. *That should do it.*

A woman came in with a makeup kit. "Hello. I'm Julia. Let's see what we can do to change your appearance." She put her hands on either side of Amber's face and lifted her chin. She took her hands away. "Look down, then up. Now to the right, left and finally straight at me, please. Do you wear glasses or contact lenses?"

"No. Neither."

"Were your eyes blue on that last passport?"

"Yes." *What is she thinking? Contacts?*

"Let's try this first." She held out a pair of thick-rimmed glasses. "These are just clear glass."

Amber looked in the mirror. "I look different already."

"I have makeup tricks that will give you a new look without drastic changes. Remove the glasses, please."

She started plucking Amber's eyebrows. "I'll just thin them out some. That will make a big difference." She handed her a tube of lipstick and a compact of blush. "See what you can do with these. Then we'll change your hair color."

Amber put the glasses back on and went over to the full-length mirror. She put on a little of the makeup. *I do look a lot different. If she does my hair dark, it will save me time in Sergiev Posad.*

She went back to Julia. "What color were you thinking of for my hair?"

"The fastest and easiest way is to go dark."

"It sounds good to me."

"Sit down, lean back and I'll get started." She applied the color. "I'll come back to check results."

Amber sat down and relaxed her body, although her mind was racing. *I hope Ari did okay covering for me. She may have to leave Russia. At least I don't have to worry about Sara or Liesel now.*

Julia came back, checked Amber's hair, and then rinsed it. "It's going to be fine. Let's get it dried."

After Amber's hair was styled, she went over to the mirror and checked her image. "I think you did a great job, Julia. Thank you. I'm sure I won't be recognized."

"You were an easy subject. I'll leave you now. Good luck!"

Amber went to be with Sara. "Look what they've done to me. I mean *for* me."

"Wow! You look like a different person."

Amber sat down across from her. "I'll be leaving soon. Even with all the problems and fear we endured, I enjoyed your company. By the way, I'm sorry I bugged you about not speaking more Polish. At that time, I thought you were Liesel, someone who supposedly speaks fluent Polish. If I ever feel safe enough, I'll contact you. I don't expect you to forget what happened. Just try to get back to your normal life."

"I will. I hope you get back safely to wherever you're going."

Amber reached over and touched her hand. "You are never to mention anything about safe houses to anyone for any reason. You will be forbidden to speak of your abduction or rescue. Leave your home address with Phillips. Someone at the agency in Washington will see that you are compensated. Not that money could ever make it okay, but it can't hurt."

Phillips knocked lightly and entered. "Ms. Thornburg, where will you be going?"

"I'd like to go to West Conshohocken, Pennsylvania, please."

"We'll get you on a flight to Philadelphia. There will be a car waiting at the airport to drive you to West Conshohocken and wherever you need to go."

"Thank you. I appreciate everything you're doing for me."

Phillips nodded. "You're welcome. You'll be home soon." He turned toward Amber. "We need to discuss a few more things. Would you come with me, please?"

He led her to a briefing room. "Have a seat." She sat in a wide upholstered armchair and put the glasses on. "Will my new appearance do?"

"Yes, if you keep those glasses on whenever possible. We'll have to take photos of you with your new look."

He sat at a desk facing her. "I checked all of the train schedules, and you were right. Leaving from Vilnius won't work. Which train did you take from Moscow?"

"I took the *Polonez*. I shouldn't take it going back."

He picked up a printout of the schedule. "There is another train that leaves Warsaw tomorrow morning, just before eleven o'clock. It will get you in Moscow at ten thirty the next morning."

"I'll need a visa to get back into Russia."

"That can be arranged. Someone will drive you to Warsaw to catch the train. Will that work for you?"

"I'd still have to catch another train to Sergiev Posad and it's imperative that I meet someone there before noon."

"If you are meeting with the person I think you are, I can call and have your contact wait until you arrive." He tilted his head to the side. "It's to do with a cobbler, right?"

"Since you know about him, then yes. That would get me back on track. Who would speak with him?"

"I would. What code should I use?"

"He doesn't know my name or code name, but he knows about Operation Winterset. Ask him to have Mrs. Winter's cover wait until two p.m. Wednesday."

He nodded and stood. "I'll take care of it immediately. Feel free to join Ms. Thornburg. I'll have more coffee sent in, and later someone will show you to your quarters."

"Thank you. I may make it in time after all." She went back and sat with Sara. "Coffee is on the way. I sure could use a cup."

"Me too. I've been sitting here thinking about my apartment, wondering if I'll ever feel safe living alone again. For now, I'm going to stay at my parents' house."

"I think that's best after your harrowing experience."

Harriet came in with a tray. "If you would like anything more, let me know."

Amber took the cups from the tray and poured their coffee. "Look at those pastries!" She took a chocolate éclair from the serving plate.

Sara reached for a raspberry swirl roll. "I haven't seen one of these in a long time." She bit into it. "Yum! It's even better than I remembered."

After they finished up all the pastries and most of the coffee, Sara pushed her plate away. "That was a real treat."

Harriet knocked and pushed the door open. "Are you ready to see your home away from home?"

Amber nodded. "Yes, thank you."

They were shown to a room with twin beds, two chairs and a desk. A wire basket holding writing paper, notepads and an assortment of pens and pencils sat in the center of the desk. Amber said, "Would you ask Mr. Phillips if I can speak with him, please?"

"I will. Extra blankets are in the closet. I'll be right back."

Harriet came back with their things. She nodded to Amber. "Come with me, please. Mr. Phillips is waiting for you."

The door to the office was open. Harriet walked away as Amber stepped into the room. Phillips said, "The photographer will set up in here. As soon as he has taken the shots I will see to it that your passport and visas are done. Someone will awaken you at three o'clock and at four o'clock you will head out, escorted by an agent.

He will drive you to Warsaw. He has been instructed to wait until you have safely boarded the train and the train pulls away from the station."

"Thanks. I'll need money for the ticket and reservation fee."

"When I bring your passport, I'll give you an envelope with enough money to get you back to wherever."

The photographer entered. He asked Amber to pose in front of the backdrop, then took the shots.

"I'll have them ready momentarily. I'll leave things set up here in case these don't meet with your approval."

Phillips walked to the door. "You can wait here for the photographer to bring you the photos. I'll check back with you soon."

In a few minutes, Phillips came back in with the photos in hand. "I stopped by and picked them up. They look fine to me."

Amber checked them out. "I'm sure they'll do. Thanks."

"Good. I'll have your passport and visa ready in less than an hour. Would you like to go back to your quarters to wait?"

"Yes. I should finish up my packing."

Sara was stretched out on a bed. She sat up when Amber came in. "Are you leaving tonight?"

"No, I'll sleep for a couple of hours, and then leave before daylight tomorrow. You'll be sleeping when I leave."

Sara got up, walked over to Amber and hugged her. "Take care, friend. I hope we can get together again someday."

"I think we will. Be safe and happy back home."

Phillips came in and handed Amber an envelope and her new passport. "To me, it looks authentic."

She looked it over carefully. "It's in order."

Phillips nodded to Sara. "I'll leave you for the night." He turned back to Amber. "I'll see you before daybreak." He closed the door behind him.

Amber opened the envelope and counted the money. "I have everything I need to get back to my assignment. I'm ready to hit the sack. Good night, Rosebud!"

"Good night, Guardian Angel!"

Harriet left the door ajar, allowing the hall light to bring a little light into the room. She touched Amber on the shoulder and whispered, "It's time to get ready. Mr. Phillips will meet you in the office in fifteen minutes. Goodbye, and be careful."

Amber dressed, took her jacket from the closet, picked up her things and went to her meeting. Phillips was sitting at one of the computers. He turned and pointed to a tea cart. "Help yourself to coffee and pastry."

She poured a cup of coffee and took a cheese Danish.

The escort came in, nodded to Amber and spoke to Phillips. "Agent reporting for duty."

"You know the drill. Coffee first, then business."

The agent poured his coffee, then went over and stood beside Amber's chair. "I'm Gilbert, your escort."

"I'm Rhonda, your passenger."

"I'll be driving the Volvo today. A food pack for you is on the stand in the foyer." He pulled his sleeve up and checked his watch. "Just ten minutes until blastoff."

Phillips turned off his computer. "I reserved a second-class, upper berth for you in the name of Rhonda Claibourne. You're all set now."

"Thanks again for your help."

He stood and shook her hand. "It's my job. Take care."

She nodded and followed Gilbert down the hall. He picked up the food pack, opened the front door for her, stepped out, and pointed to a beige Volvo parked at the end of the street. He scanned the area as they walked toward it.

The air had turned damp and much colder. Amber shivered. *Old Man Winter is here.*

Gilbert held the passenger door open for her. As soon as the engine warmed up, he headed for Warsaw.

Chapter 22

Warsaw, Poland

Gilbert parked at Warsaw's *Centralna* station. "If you feel uneasy, let me know immediately. The signal could just be bending down and pretending to tie a shoe, or zipping, and then immediately unzipping your jacket. One of our agents has boarded your train just before it left from Poznan this morning, and he will have checked out all the passengers by the time the train arrives here. He'll be waiting on the platform before you board. I'll point him out. He'll follow you onto the train, then later, he'll strike up a conversation. As a code, he'll mention something about his family and special wine." Gilbert paused to check the schedule again, and then continued. "I'll wait on the platform. As soon as you get on board, stand or sit by a window. If I wave at you, then all is clear. Otherwise, I'll get you off the train."

"I understand."

"Okay. Let's go into the station. We still have some time before the train arrives."

"I'd like to buy a watch. Mine was stolen."

"I'll go with you."

Amber chose the plainest watch she could find. *No need to draw attention to myself.* "I'm ready."

"We should pick up your ticket now."

Amber paid and put the ticket in her backpack.

Gilbert looked up at the clock above the departure board. "It's time to head for the platform. Do you have everything?"

"Yes. I'm ready to get on board. Lead the way."

On the platform, Gilbert nudged Amber and nodded toward a man in a brown overcoat. A plaid scarf dangled from a pocket as he leaned slightly forward on a four-pronged cane. He glanced at Amber. She suspected the cane was just a ploy. She waited until the other passengers boarded before stepping up onto the train.

She stood by the window and waited for Gilbert's signal. He waved. Amber nodded. *That means all clear.*

Within ten minutes after the train had pulled away from Centralna station, they arrived at Warsaw's Wschodnia station. The agent observed the passengers as they boarded. Amber waited in the corridor for him to approach.

He came up beside her. "Are you on vacation?"

"Yes. I'm traveling around Europe for a couple of weeks. What about you?"

"I'm visiting family and doing some shopping for special wines." He leaned closer and whispered, "I'll be checking out things until the train leaves. This is the end of the line for me. As soon as the conductor checks your ticket, go to the bar car. I'll find you. My name is Barry." He took the scarf from his pocket and wrapped it around his neck. *Change of signals!*

"I'm Rhonda." She went to her compartment.

After the conductor had checked her ticket, she went to the bar car to wait. *Barry had better get here soon. The train takes off again in a few minutes.* She ordered a glass of orange juice.

Barry came in and said, "I've checked all around and I'm happy to report there's nothing to report." He grinned. "You're on your own now. I have a feeling you'll be okay. I'll stay on the platform until the train pulls away. Stay safe."

"I'll try. Thanks. Goodbye."

After the train pulled away, she went to her compartment and opened her food pack. She ate a sandwich and a pear, and then stretched out on the bunk to rest. *I won't even think about the problems ahead. It will all work out somehow. I hope.*

Amber woke just before the train stopped at Vazma. She tossed the blanket aside, climbed down from her bunk and went to a parlor type car. *I can't believe I cleared customs so easily. The next stop is Moscow. Then I'll only need to buy a ticket to Sergiev Posad.*

Sergiev Posad, Russia

Amber walked past the parking lot and glanced over at the cars. *That Opel looks like Milano's. It is.* She tapped on the window, then stepped back.

Startled, Milano looked up and got out of the car.

Amber drew close to him. "What are you doing here on a Wednesday?"

"If you mean in Sergiev Posad, I have been shopping. I didn't go near the repair shop."

"It's a good thing you're here. We can expedite the getaway. Do what you have to do in order to leave Russia. We are dangerously close to being discovered. Can you wait here for twenty minutes before coming to Konstantin's?"

"Yes. I have what I need with me. I'll be ready to leave Russia whenever you say the word."

Amber walked to the repair shop and opened the door. The chimes tinkled. There was silence for a moment. Then Konstantin came through the curtains. "We were worried about you."

"You had reason to be, but it finally worked out. We have to step up the escape. Is my cover still here?"

"Yes. Go on back. She's having coffee."

"That figures. Where did you put the hair dye I left?"

"It's on the top shelf in the closet."

"Thanks. Will you call the embassy, please? My cover needs to speak to O'Bannon right away."

"Sure. Bring her to the back room with you."

Ari jumped up when she saw Amber. "You made it back!"

"Yes, and there's no time to lose. Let's call Slaney now. Tell him to bring your red-haired identification and meet you in three hours at the first Arbat place." She led her to the back room.

Konstantin was waiting by the phone. He dialed the special number. "Mr. O'Bannon, please." When asked, he gave his code name. "This is Gudok. I have Mrs. Winter waiting." Ari reached for the phone. "It's me, the cover for Mrs. Winter."

"Tell me what I need to do."

195

"Meet me at the Turkish tea shop on the Arbat in three hours. Bring my passport and papers with the red-haired photo. If I'm not there within thirty minutes, go to the church and wait. If I don't show up there soon, check for rail delays before sending out the search party!"

"Understood and will do. We're clear."

Ari put the receiver down and turned to Amber. "That's done. What's next?"

"Let's go to the bedroom and exchange clothes and shoes. I'll need my jacket back too. I don't have yours anymore. Please don't ask me to explain." *No point in telling her that some Gypsy in Poland is wearing her jacket.*

"Okay, I'll just wear the one you came back with."

While they were dressing, Amber said, "Give me my papers, then get the red hair dye from the closet shelf. Color your hair as soon as possible and wait in the bedroom for me."

Ari handed her the documents and the keys. "The mail and groceries are in the van."

Amber went back to the kitchen to wait.

The chimes tinkled again. Milano entered and spoke to Konstantin. "I was spotted in town and invited to join the Wednesday club."

"Go to the kitchen and join the meeting."

When Milano was seated, Amber said, "We must have all of our documents in order today. By tomorrow night some of us could be considered fugitives or worse, so we'll have to leave tonight. My cover should be ready to leave here soon. Can you drive her to the train station?"

"Sure. Let me know when she's ready."

Amber went to the bedroom. Ari was sitting on the bed. "I'm ready to go."

"When you get to the embassy you need to pack up and get out of Russia as soon as you can, with or without Slaney."

"I don't want to leave him. If he can't go, I want to stay."

"In this business, which you have agreed to be a part of, your dream of a picket fence, suburbia, going shopping in your SUV, and prancing around in stiletto heels is not part of it. Unless it's as a cover. You can always quit. But for now, you must do what is deemed necessary for the safety of all of us. Can you do that?"

"Okay! Yes, I can do it."

"I'm sorry, Sis. I really do appreciate you covering for me and you've done it like a pro. Let's go to the kitchen. There's someone that you need to meet. He's going to drive you to the train station."

Milano stood as they came in. Amber said, "I'm sorry I couldn't tell you that I had a twin. She has been my cover."

Ari shook his hand. "I'm glad to meet you. I think I have seen you before. Were you following me?"

"Yes. I thought you were your sister, and I was trying to figure out what was going on. Sorry about that."

"No harm done." She turned to Amber. "What are you going to do?"

"Don't worry about me. I have a plan or two. Give me a hug and get out of here."

Ari started out the door, then turned and ran back to Konstantin. "Thank you for everything."

He patted her shoulder. "Take care of yourself." He went back to the kitchen. Amber gave him the Rhonda Claiborne passport. "Please get rid of this. I'll need a new one soon. Then I'll need passports and a few other documents for some of our people."

He nodded. "Just let me know when to start on them. I have something to return to you." He took an envelope from his pocket and handed it to her. "This is the emergency money you gave me before you left for Poland. You may need it for this trip."

"Thank you. I have to get back with the supplies and mail now. I'll see you soon."

Biochemical Research Center

Amber pulled in the driveway and parked in front of the building. She checked her watch. *I'm late.*

Sabine came out to help unload the groceries. "What took you so long? Did everything work out?"

"I had some trouble with the van, but it seems to be okay now."
She tipped her head slightly to the side and nodded. "Everything is
fine. No need to worry."

Sabine visibly relaxed. *That means Liesel is safe.* "Ludmila, I
need your help in my lab."

"I'll be there in a few minutes." She went to her room and sat on
the bed. *One rescue is over and another is beginning. I feel like I'm
in a dream. How can six souls possibly make it out on the same
day? We can only try.*

Sabine was waiting at the first table. She motioned for Amber to sit
next to her and whispered, "I understood your signal. Where is
Liesel now?"

"Your daughter was not taken. The agents kidnapped a young
American tourist by mistake. It took me a few days to find her and
get her out of the Kaliningrad Oblast."

"That poor girl! But now they will go back after Liesel."

"If they do, they won't find her. Agents were sent to take her to a
safe place. When you get back to Maryland or wherever, they'll
contact you about it."

Sabine heaved a sigh of relief. "Thank you!"

"Now we have to figure a way to get ourselves out of Russia.
We're the ones they'll come after, and soon, I'm afraid."

"We have to get passports and visas."

"I'll have that taken care of when I get back to Sergiev Posad.
Have the little girls ready to go, right after dinner. What name and
birth dates do you want on the documents?"

"The names won't matter as long as Darya and Cassandra have
the same last name that you choose for me." She tore a sheet of
paper from her tablet, wrote down the birth information and gave it
to Amber. "I'll need birth certificates for them. Can the cobbler
handle that?"

"Yes. I assure you that he is capable."

"Now we'll need an excuse for you driving back there."

"I did say the van had given me trouble, even though it was fine.
I'll just say I'm taking it to be repaired."

"That should work. You didn't give me the keys back, so just
leave. If anyone notices you driving away, they'll ask me about it.

By the way, I still have the money your sister gave me in case we had to leave in a hurry."

"Keep it. You'll need it for the escape. I'll see you later."

Sergiev Posad

Amber drove the van to the lot, careful not to park too close to Milano's car. *Good. He's still here.* She walked to the shop. Konstantin met her at the door. "I'm expecting a customer. Please go to the kitchen. Milano is there."

"Okay. May I use your computer?"

"Yes, take Milano with you to the back room."

She put her forefinger to her lips and motioned for Milano to follow her.

In the back room, she sat down at the computer and checked train routes and schedules.

Milano whispered, "What about a flight?"

"That won't work for any of us. We can't risk being spotted. As you know from your experience, security is tight there."

Konstantin joined them after his customer left. "Have you decided on a route yet?"

Amber said, "For the woman and the little ones, I think a train to Riga, Latvia would be best." She turned to Milano. "If you could drive them to Rzhev to catch the train, it would be a direct route on to Riga. That's about three and a half hours driving time. It's too risky for them, or any of us to leave from Moscow."

"I can go with them to Riga. I'll drive them to Rzhev, ditch the car, and then we'll all take the train to Riga."

"That would be great!" She looked over at Konstantin. "Could you do American passports for them?"

"Sure. I have their photos. Give me the names."

She gave him the note from Sabine. "That lists the birth date information. Let's say the woman is Wanda Reynolds, born in Illinois. The girls can go with the first names they have, Darya, and Cassandra. Give them the same last name and place of birth as Wanda's."

Milano said, "Konstantin, can you take the photos of me?"

199

"Sure. First, we'll do something about your hair! It's too noticeable. Come with me." He turned to Amber. "Let me know if anyone comes in."

In an hour, Milano came back to the kitchen wearing a woolen hat. He slipped it off and laughed. "How do I look now?" With the help of Konstantin, he had shaved his head. He looked like a different person.

"Who are you now, besides a bald guy?"

"I'm Mr. Rodney Gardner, born in West Virginia, USA." He bowed. "At your service."

Soon Konstantin came in holding up three passports and handed them to Amber. "Since they will be traveling with Milano, I used the last name of Gardner for them, instead of Reynolds."

Amber grinned at Milano. "So, there is now a Mrs. Gardner traveling with you. And you have children! Congratulations."

He shook his finger at her. "Don't press your luck!"

"I know when to quit!"

She nodded to Konstantin. "Thanks. I'll see you later."

Biochemical Research Center

Amber pulled into the driveway and went to find Sabine. Just as she got to the hallway, Svetlana came up to her. "I suppose the van is okay, now?"

"Yes, it's fine. It was only a minor problem." *I knew Svetlana would be curious about my time away.*

"That's good. If you're looking for Sabine, she has been in her private lab most of the day."

"I'll go check. Thanks."

Sabine answered Amber's knock and waved her in. She locked the door and turned up the radio. "How did it go?"

"We got some of the problems straightened out. I have the documents for you. They're American."

Sabine flinched. "Why American?"

"With American passports, you won't need adoption papers or birth certificates, because applicants have to submit them when applying for passports in the States. You'll still need a visa to exit Russia. The cobbler added the date as if you had been in the country for the last two weeks. With Russian passports, it might not be so easy to enter any of the Baltic States now. Our plan at this time is getting into Riga, Latvia. Do you remember the man Darya saw peeking in the sunroom window?"

"Yes. You said he had been looking for you, or any agent."

"He is an agent who ended up trapped in Russia, and I was to help him get out. I hope you'll agree with the plan we came up with. The cobbler made passports for you and the girls with the same last name as the agent's. You four can travel as a family."

"Without consulting me?"

"You weren't there! We had to think of every alternative to get you and the girls out safely." She gave her the passports.

Sabine looked them over. "I'm Mrs. Wanda Gardner and the girls are Darya and Cassandra Gardner. That's fine. I didn't mean to sound ungrateful. I was taken by surprise."

"That's okay. I have to pick up Fyodor shortly, but I can't bring him here. I'll take him with me to Sergiev Posad. I'll stay there and discuss ways for us to get out. We'll have to rush it up. It looks as if we'll have snow before nightfall."

"We must leave tonight, no matter the weather."

"Right. When I get back we should wind things up. We'll wait until Svetlana goes to her cottage before we do the last-minute things. She's in her lab now, so I'd better hurry before she comes out." Amber stepped close. "Sabine, could you put something in Svetlana's coffee at dinner? You know, just enough to make her sleep soundly for twelve hours, or more?"

Sabine laughed. "Oh, you naughty girl! That's a great idea!"

"I thought so."

Chapter 23

Dmitrov

Amber parked near the spot where she and Fyodor had ended their walk, went directly to his room and knocked lightly. He pulled the door open.

"Fyodor, it's me, Ludmila." She stepped in, closed the door, touched his shoulder and whispered, "It's time. I'll take you to the cobbler. He'll make the proper documents for you. You won't be coming back here, so we'll slip away during our walk. Are you prepared to leave?"

"Yes. Everything is in order." He put his jacket on, then reached for his balalaika.

She said, "I'll wear your backpack. Anyone who sees us will assume it's mine. You left some clothes hanging in here."

"Leave them. I need to travel light." He put his dark glasses on and took his cane from the corner. "Now I'm ready."

She checked the hallway near the side door. No one was in sight. They slipped out without making a sound. When they reached the path, no longer needing to whisper, Amber said, "Will they miss you if you don't show up for dinner?"

"I doubt it. I have a small refrigerator and I often make a sandwich for dinner instead of going to the dining room. I usually fix my own breakfast here too. My friends never come to my room. We meet in the recreation area or the Braille and audio book library. It will be several days before anyone notices my absence."

"Good. We'll just vanish after we pass that wall we walked by the last time I was here. I left the van near there."

Sergiev Posad

Amber parked the van a block from the repair shop. "We'll walk from here." She checked her watch. "The shop is still open. If

202

there's a customer there I'll nudge you. We'll wait until they leave. Let me do the talking."

"You secret agents are so precise about the least little thing."

She laughed. "It's part of our training."

"If you'll walk around to me, I'll offer you my arm so you can direct me, then I won't need the cane. It folds up." He took the dark glasses off.

She quietly warned him of anything that could trip him up along the way.

She opened the door to the familiar sound of the chimes and introduced Fyodor to Konstantin. He came out from behind the counter and shook Fyodor's hand. "I'm glad to finally meet you. Milano is in the back room. Please follow me to the kitchen."

Amber led Fyodor through the curtains, showed him to a chair at the table and stood behind him.

Konstantin said, "Coffee, tea, anyone?"

Fyodor nodded. "I would like a cup of tea, please."

Amber shook her head. "Nothing for me, thanks."

When Milano came in, Amber reached over the back of Fyodor's chair and touched his shoulder. "I would like you to meet Milano, another agent."

Milano walked over. "It's good to know you. I understand that you'll also be leaving here tonight."

Fyodor extended his hand toward the voice. Milano took the hand, shook it firmly, and then sat down next to him. Fyodor heard the movement and turned his face in the correct direction. "I do hope to leave tonight. We just have to decide on our route."

Konstantin put the kettle on.

Amber sat down across from Fyodor. "Any ideas?"

"I would like to go from Saint Petersburg into Finland."

"That will probably be the first route they check when they find you missing." She turned to Konstantin. "I'd like to use your computer, please."

"Sure. Help yourself." He brought a pot of tea to the table, poured a cup for Fyodor and one for himself. "Tea will be a good respite from all the coffee I have indulged in lately."

Amber came back with a list of routes. "Fyodor, we should have American or Canadian passports. Then we could cross into Latvia,

Lithuania or Estonia without an entrance visa. We'd just need a visa that shows a date we entered Russia."

The chimes sounded. Konstantin whispered, "Stay quiet." He went to the front room and spoke to his customer.

When he came back to the kitchen he said, "That was probably the last customer for the day. I close in ten minutes." He took his place. "Please continue."

Milano said, "I was planning to drive my group to Rzhev and ditch my car somewhere. Then I'll board the train with them. There is no way for the authorities to trace the car to any of us. I bought it from someone who had registered it in a false name. He didn't report selling it to me and he has no idea who I really am." He looked over at Amber. "If you drive us to Rzhev, you and Fyodor could drive on to wherever you like, get rid of the car, then sneak across the border."

"That's an idea, but it isn't safe for all of us to be in the same car. If one gets caught, we all get caught. I won't jeopardize the children. Maybe I can come up with a vehicle." She turned to Fyodor. "I think you and I should get out through Latvia too. What about it?"

"Yes. I know the area. That is definitely the best way. By vehicle, not rail."

Konstantin pushed his chair back. "I'll be right back. It's time to lock up. Then I'm going to get started on the documents. Later I'll fix dinner for whoever is here."

Amber said, "Milano, I'll bring the rest of the Gardner group to you in a couple of hours or so." She touched Fyodor's arm. "I'll see you later." She walked back to the van.

Biochemical Research Center

Amber left the van in the driveway and went directly to Sabine's room. She knocked lightly. No answer. She tapped on the door of her private lab and waited.

Sabine opened it and whispered, "Pavel is here with me. I'll meet you in your room in a few minutes." She went back to Pavel. "When the authorities discover that Doctor Kirsinova and I are

204

missing, they'll assume we have absconded with the cloned embryo of the Czar. How will you handle that?"

"There is no need to worry. When they find out the embryo is safe, they'll find another surrogate to bear him."

"I'm sorry to leave you to face it alone." She pointed to one of the other tanks. "That little guy has been a problem from the beginning. I don't know what I could have done differently. I do know that he will never survive in the womb. I was afraid I'd have to make a decision someday. That day has come. It's breaking my heart. That's what I get for playing God."

Pavel held her close in his arms and stroked her back. "You weren't in this alone, you know. I have to share the blame."

She pulled away from him. "Am I an angel of mercy or a doctor of death?" She reached for the tank but quickly pulled her hands back and put one hand on her heart, stifling a scream. "God forgive me! I just can't do it!"

"Sabine! Calm down. You're breaking my heart, too. Leave him. I promise you I will do everything in my power to save him. If I can't, then the outcome will be on my conscience, not yours."

"Maybe you can find something in my notes that could be changed or modified to solve the problem. Pavel, I can't thank you enough for giving me this hope."

"You have enough responsibility getting Darya and the baby out. Go now, get everything ready."

"Okay. We've figured out how to get Svetlana to stop nosing around. We'll add something to her coffee tonight. Even if she wakes up before we are safe, she will assume Ludmila and I are in my private lab. Meet me in the sunroom in an hour." She walked to the door, turned back and said, "I love you. Don't ever forget that."

Sabine knocked on Amber's door, opened it and stepped in. "Are you ready for dinner? The rest of our group will be ready for dessert." She drew close to Amber. "I'll have to make that special pot of coffee. Don't drink any! Add something for me on your tray. You know what I like. Hurry before the kitchen staff puts all the food away. It's almost time for them to leave for the night."

"I'm right behind you. Go ahead."

Alena was sitting with Darya and Svetlana. She held Cassandra against her shoulder, patting her gently on the back.

Darya waved at the doctors as they came in. Sabine sat down beside her and planted a kiss on top of her head.

Amber went straight to the buffet, dipped a bowl of soup and a plate of vegetables for herself and made a salad for Sabine. Back at their table, she set Sabine's plate in front of her and sat down across from her.

Svetlana grimaced. *Now she's waiting on Sabine hand and foot. What next?*

Sabine smiled at her companions. "I'd better go pick out an assortment of desserts for us." She went over to the sideboard, lifted the coffee pot and shook it. Although it was full, she emptied it and started a fresh pot, careful to add just the right amount of the drug. Then she went to the buffet, loaded a tray with desserts and took it to their table. "Take your choice."

Darya picked a dish of pudding and a slice of cheesecake.

Svetlana went to get their coffee. She came back and spoke to Sabine. "Why did you dump the coffee out? We haven't had any yet."

"It smelled too strong. I've made a fresh pot. It will be ready to drink momentarily." She looked sideways at Amber.

Amber lowered her head slightly. Her eyes communicated that she understood.

Sabine brought the coffee pot to the table and poured a cup for Svetlana and one for Alena. "That's much better." She stopped behind Amber. "Would you like a cup, Ludmila?"

"No, thank you. I've had too much coffee today."

Sabine poured herself a cup but didn't drink from it. She sat down next to Alena and reached for Cassandra. "Ludmila, since you aren't drinking coffee, would you hold the baby?"

"Sure." Amber took the sleeping Cassandra from Sabine's arms.

When Alena finished her third cup of coffee, she rose and said, "I'll see all of you tomorrow."

Sabine nodded. "Thanks for staying with the girls so long. I really appreciate your help."

"I know you do, Doctor. Good night, all."

After Svetlana left, Sabine checked the coffee pot. It was nearly empty. *That should do it.* She went back to Darya. "How would you like to sleep in the sunroom?"

"Oh, I would like that very much!" She picked her doll up from the chair. "Anna Jelina wants to sleep there too."

Sabine took Cassandra from Amber. "Ludmila, would you throw away the coffee grounds and clean the pot, please? We'll be waiting in the sunroom with Pavel."

"I'll take care of it." Amber took the trays and dishes to the sideboard, washed the coffee pot, and then went to meet Sabine.

Cassandra was sleeping in Sabine's arms. Darya tossed and turned on the sofa, until she finally got up, went to the window, and squealed. "Look! It is snowing!" She jumped up and down. "Can we go out and make a snowman, Doctor Heitbrock?"

"It is too late tonight, Darya." She led her back to the sofa. "You need to sleep now."

She switched to English. "Ludmila, what's the plan?"

"What about taking the van? I'll drive you and the little ones to the rendezvous and someone there can follow me back here. I'll leave the van and ride back with him."

Pavel said, "You can take my car. I can always claim that you stole it."

Amber laughed. "Thanks, but I don't want to add a felony to the other charges."

"I offered. Just decide soon."

Sabine looked at Amber. "Which vehicle?"

"Pavel's car would save us some time." She turned toward him. "I assume it's insured against theft."

"Yes, it is." He took the keys from his pocket and handed them to her. "It's the Lada. The tank is full. You're welcome to take it as far as you need to. Then just leave it." He turned back to Sabine. "I guess this is farewell."

"Not just yet. We need to make coffee for the guard. Then we'll have to make sure you're zonked out until morning."

"Just put some of that drug in my coffee. I promise I'll sleep."

"Okay. We need you to watch the children while we make more of the magic sleeping potion."

"I will stay as long as you need me."

207

Sabine turned to Amber. "Go to the dining room and make two pots of coffee." She handed her a small bag with two doses of the drug. "Add the contents of one packet to each pot after the coffee has brewed. Stir it slightly. Bring both pots back here."

Sabine went to her room, took an eight-quart cooler from the closet, and hurried to the dining room. As she passed by Amber she said, "I have to get the dry ice. I'll meet you back in the sunroom." She went into the kitchen, opened the door of the huge walk-in freezer and filled the cooler.

In the anteroom, she took the liquid nitrogen tank that held Alexei's sperm down from the shelf in the closet. She dispersed the vials among the dry ice in the cooler, took it to the sunroom, and then set it down by the sofa.

Pavel said, "I can guess what's in there. If anyone asks you to open it, tell them it's a human heart. And whatever you do, don't let the cooler go through x-ray." He stood and took her in his arms. "I love you. Take care until we meet again." He stepped away. "I'm free to leave whenever I decide to. I'll wait until my work is finished, though. I think I know how I can find you. Stop me if I'm out of line. Is Ludmila with one of those … shall I say … agencies?"

"Yes, she certainly is. You're right, Pavel."

"I also believe she is an American and not exactly a doctor."

"Right again, and her name is not Ludmila Kirsinova."

"It was you that made me think something was amiss. You have sent her out on too many errands when she should have been working in the lab."

"I didn't send her. I just arranged for her transportation and time off. She wasn't much help in the lab anyway."

Amber came in and set one pot of the coffee down. "Here you go, Pavel. Enjoy!"

Sabine said, "The other pot is for the security guard. He'll be checking in any minute. You can take it to him now."

Amber slipped out the door. Snow was still falling and the wind had picked up.

Pavel put his arms around Sabine and whispered, "I guess this is really goodbye."

"No, it's au revoir. We will meet again someday." She laid her head on his shoulder. He kissed the back of her neck, and then stepped back. "I love you, and I believe that we were meant to be together. We have to make it happen."

"We will." She squeezed his hand. "Now, I need to get back to the business of getting out of here."

"I'll retire to my room and get started on the sedative." He grinned and shook his head. "Oh, the things we do in the name of love!" He blew a kiss as he stepped out.

The guard was checking in at his post. He watched as Amber approached the building with the pot of coffee. "That is a welcome sight. Thank you."

"I figured you would need a lot of this tonight. The snow is only going to get worse."

"It looks that way. I had better make a trip around the grounds. I will need some of that coffee when I get back here. Thank you."

Amber nodded and went back to the sunroom.

"Sabine, the guard will surely drink that whole pot of coffee when he gets back from his rounds. It's freezing out there. My things are sitting just inside my door. Shall I bring them now?"

"Yes, and hurry while the little ones are still asleep."

Amber went to her room and looked around. She left her empty suitcase in the closet and transferred the few things that were in her purse to her backpack, leaving the empty purse on the desk. She put her jacket across one arm and went back to Sabine.

As soon as Amber entered, Sabine got up. "Now it's my turn." She went back to her private lab, took the tea can and went to her room. She put the can in her bag, picked up the rest of her things and closed the door gently.

In the sunroom, Sabine took the tea can from her bag. "This holds Alexei's ashes. I hope they will stay safe. I taped it closed when I transferred them from the urn." She pointed to the cooler. "And that holds his issue. I'll be carrying with me the beginning of life and the end of life." She held the tea can close to her heart.

There was nothing Amber could say. She went to the window and watched the snowflakes falling. *I was to get Sabine out before winter sets in. I guess I'm running late.* She turned back to Sabine. "Are you okay? It's time to go."

"Yes. I'll be fine." She wiped her eyes, then put the tea can in her backpack. "You have the keys." She pointed to the suitcase and the bag of clothing. "Put those in the car, please."

Amber came back in and asked, "Could we take the ambulance or the truck? They both have four-wheel drive."

"That ambulance was converted from an older Chaika and it would get too much attention. The truck hasn't been used for a long time. We can't trust it. If we leave now, we'll make it before the roads get too bad." She handed Darya her coat and boots. "Here, put these on. We are going for a ride in the snow."

Sabine put the diaper bag across her shoulder, wrapped a blanket around Cassandra and carried her out to the car.

Amber took Darya's hand and picked up the cooler. She put Darya in the back seat next to Sabine, then slid into the driver's seat. She eased the car out of the driveway and past the cottages before turning on the headlights.

Sergiev Posad

Amber parked the Lada in front of Konstantin's shop, opened the back door and helped Darya out. Sabine slung the diaper bag over one shoulder, picked up Cassandra and followed Amber and Darya to the entrance.

The door was locked and the buzzer was off. Amber knocked lightly.

Konstantin opened the door. "Come in out of the cold." He stepped away from the entrance until they were inside. "Welcome. Follow me, please." He led them to the living room.

Amber introduced Konstantin to them. Then she said, "Excuse me for a few minutes, Sabine." She went back to the kitchen to speak with Milano and Fyodor.

Konstantin smiled at Sabine. "You may lay the little one down on the sofa if you'd like."

She laid Cassandra down, adjusted her blanket, and then led Darya to a chair. "Sit here for a minute." Sabine sat on the sofa beside the baby. Turning to Konstantin, she said, "Thank you so much for helping us. You are the famous Gudok, I believe." He shook her hand. "Famous? Infamous, perhaps. Welcome, Doctor Heitbrock."

Darya tipped her head to one side and looked up at him. "I have seen a man like you in my Heidi storybook. You are a grandfather."

"I am sort of a grandfather. You are a very clever child. Can you speak English for me?"

She paused, nodded and said, "How are you?"

"I am fine and I am happy to meet you. I think you speak very good English." He switched back to Russian. "Would you like something to drink or eat?"

"Only if you have chocolate candy, thank you."

He looked at Sabine. "Is that okay?"

She nodded. "Sure, it's fine."

"Shall I make coffee? Tea? Sandwiches?"

"We have packed sandwiches and snacks, so just coffee, thank you."

"I'll be right back."

Cassandra woke and whimpered. Sabine picked her up, put her across her shoulder until she was calmed, then changed her diaper. Then she wrapped the blanket back around her and held her on her lap. She leaned toward Darya. "Soon, we will take a train ride in the snow and we will sleep in a bed on the train, all night."

"Where is the train taking us?"

"It's a secret. You will like the places we go. While we are on this trip, we will play a game. A secret game. You can practice your English, because we will speak only English when others are near. When someone asks you a question, you must answer in English. If you do not know the English, do not answer at all. I will answer for you."

"That will be fun. I hope there will be lots of other children on the train for me to play with."

"The first trip will be at night and the children will be asleep. Very soon, you will have lots of friends to play with and we will go to a park where you can swing and go down the sliding board."

Darya got up from the chair and came close to Sabine. "Could we have a picnic at the park?"

"Oh, yes my darling girl. We will have many picnics and you will ride a carousel. And we will go to the movies too."

"This is already like a movie! I am very happy." She went back to her chair as Konstantin came in with a tray.

Sabine said, "Will you sit with the little ones while I wash up?"

He nodded, set Sabine's coffee down on a table and put a Hershey bar, a glass of milk and a napkin down for Darya. "Here you are, young lady."

"Thank you, Sir."

"You may call me Grandfather. I would like that." He sat down on the sofa and picked up Cassandra. *I have never had the joy of holding my own little one in my arms. These times with my new friends have been the happiest since my youth.*

When Sabine came back in, Konstantin handed her the baby and went back to the kitchen to join the others. He reached in his pocket and took out Amber's passport. "See if this will pass inspection."

"I'm Beverly Jamieson, born in North Carolina, USA. Yes, it looks fine." She leaned toward Fyodor. "Are you English or American?"

"I'm Stanley Watkins, born in Arizona, USA."

"So, we're not related, just traveling buddies. I'm ready now to hear your decision. Which route?"

"With the help of Konstantin, we've mapped out a route to the Latvian border. Before I lost my sight, I traveled through every foot of the area, many times. I can direct you to the least patrolled areas after we leave the vehicle." He slid the paper across the table to her. "That shows the roads we should take."

She studied the hand-drawn map and the notes. *Crossing at Zasitino and Terehova.* "It's worth a try."

Konstantin pushed his chair back and stood. "Now it's time for you people to get started. Fyodor, I'll be right back."

He nodded. "I'll be ready to go."

Milano followed Konstantin and Amber to the living room. He went over to Sabine. "Hello. I'm Mr. Rodney Gardner."

"I'm Mrs. Gardner. You may call me Wanda." She nodded toward Darya. "And this is our Darya."

She pointed to the baby. "This is Cassandra."

Darya looked up at Milano. "I saw you peeking in our sunroom window! Are you my father?"

He looked at Sabine for help.

Sabine said, "No, Darya, he is not your father. He is going on the train with us. He will be your pretend father for the secret game we are going to play. You may call him Daddy. Is that okay?"

"Yes. Shall I still call you Doctor Heitbrock?"

"No. You must call me Mama."

"Okay. You will be my secret mother."

"And Cassandra is your secret baby sister."

Milano held Darya's coat out to her. "We must leave for our adventure now." He helped her on with it and buttoned it up. He looked at Sabine. "What do you need help with?"

Sabine nodded toward the coffee table. "Would you add that thermos to my backpack and carry it to the car for me?"

"Sure. We will be traveling together, as a family."

"That's fine. I left some of our things in the Lada."

Milano transferred Sabine's things to his car, and then went back in the shop. "I've taken your things to the Opel."

Sabine put her jacket on, wrapped Cassandra with an extra blanket and reached for the diaper bag. "I'm ready."

Konstantin patted Darya on the shoulder. "Have a good train ride, little one." He shook Sabine's hand. "Take care."

Amber turned to Milano. "We'll be right behind you but wait until I introduce the others to Fyodor." She went back to the kitchen. "The others are ready to leave. You need to meet them. Grab your backpack and balalaika."

Amber introduced Fyodor to Sabine and Darya. He shook hands with Sabine, and then took Darya's hand. "I am glad to meet you, Darya. You will have a lot of fun on your trip. Maybe I will see you some other time."

"I would like that. Goodbye."

Konstantin met Fyodor and Amber at the door with a thermos of hot coffee and a bag of sandwiches. He shook hands with Fyodor and hugged Amber. "It's going to be lonely around here without you people."

"Don't forget. We may meet in Paris one day."

He grinned. "It's a date!" He held the door open, watched them load up and pull away, and then closed and locked his door. *I had a family again for a little while. I'm a lucky man.*

The night air was biting cold and snow was still falling. Amber turned the heater on. She accelerated just enough to catch up with the others on the highway and blinked the lights once. Milano answered with a double blink and drove on.

Amber glanced at the dashboard clock. "We're cutting it too close for them to catch the train in Rzhev. Hold on, Fyodor, I need to hurry Milano up." She pressed down on the pedal, caught up with the Opel and drove alongside. Milano turned his head her way. She made a circular motion with her hand. He nodded. She slowed, allowing him to get back in the lead, and then took her own lane again. He sped up.

She leaned toward Fyodor. "Can you reach the thermos? I could use a cup of coffee."

He felt behind his seat. "Yes, I have it."

"Snowflakes are falling faster and faster, whirling around as if they are propelled by a strong wind. The snow is getting very deep on the sides of the road and it glitters like diamonds when the headlights shine on it."

"Thank you. I can picture it in my mind."

Several miles down the road, Fyodor said, "I hear a truck coming up behind us. Fast!"

The truck's headlights were shining in the rearview mirror.

She got on the brake as hard as she safely could. "He's going to pass us!" She had to leave more space between their cars. The driver started to go around them, his turn signals blinking. He didn't see the Opel in front of them soon enough.

Milano tried to get out of the truck's way but it swerved toward them, forcing the car into a shallow, snow-filled ditch.

The truck raced onward. Amber pulled off the road, jumped out and charged into the ditch. Throwing open the back door of the Opel, she called, "Is anyone hurt back here?" No one answered.

Sabine sat holding Cassandra. Darya had fallen onto the floor.

Amber took the baby from Sabine's arms. "Help Darya up! I'll be right back to get you out." She carefully stepped out of the ditch with Cassandra in her arms and opened the front door of the Lada.

"Fyodor! Hold the baby." She went back and helped Sabine and Darya out. "Hurry! Get in the back seat of the Lada. I have to check on Milano." Wading through the deep snow again, she made it around to the driver's door. Milano's head was against the steering wheel, yet he had managed to turn the engine off before he passed out. She pulled the door open, felt his pulse and lifted his head back. Blood dripped from a deep gash on his forehead. "Milano! Wake up!" He stirred slightly and said, "What the hell happened? Are the others okay?"

"Yes. They're fine. You aren't! Your head is bleeding. Do you have a clean tissue?"

He reached in his pocket, pulled a tissue out and rested it firmly against the gash. Amber said, "We have to get out of here!" She took his arm and helped him out of the car. "Can you make it to the Lada?"

"Yes. Take everything out of the car."

Amber handed him the backpack and the diaper bag. "I'll get the rest."

Milano carried the things to Sabine and got in beside her.

Amber took the papers from the Opel's glove compartment and stuffed them in her pocket. She picked up the cooler and set it on the ground by the road, then took everything out of the trunk. She climbed out of the ditch, put the things in the Lada, and then got back behind the wheel.

Fyodor was holding Cassandra. He leaned toward Amber. "Do you want Sabine to take the baby?"

"Yes. She might be safer in the back seat."

Milano took Cassandra from Fyodor and said, "Sabine, here's your girl. Safe and sound."

She reached for Cassandra. "We're good to go back here." She patted Darya's hand. "Everything is okay, now."

Fyodor said, "I can hear more trucks coming from way back. We'd better get started."

Amber eased the Lada back onto the road. "That's one way of ditching your car, Milano!"

"Yes, and now we won't have to find a parking place at the station. See how clever I am?"

215

She nodded. "Milano, you're a real genius when it comes to defensive driving!"

"Don't rub it in!"

"Joking aside, you managed to keep everybody safe. It was a miracle you kept the car from turning over. We ended up in one car, after all."

Fyodor cut in. "There's a train coming, and it won't be long before it gets to Rzhev. You need to speed up."

"Maybe it's a freight train." She pushed the pedal down harder. They heard the train rumbling down the track.

Fyodor touched his hand to the window. "You're right, it's a freight train. I can feel the vibrations. It's a long and heavy one."

Chapter 24

Rzhev, Russia

The lights of Rzhev came into view. Amber said, "Okay, Gardner family, gather up your stuff and be ready to get out." She touched Fyodor's arm. "You can wait in the car. I'll be back right after the train leaves."

She pulled into the station. "What about tickets, Milano?"

"Secure. I bought them today. Fyodor, I hope to see you again somewhere." He looked over at Amber. "That goes for you too, Pavlova." He jumped out and held the door open.

Sabine handed the diaper bag, and then Cassandra over to him. She helped Darya out of the car. "Stay beside me." She strapped on her backpack, then picked up the cooler and the suitcase. "Goodbye, Fyodor." She nodded to Amber. "See you soon, friend."

"Right. In Washington! Fyodor and I will follow the rail route until you're safely through the Russian checkpoint." She got out and kissed Darya on the cheek. "I will see you in a few days. Now we have to keep playing our secret game. If you see me at the station, pretend you don't know me. Okay?"

"Yes. You can be my secret stranger!"

Sabine and Darya walked with Milano to the station and on to the platform. The train was just pulling in.

Amber followed a few paces behind them, and then began her surveillance. Nothing seemed out of the ordinary. She waited until all the passengers boarded and the train had pulled away. Then she went back to the Lada and drove on.

Darya was sitting by the window in their compartment holding her doll and her teddy bear. She was watching the snow fall. "Snowflakes look just like fluffy feathers."

Sabine sat with the baby in her lap. "Yes, they do. Soon you will build your snowman, but now you must lie down and rest."

"Wake me up when it's time to start the snowman."

"I promise."

Milano stepped back into the compartment. "I checked all the corridors. Should we finish off that thermos of coffee?"

"Sure. I might even eat a sandwich."

Darya sat up. "I am hungry too. May I have a sandwich?"

Sabine smiled at her. "You don't miss a thing, little girl." She took the sandwiches out and let Darya choose one. "When you finish eating, you should sleep."

The train stopped in Velikiye Luki just after three a.m. Milano watched from the window as the passengers boarded, knowing that Amber was nearby and watching too. *The next stop is the Russian checkpoint at Sebezh. No more stops in between.*

Sebezh, Russia

Amber parked near the train station. "Fyodor, we're in Sebezh. I'm going to check out the area. I'll be back within ten minutes after the train leaves."

"Okay. Be careful."

"I will." She looked around the parking area, stepped out, and then walked quickly to the station.

The train pulled in. *This is it. If they make it through this checkpoint, they're home free.* Amber stayed back from the platform and watched.

Darya sat up and yawned. "Are we there yet?"

Sabine said, "No, not yet. We are at the border and soon some men will come in and ask us our names. You must answer only in English. Say your name is Darya Gardner. If they ask anything else, let me answer for you." She heard footsteps in the corridor. Two men entered the compartment. One of them checked their documents and looked at the children. He smiled at Darya, but he didn't speak to her. He nodded to Sabine, and then turned to Milano. "Where are you and your family going?"

"We are going to Riga to finish up our vacation."

"Have a nice trip." He handed the documents back to them, and then stepped back into the corridor while the other man searched the luggage. Then they both disappeared down the corridor.

Cassandra woke and started to cry. Sabine held her across her shoulder and quieted her. After she changed the baby's diaper, she said, "Milano, will you hold her while I go wash up?"

He reached for Cassandra. "Sure. Go ahead."

When Sabine returned, she mixed the baby's formula and asked Milano to have the attendant warm it.

He said, "The customs agents are in the last car now, so we should pull out soon. Then I'll ask the attendant to warm the bottle. I'll order our breakfast while I'm at it."

When the train pulled away, Amber went to the platform and checked the area. There was no one about. *It looks as though no one was taken from the train. They made it. I'm sure they won't have any problems with the Latvian officials.* She went back to the car. Fyodor was awake and anxious. "Is everything okay?"

"Yes. Apparently, there were no problems. We're free to carry on. Which way?"

"Continue toward Zasitino. The checkpoint for vehicles is there. Pull over when we're about ten kilometers from it, and you'll see an abandoned roadhouse, on your left. If I'm sleeping, wake me. I'll need to direct you the rest of the way."

"Okay. Are we going into Latvia near Terehova?"

"Only if it still feels safe when we get close to Zasitino. We'll leave the car somewhere and sneak across the border on foot."

"There's a safe house at Rezekne. I know the directions from the edge of town. The chief agent will find out where your family is."

"I can't ask for anything more." He leaned back against the seat.

"Wake me if you need me."

Amber gently touched Fyodor's arm. He leaned forward, rubbed his eyes and yawned. "Where are we now?"

"There's a sign saying Zasitino, with an arrow pointing to the right."

"You woke me just in time. The checkpoint is just a little further to the right."

"I must have missed the roadhouse."

"It might have finally collapsed in on itself. We'll keep going straight ahead until you find a good place to hide the car. What does the terrain look like?"

"I see lots of evergreen trees, a few other trees with dead leaves, and some bushes on both sides of the road. I can see a wooded area with tall trees a couple of hundred meters ahead. There's a clearing, then a narrow path that looks as if it goes into the woods."

"I know where we are. Drive the car as far as possible, then we'll hide it as best we can."

The early morning light crept across the sky, filtering through the trees. Amber concentrated, driving steadily where the wind had whipped the snow almost clear. "We made it across the clearing. Now we get out and push." She turned to Fyodor. "Leave the balalaika until we get the car as far into the trees as possible."

Fyodor felt his way to the back of the car and put both hands on it. "Say the word when I should push."

Amber reached in the open window and put one hand on the steering wheel. "Okay, Fyodor, let's push." She pushed hard with her other hand. The going was difficult. They finally got the car in between two trees. Amber eased the door open just wide enough to pull the balalaika out and handed it to Fyodor. Then she removed all of the papers and documents from the glove compartment and put them in her pocket. She twisted off some of the lower branches from a couple of evergreen trees, laid them across the top and back of the car, and then broke off the tops of several bushes to cover the bare spots. "That's the best we can do. The snow will cover it soon anyway. Hold onto the back of my jacket with one hand and walk behind me."

She warned him whenever the ground was uneven or when a branch was too low. As they moved onward, she took the papers from both cars out of her pocket. She tore them into tiny scraps and dropped them piece by piece at intervals as they plodded through the snow.

Soon, Amber slowed. "Let's hold up for a minute." She slid her backpack off and drew out a hat and a scarf. She handed Fyodor the hat and pulled the scarf over the lower half of her face. They walked on toward the border.

Fyodor sensed the traffic before they heard the engines. "We must be walking parallel to the checkpoint. Those vehicles will be backed up for a long time, waiting to cross. We need to keep to the way we're headed. There is a point less than half a kilometer ahead where you'll see a path and two striped posts marking the borders. Signs will say no trespassing in both languages. We should go on anyway. That's our escape route."

They went on dodging trees until they came to the path. After a few steps, Fyodor froze. "Stop! Stay perfectly still. I know there is a guard shack near here. I can almost taste the smoke from a fire. There is usually one guard per shift."

Amber pulled him behind a tree. "What do you suggest?"

"We go on. Be as quiet as possible. When you spot the shack, nudge me or grab my arm."

They walked on, following the smell of the smoke until Amber spied the shack ahead. She nudged Fyodor and whispered, "I see it. We're close."

He stopped. "Sneak up and look in the window. There should be a cot at the back of the shack. The guards are supposed to check the area every half hour, although at times, some of them goof off or nap."

"Why don't we just go on toward Latvia?"

He lowered his voice. "Because there will be at least one more guard, with dogs. You may need a weapon." He paused. "Go in and tell the guard that you and your friend are lost. I'll follow you in and distract him while you take his gun."

"Oh, right. That ought to be easy."

"You're an agent. You've had the proper training. I can't get it or I would. It's up to you to try."

"Okay. I have come this far into my assignment with more problems than I could ever have imagined, so let's move out."

Amber could hardly see as they trudged on to the shack. She went to the window, wiped the snow from it and looked in. A man wearing a military jacket was lying on a cot. His rifle was propped against the wall next to him. Amber handed Fyodor her backpack and said, "You'll have to take this."

He slung it across one shoulder. "Okay. Ready. Go in."

The door was unlocked. Amber eased it open a crack. "Hello." No response. She pushed it open and stepped in. The man was snoring, his mouth wide open. Drool slid down one side of his chin and he reeked of alcohol. A bottle of vodka sat on a small table and an empty bottle lay on its side on the floor. She reached back, took Fyodor's arm, pulled him in and whispered, "Stand here. There is one man, sound asleep on a cot." She went over to the wall, eased the weapon away and slung the strap over her shoulder.

She checked out the weapon. *A Kalashnikov. Easy for me to handle.* The guard still hadn't stirred. She went back to Fyodor. "I have his Kalashnikov. The man is stoned out of his mind. He'll sleep for hours." She added wood to the fire. *That should keep him warm until he wakes.* She touched Fyodor on the arm. "Wait outside while I check around and behind the building."

Amber lost her footing in the deep snow before she rounded the first corner of the shack. She managed to get back up and search further. *Pay dirt!* Excited about her find, she made her way back to Fyodor. "There's a motorcycle with four-wheel drive in a shed out back! Shall we take it?"

"Absolutely! We may not be able to walk much longer in this weather. Look for goggles. You'll need them."

"Hold on a second. I need to go back inside."

The guard was still snoring. Amber searched his pockets. She found the keys, and then eased the door to. Fyodor was still holding his balalaika. Amber said, "I've got his keys! Take my arm. We'll get the motorcycle."

"We aren't far from those border posts. I think we can make it across before the weather gets much worse." He paused. "Listen a second. I hear something."

"I don't hear a thing but keep an ear tuned. You'll have to keep my backpack. I can't drive with it on." She found a pair of goggles in one of the saddlebags, put them on, and then climbed on the motorcycle.

Fyodor didn't waste any time. He got on the back, squeezed her backpack between them and balanced his balalaika on it.

"I hear the snow crunching. It sounds like footfalls." Then all was silent. "It's too quiet. Someone is waiting and listening. I sense there is at least one dog standing by."

Amber felt a chill creep down her spine. "Hold tight." She started the engine and warmed it slightly. Then she took off as slowly as possible. The snow lay deeper on the ground now. She couldn't tell where the path began. *I'll have to depend on Fyodor's extra senses and his memory of the area to get us to safety.*

He leaned toward her. "Keep in a straight line. The posts should be up ahead."

A shot rang out. *That's a warning.* Two more shots were fired. She swerved, barely missing a tree. A volley of bullets whined through the air.

The goggles had clouded over. Amber pulled them off and threw them toward the trees. She brushed the snowflakes from her eyes and kept searching for the posts.

The border guard unleashed a German shepherd.

Fyodor yelled, "Someone is behind us in a jeep. He's closing in on us! And the dog is loose."

Amber went full throttle through a clearing. She spotted what looked like tall posts about fifty yards ahead. "I see the border! Hang on!" The dog was chasing the motorcycle, snarling like a wolf. It caught up to them and snapped at Fyodor's heel. As Fyodor pulled his leg away, the balalaika slid off onto the snowy ground.

Amber shot across another clearing and crashed hard into a border post. She flew off the motorcycle. Her head was reeling. She lay on the ground holding her hands over her face.

Fyodor lifted his head out of the snow, shielding his face with his forearm until he sensed the dog had backed off. Then he whispered, "Where are you? Are you alive?"

Amber sat up. "Yes, and we made it across. I slammed into one of the posts!" She stood up, picked up the Kalashnikov that had fallen to the ground and pointed it toward the Russian side.

A guard dressed in winter camouflage drove a jeep up to the border, jumped out and aimed a rifle at them. "Lay your weapon down! I am coming across to get the motorcycle. Stand back or I will shoot."

Amber yelled, "No, you will not! We are on Latvian soil!"

"Either you bring the vehicle to me or I will send the dog over. He is fast and vicious."

Amber whispered, "Fyodor, can he do that? Or is he bluffing?"

"I suspect he's bluffing, but since there is no one around to witness, he just might follow up on his threat. I have an idea. My balalaika slid off back there. Maybe we should offer to exchange the motorcycle for it."

"That idea sounds far-fetched, but it just might work."

The guard was waiting with his weapon still aimed their way.

Amber looked at him through her scope. She yelled, "If you shoot me, my fingers will automatically squeeze the trigger, and you're dead too. There are two of us! You are alone. Perhaps we can make a deal. You search for a musical instrument in a black case. Bring it as an exchange."

"That is a ridiculous offer, but it will spare us a shooting contest. It is a deal."

"It is a deal only if we lower our weapons, and then lay them down. Consider it a truce. Will you comply?"

"Yes. Truce." They lowered their weapons.

Amber said, "Now we lay the weapons down. On the count of three. One ... two ... three!" She laid the Kalashnikov down, staying ready to grab it. Simultaneously, the guard put his weapon down, keeping one hand on his jacket pocket where his pistol was hidden. He had no problem spotting the balalaika with its black case in the snow. He picked it up, brushed it off, walked as close as possible to the Latvian side, and then laid it down.

Amber pushed the motorcycle over to the edge of the border. As the guard reached for it, she reached for the case.

He pulled the motorcycle over, turned back, and saluted.

Amber returned the salute, and then waited until he drove away. She handed Fyodor the balalaika. "That was an ordeal. What shall I do with the weapon?"

"Leave it. The snow will bury it."

Amber unloaded the Kalashnikov and hid it under a bush. She scattered the cartridges among the trees as they walked.

She looked down at her watch. The crystal was shattered and the hour hand was missing.

Soon, they reached an asphalt road. Signs were in Latvian. They were still heading in the right direction.

Fyodor heard the sound of an engine. "A vehicle is headed this way." He put his thumb up. A Volkswagen bus slowed and pulled over. The driver rolled the window down and spoke in Latvian.

Amber shrugged her shoulders. "Do you speak English?"

The man nodded his head. "Get in before you freeze."

Amber climbed into the back seat. Fyodor sat next to the driver and said, "Where are you headed?"

"I am going to Ludza. Where would you like to go?"

"We need to get to Rezekne. Could you drive us there, please?"

The man hesitated. Then he said, "I will take you."

Rezekne, Latvia

In less than an hour, they were in Rezekne. Amber leaned forward and spoke to the driver. "Could you take us to the Museum of Culture, please?"

"Yes. It's just around this corner, and then two blocks down." He pulled over in front of the museum and pointed out the building.

Amber folded three twenty-dollar bills, leaned across the seat and put the money into the driver's hand. "I insist on paying you for going out of your way. We appreciate it."

"Thank you. It was my pleasure."

Fyodor got out and held the door open for Amber. She handed him his backpack and balalaika, then stepped out. His cane was still folded and in the pocket of his jacket.

Amber took his arm. "I can find the safe house from here. First, we go to the street behind the museum. I'll guide you."

From there, they walked several streets west, turned down the next street and stopped in the middle of the block. Amber looked at the apartment building directly across. She had only seen it on film. "There's a curb right in front of us. Step down." She led him across the street. "There's another curb here. Step up."

She stopped in front of the building. "We're here. Give me your passport. I'll show it along with mine when needed."

He took it from an inside pocket and handed it to her.

She took a deep breath and blew it out slowly. *There's the small rounded landing after the top step. This has to be the place. The mission is almost completed!* "Fyodor, five narrow steps lead up to a landing. I'll tell you when to step." She led him to the door and rang the bell for the second floor. A woman leaned out the window and nodded. Almost immediately, a man opened the door and ushered them into the hallway. Amber noticed that he kept one hand on his hip. *So, he wears a gun to greet his guests. Why not?*

Another man was standing by. He searched Fyodor first, then Amber. After checking their backpacks, he opened the balalaika case and checked inside. Then he motioned for them to follow him into the elevator as the other man disappeared through a doorway. The elevator was one of the old ones with bars for a door, looking and feeling much like a jail cell. As it ascended, it groaned and whined, as if it might be about to expire.

In the first room down a long hallway, they were seated across from the chief agent. He said, "I must see your papers now."

Amber nodded and handed them to him.

He checked each page of the passports. "Do either of you have a different name that I should know about?"

Amber spoke up. "These passports were done by one of my agency's cobblers. None of the information is correct. We are not to state our names at this time. I'm an agent working for PDI and I have been on a mission in Russia, which includes my companion. Are you aware of Operation Winterset?"

"No. I'll call Moscow."

"Ask for Mr. O'Bannon, please."

The agent came back in a few minutes. "Mr. O'Bannon would like to speak with you."

She followed him back to another room and picked up the receiver. "I'm here, O'Bannon. What's next?"

"First, tell me who is with you, and then tell me why."

"I'm with Fyodor Kirsinov, the brother of Ludmila Kirsinova, the doctor your wife and I were impersonating. I was asked to bring her brother out safely, and I have done that. Now, he can't go back to Russia. He needs to be reunited with his sister and his mother. I have no idea where they were sent. If you don't know, then I'll have to check with the embassy in Helsinki. I'm exhausted, and I need to get back home. I'm so tired of running and hiding."

226

"I do know where they are. I'll send a couple of agents to get Fyodor, and you too if you're finished running."

"I'm finished, but I'd rather get back on my own. I just needed to know that Fyodor will be safe. Is my cover safe?"

"Yes, she is. Don't worry about her, just be careful when you leave there. Give me the agent again, please."

She handed the receiver to the agent and went back to Fyodor. "My contact at the embassy is sending people to take you to join your family. I'll wait until they arrive, then I will leave you. I'm going home."

"Because of you, I will be going home too, wherever that may be." He squeezed her hand and held it against his cheek. "I no longer need to call you Ludmila. To me, you will be Kalinka until I can know your real name."

Amber hugged him. "We will get together again someday."

The agent came back in. "Help is now on the way."

When the *Latvian Express* had stopped in Rezekne, neither Milano nor Sabine suspected that Amber and Fyodor were also in Rezekne. Milano came back from his rounds. "Is anybody ready for their second breakfast besides me?"

Darya said, "I am! May I have eggs today?"

"Yes, and I will bring you some toast with orange marmalade." He laid his jacket across his bunk. "Sabine, what would you like?"

"Coffee and a pastry, please." She thought about the other children on the train. *They don't have to stay cooped up in one small room. Very soon Darya will discover all of the things that many children take for granted.* She leaned over and patted her on the shoulder. "In a few hours, we will be in a big city and we will find a big pile of snow for you to play in. I promise."

"I am very happy. I will build a happy snowman, too. And I like this train and the noises it makes. I once read a book about a tiny toy train. Now I am on a real one. A giant one!"

Chapter 25

Riga, Latvia

The train pulled in at 10:05 a.m. Milano carried the cooler and the suitcase out to the taxi stand in front of the station. Sabine followed with the children. Milano turned to her. "It would be better if you go to the embassy without me. There is no need for them to know anything about me at this time. I'll contact PDI as soon as I get back home. Someone at the embassy here will see that you get safely to your home in America. Now that I'm out of Russia, I'm safe too. I'll spend the night in a hotel here and tomorrow I'll go sightseeing like an ordinary tourist. With this passport, as Rodney Gardner, I can get a flight out to New York and on to Canada. I'll get a passport in my own name in the embassy there. Then I can resume my life."

"Thanks for your help and your company. I plan to get back to my life too, Milano. Maybe I'll come to hear you sing at one of the famous opera houses someday."

"Someone at PDI will know where to find me. If you keep in touch, I'll send you complimentary tickets for any opera that I'm affiliated with."

"That would be great. Thank you. Take care."

"You take care, too."

When the taxi pulled up, Milano waited until the driver placed Sabine's things in the trunk, and then he kissed Darya on the top of her head. "You can build your snowman soon." He helped her into the back seat. Sabine sat down next to her and held Cassandra on her lap.

Milano watched until the taxi was out of sight then went to find a hotel. *A few more days of traveling as Rodney Gardner, tourist. Then I'll be Grayson Montgomery, opera singer again.*

Chapter 26

Washington, D.C.

Amber walked out of the airport into a flurry of snow. Tiny flakes were swirling around in the wind, hinting of a white Christmas. She slid into the back seat of a waiting taxi and gave the driver the address of the Potomac Decorating Institute. She leaned back and relaxed. *My last debriefing for a very long time, I hope.*

In the lobby at PDI, she dialed Willoughby's office number. As soon as he answered she said, "Amber here. Arrival on the second level in two minutes."

Willoughby was in the hall waiting for her when she stepped out of the elevator. "I've been expecting your call. Today we are having our meeting on the third floor."

Amber was too tired to feel elated. "Lead the way."

He opened the door to his private office, reached under the desk, pushed a button and the bookcase on the back wall slid silently open, revealing a staircase. "Step into my parlor." He pointed to the narrow steps. "Welcome to the third floor!"

She followed him up and stood with her mouth open for a second. "So, this is your private lair. It's certainly hidden from us lowly ones."

"You've been promoted. Let's sit." He led her to a long conference table and pulled a chair out for her. "I know you're tired, but we have to get this over with. All of the agents that were working with Operation Winterset have been accounted for and several of them, including your sister, are waiting in other rooms."

"Thank heaven for that!"

"You have to keep a low profile, just to be on the safe side. We can offer you a place for as long as you need it."

"I know. I'm not sure yet where I want to be. By the way, there's the matter of Sara Thornburg's compensation."

"It has been generously taken care of."

"Thank you. I have one more request. Can you or the agency get my travel book published?"

"What book? Amber, *travel writer* was just your cover. What is there to be published?"

"Plenty. On all the days and nights on trains, boats and buses, and on all those nights in between deliveries when I couldn't sleep, I jotted down everything I had learned about train travel. I can have a book ready in a couple of months or so."

"What name would you use as the author?"

"A pen name, I guess. I don't know who I am. I'm no longer Amber Haworth, and I'm not sure it's safe to be Amber McFarland anymore. Just give me a name and I'll be her."

"You can be anyone you want to be. *You* give *me* a name and I'll make it legal for you."

"Thanks. I'll think of something and get back to you. Now, what do you want to know about the operation?"

He handed her a sheaf of papers. "This is Doctor Heitbrock's account of the action from the time of your arrival in Russia, until she left you in Latvia."

Amber leafed through the papers. *No mention of the clones, but it's not my call to mention them.* She put the papers down in front of him. "It works for me. Do I fill out a report?"

"Not unless you can account for the money Slaney sent you."

"I can. About half of it was used for our escape."

"And the other half?"

"Stolen by Gypsies."

"Very funny!"

"I'm not joking, Willoughby. Sara Thornburg can vouch for that. She was with me in Poland when it happened. Her money was also taken. It's a long, unbelievable story."

"I'll believe you. It's probably something that could only happen to you! Let's go down and join Ari and Slaney."

Amber ran over to Ari and hugged her. "I'm glad you made it home safely." She looked over at Slaney. "Are you going to take some time off now?"

He nodded. "Yes. Ari and I just might go on a real honeymoon. Somewhere warm and sunny."

Amber sat down next to Ari. "I see you've done your hair back to its natural color. Now we look like twins again."

A door opened and quickly slammed shut again. Amber said, "I'll be right back." *I think I heard Darya in the hall.* She looked up and down the hallway, and then went into another briefing room. Sabine was sitting on a sofa with Cassandra on her lap. "Amber! See, I finally know your real name, thanks to Mr. Willoughby."

Amber chuckled and took Darya's hands. "What a surprise seeing you today! We are going to have lots of fun." She kissed Cassandra on the forehead, and then sat down next to Sabine. "Tell me about your arrival in Riga."

"Milano didn't want to go to the embassy with us. He put us in a taxi and said he was going sightseeing. Then he planned to go back to his life in Canada. When the girls and I got to the embassy, they gave us a room in a fancy hotel. They had a guard posted outside our door. Imagine!" She shook her head. "I didn't expect that. And when the guard overheard Darya asking me if she could build a snowman, he took us outside and found a pile of snow for her. She built her snowman. I stretched out in the snow and showed her how to make a snow angel! Darya even helped her doll make an angel in the snow. I have never seen the child so happy. The next day a man from the embassy picked us up and put us on a flight to Washington, via New York. Willoughby met us at the airport and took us to a safe house in Chevy Chase, Maryland. Today he sent a car to bring us here for our special meeting."

"Things worked out, after all. I should probably get back to the other room now." She opened the door just as Slaney and Ari walked by.

Sabine gasped. "Who is that man with your sister?"

"That's her husband. He works for PDI."

"He was the first one to approach me about Alexei. Get Willoughby!"

Amber found him and told him what Sabine had said. He threw his hands up. "What the hell else went wrong on that operation?"

"Believe me, you don't want to know the whole story."

"I'll have to hear all of it eventually. Now let's go to Sabine."

Back in the other room, he spoke to Sabine. "Please come with me to the debriefing room. I want you to meet the agent who had you taken to Russia." He looked back at Amber. "Watch the little ones for us."

When Sabine was seated, Willoughby went down the hall to Slaney. "Go to the debriefing room. Pronto!"

"If this is about Operation Winterset, I want Ari to hear what I have to say."

"Bring her with you."

When they came in, Willoughby motioned for them to sit across from Sabine. He sat down at the head of the table.

Slaney looked straight at Willoughby. "Hear me out before you judge me. I was married to a Russian woman, long before I met Ari. Her name was Illona Zabinskaya. She was a conductor on a train that ran between Moscow and Budapest, and we first met on that train." He paused to glance over at Ari before he continued. "I was on a mission in Syria when our daughter was born. When I got back to Moscow I was told that my wife had died in childbirth."

Ari turned away in shock.

Slaney sighed. "They told me that my baby girl died right after her birth. I should have been there! Illona knew nothing of my work. I had a cover, you know, and that's the only name and job she ever knew me by until we were married. I have never delivered anything in Budapest or anywhere else. I was not a courier. What I needed to report was kept in my head."

"Marrying her was against the rules! You knew that. Have you ever thought that they might have known who you were, and killed her because of it? Or that she might be alive somewhere?"

"I saw her grave! Her name and date of birth and death were on the tombstone. I laid flowers on her grave. No one would tell me where my baby daughter was buried."

Willoughby shook his head and frowned. "You could have compromised yourself, and others. You knew it was dangerous to take up with someone you met on a train, much less marry her. She could have been a plant. What were you thinking?"

"I don't know. We fell in love."

"That's no excuse, Slaney! You should have resigned from the agency, immediately."

"Well, I didn't." He turned to Sabine. "I agreed to recruit you for the Russians because I knew of your research. My wife was from an area in Siberia where cretinism was prevalent and I had been told that my baby girl was born with cretinism. I hoped you would find a cure for others. Also, I was told that you were needed to care for your son. Still, I had no right to take it upon myself to disrupt your work and your life. I'm sorry."

"What you did was wrong, but I do understand your reasons. I'm glad that I was with my son when he died. I'm only sorry that we caused so many problems and such expense for others."

Willoughby stood and faced Slaney. "Did you also take it upon yourself to send the Canadian agent away after you got him to Moscow?"

"I had no idea he would be stuck in Russia. I gave him plenty of money and a false ID to get out on the next flight."

"That agent was supposed to bring Doctor Heitbrock home! Because of your actions, Amber and Ari had to take over his mission. You endangered their lives, Slaney! That's a case of insubordination, or worse. Big time!"

They were interrupted by the tinkling sound of a music box. Darya came skipping in. She gazed at Ari for a moment. "I thought there were two of you. You acted different than the other one."

Amber came in with Cassandra in her arms. "I'm sorry. Darya got away while I was concentrating on the baby."

Slaney stared at Darya. "Little girl, where did you get that music box?"

"From my real mother in Russia. She left it for me when she went away." She handed it to him. He looked at the one-armed ballerina, and then opened the drawer. The arm was lying there, just as it had always been. "This is exactly like the music box I gave to Illona." He looked up at Darya. "May I see that pendant?"

"No. It is mine! Forever and ever."

"Please let me see it. It looks so beautiful on you."

She frowned. "Okay." She lifted it from her neck and handed it to him. "Just for a minute though."

He turned it over and read the inscription: To Illona, my own Mona Lisa. *My God! Could it be? Is my baby alive?*

Darya smiled at him, showing a single dimple in her left cheek. The dimple was low, near her mouth, just as Illona's had been. Slaney reached for her hand. "I am your father, Darya."

"I knew we would find you some day!" She stepped back as tears rolled down Slaney's cheeks. "You should not cry, Father. You should be happy like me."

Ari couldn't hold back the tears when Slaney stood and put his arms around Darya.

Sabine just sat there in awe.

Amber was standing with Cassandra in her arms. *Did I miss something here?*

Willoughby shook his head over and over again. "You people never cease to amaze me. This should not be happening in an agency briefing room!"

Darya wound the music box up again. "Doctor Heitbrock, may I dance for my father?"

Sabine nodded. "Of course, you may."

Darya danced, almost keeping time with the music. She did her usual whirling, grand finale. They all applauded.

Willoughby said, "Amber and Ari, please take the little ones back to the other room. I need to speak with Slaney and Sabine."

Slaney nodded to Ari. "I'll see you in a few minutes."

Willoughby sat down at his desk. "Sabine, you did steal medicine and equipment for the Russians. I understand it was under duress, so I don't think you will be charged with a crime." He turned to Slaney. "You are responsible for the theft of that equipment and for the disappearance of Sabine and of Milano. You stepped way over the line. I'll ask for impunity for you, although I think the minimum punishment you can expect is early retirement, without severance pay. And probably no pension!"

"That would be acceptable. But if I'm threatened with prison, then I won't hesitate to fight it."

"That's up to you. For now, you can go back to Ari."

After Slaney left, Willoughby spoke to Sabine. "You and the children will have to remain at the safe house for at least a month. Then, if you are not charged with theft, you can work for us."

"I would like to continue my work. First, I want legal adoption papers for Cassandra. If it doesn't work out with Darya going to

Slaney and Ari, I'll want papers to adopt Darya, too. I want unlimited visitation rights if they are given custody of her."

"I'll see to it. Let's get back to them."

Darya was sitting between Ari and Slaney, telling them about her train trip.

Sabine took the baby from Amber. "Will you come to the safe house with us, please?"

"Not right now. I'll get back to you."

Willoughby said, "Anything that has been said today about Operation Winterset is strictly confidential. Let it go no further than this room, people!" He walked over to the door and put his hand on the doorknob. "I had a special phone call this morning. Another of your co-conspirators will arrive soon." He went out the door, closing it behind him.

Ari asked Sabine to excuse her for a minute. She motioned to Amber. "Can we speak in the hallway?"

Amber nodded and followed her out.

Ari said, "Will you talk to Sabine? You know her better than I do. I think she is planning to adopt Darya. The child belongs with Slaney and me. I want to be her mother."

"Are you sure about accepting her as your daughter?"

"Yes, I am. Just in the week I was covering for you, I became very fond of Darya. She is the same age as my Roddy was when he died. Anyway, all I had ever wanted was to be a wife and a mother. When Evan and Roddy were taken from me, it was hard to face the horror of their violent deaths. Sometimes, at night I lay in bed and imagined different, easier deaths for them. I'd tell myself they had been on a skiing trip, trapped by an avalanche, and that they froze quickly and painlessly." She paused and caught a breath. "After four lonely years, I met Slaney and we have been happy. What do you think will happen to him?"

"I'm sure Willoughby will request impunity for him. Slaney can always threaten the authorities with graymail."

Ari squinted. "What's graymail?"

"It's when a defendant threatens to expose highly classified intelligence activities or information."

"That sounds scary. Slaney and I can't go back to California until this whole thing is over."

"For now, why not stay with Willoughby and Mom? She needs to know what's happened. You can fill her in."

"That may be best. We'd better go back inside."

Willoughby came in shortly after. "Since this seems to be a reunion of spies, welcome your friend from Russia."

Darya squealed. "Grandfather! You found us again!"

All eyes turned to the newcomer. Konstantin stood in the doorway, grinning. "Hello. I retired. Willoughby and I are old buddies. We go way back in this business. Back to the cold war days."

Amber asked, "What are your plans now, Konstantin?"

"Traveling. That's what I'm going to do. For now, I'm staying at the Ambassador Hotel in Washington. Maybe we can all get together there. I'll keep in touch." He patted Darya's cheek. "I will see you soon, little one." He looked over at Amber. "Don't forget about Paris!"

She smiled and nodded. "I won't. I'll remember our promise to meet there someday."

"Good, but don't wait until then to see me again! I'll be around for a while."

After all of the others had gone, Amber said, "Willoughby, please promise me that you will introduce Konstantin to my mother."

"I sense a conspiracy, but I promise."

"Thanks. It's hard to believe the mission is over and that I'm still among the living."

"I know. Let me take you to a safe place."

"I would rather go somewhere on my own. I don't know where to go to feel safe. I don't know anyone other than my family, my friend Claire and a few PDI agents."

"I'm family now, so why not come home with me? Your mother and I want you to stay with us. That's as safe as it gets."

"I know, but I'm not sure where I want go. Now, I'm going down to the cafeteria and untangle the thoughts that are spinning around in my head. Then I'll decide where I want to go."

"Okay. I'm going home. Take care."

"I will. I'll let you and Mom know where I'm staying. Bye."

Amber took the elevator down to the cafeteria. She sat at a table with a cup of tea and thought about the last few weeks of her life. *After all that's happened, I feel a deep coldness inside. I feel fear. Maybe I need to be held. I need to be held by a man who loves me. Will Cotter still want me?*

She remembered his words. 'I have loved you since the day we first met'. *I do have a place to feel safe!*

She dialed Cotter's number. "It's Amber. I need a safe house. Can I come to you?"

"Always! Tell me where you are. I'll pick you up."

"I'll take a taxi. It will save time. Make a fresh pot of coffee, please. And Cotter, don't forget to put the umbrella up on your Parisian cafe table!"

****

Other books by Mona MacDonald Tippins

Tomorrow the Train: Journey to the World Record

European Train Travel Tips

Books are available in Large Print and e-book